# REDs Dreams

## KETLEY ALLISON

# 1

# LAYLA

The zip ties cut deeper as Cassie explains exactly how she'll break her father, starting with me.

"Poor little Layla," Cassie coos. "You're looking a bit worse for wear."

She wraps her hand around my throat, hoping for a reaction. Those eyes, so much like Kaden's, scrutinize my exposed, abused body. There are angry welts across my back from the lash of a belt, deep purple contusions on my stomach from the toes of Cassie's shoes, and raw, weeping cuts from her gleaming blade.

I try not to flinch, not to swallow, but her grip tightens, forcing me to choke before her hand falls away, and I slump forward, coughing up blood.

Laughing under her breath, she circles me slowly, her heels clicking against the marble floors. I keep my attention down, tracing the swirling patterns in the expensive stone. Anything to avoid seeing my broken reflection in all the polished brass adorning the private suite.

"I really thought you'd last longer," Cassie muses, trailing a perfectly manicured nail down my spine. I shudder, goose bumps erupting across my skin.

She lingers on a particularly vicious gash at the small of my back, the edges ragged and inflamed. I remember the searing pain as she carved into my flesh, her knife as sharp as her smile. Each cut was deliberate, placed with surgical precision to maximize the agony without allowing me the mercy of unconsciousness.

"You know, I'm almost impressed," Cassie remarks. "Most people would've blubbered by now. Begged for death. But not you." She leans down until her mouth is hot against my ear. "No wonder Daddy likes you so much."

I want to spit in Cassie's face, to tell her to go to hell, but my throat is raw from endless hours of screaming. The salty, metallic taste of blood coats my tongue. How long has it been since she ripped me from the illusion of safety and threw me into this nightmare? Days? Weeks? Time blurs together in an endless cycle of agony and humiliation.

Cassie straightens, her movements feline as she stalks back into my line of sight. She's stunning in a cruel, twisted way that reminds me of the unforgiving cliffs of Greycliff. Her eyes, a piercing steel blue that could cut through bone, lock against mine with an intensity that sends ice water trickling into my stomach.

Water would be nice, actually. Or food. Clothing. It'd be especially great if she'd loosen the zip ties binding my wrists together behind my back.

Cassie's full lips, painted a deep crimson, curve into a smirk as she notices the thoughts playing across my features. She tosses her head, her glossy raven hair cascading over her shoulders like a polluted waterfall.

"I see you've noticed the family resemblance," Cassie purrs. "Tell me, does it make it harder, knowing that the man you're so desperately trying to protect shares my blood?"

I glare at her, rasping, "Kaden is nothing like you."

"Oh, but he is."

She crouches down in front of me, her tight leather pants protesting. Cassie's perfume, something strong and spicy, invades my nostrils. "What is it about my father that inspires such loyalty in you? Is it the way he fucks you? The way he makes you feel special, like you're the only one who truly understands him?"

"Go to hell."

Cassie laughs, a cold, brittle sound.

"Hell is too good for me," Cassie says with a wink. "Besides, we have so much to talk about. Does Daddy still go for those ridiculously long runs every morning? Along the cliffs, no doubt, so he can brood in peace."

"I don't know what you're talking about," I snap, but my voice wavers. I know for a fact he no longer runs because the last time he did, his daughter was killed. No, kidnapped. Cassie's not dead. Ten years later, she's right here, playing mind games and enjoying every fucking second of it.

"Of course you do, Layla. You know everything about him, don't you? Like how he takes his coffee. Black, two sugars. And let's not forget about your charming little lighthouse cottage that he converted into your little love nest. Did you think those cameras were for your protection?"

Cassie's lips curl as she circles me again.

"Every single one, positioned exactly how he always does it. Three feet above eye level, angled down at precisely thirty-seven degrees. He's been doing security installations the same way since his military days."

Cassie pauses, running a finger along the crystal decanter near the fully stocked antique bar I've never been allowed to get close to. "The way he tested each sensor twice. Checked the motion detectors three times. He's obsessive like that. Has been since I was taken. But my favorite part?"

"Stop," I whisper.

She doesn't. "How he made sure the primary camera in your bedroom had the perfect view of your bed. Oh, he told himself it was for your safety, but we both know better, don't we? The way he'd watch you sleep for hours through that feed. Did you know he'd break in and adjust your covers if you kicked them off? Such a protective Daddy."

Cassie strolls in front of me, propping her hands on her slender hips. "He installed that system thinking he was keeping his precious Wraithling safe. Never realizing he was just giving me a front-row seat to your little love story. Every touch, every kiss, every time you spread your legs for my father—I saw it all. Rather kinky, wasn't it? The way you let him watch you pleasure yourself that night?"

I raise my head and spit out, "You're *lying*!" but the movement only triggers the tears building up in my eyes to escape.

Cassie's voice drops to a whisper. "But here's what you don't know, Layla. While Daddy dearest was getting off to your little show, I was in the warehouse with him. Just a few feet away, hidden in the shadows. Close enough to smell his sweat, to hear those pathetic sounds he made when he came. Quite the family reunion, wouldn't you say?"

Cassie spins, unbothered by my trying not to puke, and walks to a nearby coffee table. "You know what's truly pathetic? The way he cared for that mangy cat and her kittens. The great Scythe, feared assassin, hand-feeding strays. Did you think that made him soft? Human?" She picks up something from the table—a rope of red licorice. "The same way he always has these on hand when he kills. You see, I used to love red licorice. He'd bring me a pack every Friday after his morning run."

I say through trembling lips, "He never told me that."

"Of course not." Cassie takes a deliberate bite, chewing slowly. "Just like he never told you how he'd force his marks to gag and choke on this stuff until they died. Or how he'd revive them and do it some more, depending on his mood that day. But that's the thing about Daddy—he keeps the most important secrets to himself. Like how many times I've watched him break down at his surveillance monitors, torn by his obsession with you and giving zero shits about me."

"He loves you," I plead, my voice cracking. "Everything he did—"

"Was for me?" Cassie cuts me off with a snarl. "No, Layla, baby. Everything he did was for himself. His selfishness. His denial. And you? You're just another failed attempt."

The cold floor seeps into my throbbing, battered knees. The zip ties ate through the skin of my wrists a while ago, but it's nothing compared to how her words tear into me.

I taste copper. I've been biting my cheek to keep from screaming in terror, frustration ... and defeat.

"Like father, like daughter," I manage to retort. "You're just as obsessed with him as he is with me."

Her hand whips out, cracking across my face. The sting brings fresh tears, but I refuse to look away.

"Did it hurt?" I ask, watching her face carefully. "Seeing him care for someone who isn't you?"

Cassie's composure slips for just a second—a crack in her professional veil of cruelty. But then she smiles, and it's worse than any slap across the face.

"Let's watch a movie, shall we?"

Cassie pivots, reaching for a remote on the table. Directing it to a wood-paneled wall, she clicks it. A large white screen unrolls from its hidden port in the ceiling, the buzz of its mechanics mimicking the grinding of my joints every time I shift.

The mounted screen flickers to life, to a drone view of Kaden and me at the top of the lighthouse widow's walk, his knife at my throat as he pushes me against the railing and his fingers claim me. I remember the salt spray on my skin, the way his touch burned hotter than good sense.

"Look how easily you gave in to him," she taunts. "The daughter of an absent father desperate for a big, strong man's approval."

"You don't know anything about us," I grit out, but my heart hammers against my ribs as she flips to more footage.

"I know a whole fucking lot," she says, stopping on a video of Kaden in his warehouse, watching my staged performance in bed, the straps of my nightgown sliding down, my fingers...

"This was my favorite part," Cassie muses. "The way you thought you were so clever, creating that loop to escape. But you weren't trying to run, were you? You wanted him to catch you. Needed it. Just like he needed to own you."

"That's not—"

"True?" Cassie laughs. "Let's see what else I have."

I close my eyes, remembering how powerful I felt that night, how in control. Now that arrogance turns to ash in my mouth.

Cassie grabs my chin, forcing my eyes open.

"Watch," she commands, and I see myself cradling a bleeding Kaden, confessing my love. The video is crystal clear, my tears cutting tracks through his blood on my face, my fingers desperately trying to stem the flow from his wound. Even through the screen, I spot the exact moment his eyes started to glaze, when the poison began taking hold.

"I love you," my recorded self whispers.

The raw devastation in his eyes haunts me now as it did then. After ten years of being the Scythe, of carving his emotions out alongside his victims' hearts, those three words from me shattered him.

I strain against the zip ties, needing to touch the screen, to somehow reach through time and hold him again.

"Did the antidote work?" I ask Cassie. My voice is unrecognizable, even to me. "Is he even alive?"

Cassie's closed-lipped smile tells me she won't answer, and that uncertainty is another form of torture.

The footage continues, showcasing how they dragged me away from him, his blood bright on my skin as I fought to stay by his side. His hand reaching for me, my name on his lips even as he collapsed.

The last thing I'd seen was Kaden's face twisted in

anguish. The last thing he'd seen was his daughter orchestrating my abduction.

Both of us helpless to stop it.

A sob rips from my throat, but I force myself to keep watching. To witness every second of our separation, to burn it into my memory in case it's all I have left.

"Your biggest weakness?" Cassie prods. "It's not your fear. It's not even your need for him. It's that you actually believe love can save a monster like my father."

"You're wrong," I whisper, but the words catch in my throat as she pulls out a rope of red licorice and chews on it like she's eating movie theater snacks. "The real monster is what Morelli turned you into."

Her face contorts before she spits a wad of chewed-up licorice at my face. It lands against my cheek with a wet smack before sliding down my chest and landing between my knees on the floor.

"I've seen *everything*," Cassie seethes. "Every nightmare he gave you, every time he made you come. And now?" She trails a finger down my cheek, following the path of her sugar-sweet saliva. "Now I get to break you the same way Morelli broke me. Only this time, Daddy gets to watch."

# 2
# KADEN

The bullet in my shoulder burns like hellfire as I force myself back to consciousness. Layla's scream as she was dragged away echoes in my mind; the last thing I heard and saw before everything went black. As I blink awake in what seems to be a basement, panic grips my soul.

*Where the fuck is Layla?*

I try to sit up, but a wave of dizziness slams me back down onto the couch. The room spins, and I clutch the torn upholstery, willing the nausea away. I need to move. I need to find her.

A figure stirs in the dim light. For a moment, hope surges —*Layla?*

But as my vision clears, I see it's Ethan, hunched over a neon-orange plastic desk and sitting in a tiny yellow chair, the glow of his laptop illuminating his haggard face.

"Ethan," I say, my voice one notch above a rasp.

He jumps, nearly knocking over an energy drink can. "You're awake!"

He scrambles over, worry etched on his face. "How—how are you feeling?"

"Like shit." I wince, fighting the endless agony as I push myself up. "What happened? Where's Layla?"

Ethan's expression falls, and my stomach drops.

"I don't know," he admits. "When I got to Pulse, it was chaos. Alarms blaring, security everywhere. I found you unconscious in a service corridor near the server room. Layla was ... gone."

The amount of air in the room suddenly shrinks.

I grunt, grimacing as I shift on the couch. "You patch me up?"

Ethan nods, pushing his glasses up. "Yeah. CIA recruitment wasn't all computers. Basic field med was part of the training. They don't tell people that, though ... I'm probably not supposed to tell you that."

It's too easy to forget that the kid's got some skills beyond hacking, and that a dumb college prank kicked him out of likely becoming a successful spook. The way his stolen records explained it, Ethan never made it to the recruitment phase. Yet my stitches say otherwise. He could be an asset going forward. But then reality crashes back.

"How long?" I demand.

"You've been out for almost seventy-two hours," Ethan says, his voice barely above a whisper. "I brought you to my cousin's place."

I blearily glance around the room with small rectangular windows near the ceiling. A basement, then. In one corner, a plastic play kitchen overflows with miniature pots, pans, and brightly colored fake foods. Nearby, a tower of wooden blocks teeters precariously. A worn, patterned carpet stretches across the floor, its once vibrant colors now muted by years of spilled juice and stomping feet. The walls are a warm, inviting shade of yellow, though the paint is chipped in places.

Ethan adds, "He and his family are out of town, and I knew we needed to lay low."

I tear my gaze away from a child's prized doodles adorning the walls.

Seventy-two hours. Seventy-two fucking hours of Layla missing. The thought makes me sick.

"We need to move," I say, standing despite the room's sudden tilt. "Every second we waste—"

"Is a second Layla could be in danger, I know." Ethan surprises me with his boldness. "But you're no good to her if you tear those stitches and bleed out before we even start looking."

I hate that he's right. I slump back onto the couch, letting him check the wound just above my armpit. Every second I lay here feels like a betrayal to Layla, but I force myself to breathe through the pain.

Ethan mumbles to himself as he peels back the bandage, his brow furrowed. "Okay, okay, it doesn't look too bad. I mean, it looks bad, but not, like, life-threateningly bad. I think."

"You sure you know what you're doing?" I ask, my voice tight.

"It's not like we have a lot of options here. Just ... try not to move too much, okay?"

I bite back a retort, reminding myself that Ethan's out of his depth here. We both are.

"Just clean it and wrap it up," I grunt.

I grit my teeth as he dabs at the wound with a damp cloth, the cold water sending spasms down my spine. Ethan works in silence, his face scrunched up in a mixture of concentration and mild nausea.

"Talk to me," I demand, needing a distraction. "What do we know?"

Satisfied with his emergency triage for the moment, Ethan straightens and returns to his laptop. "Not much, unfortunately. I've been monitoring police scanners, traffic cams, anything I can access remotely. There's no sign of Layla anywhere. It's like she vanished into thin air."

A cold dread settles in my gut. "And the woman? The one who shot me?"

Ethan hesitates, the confusion clear in his eyes. "I don't know anything about a woman. When I found you, there was no one else there. Mr. Black, what happened in that server room?"

I close my eyes, the memories flooding back. Cassie. My daughter. Alive. The baby girl I thought I'd lost, now a creature of Morelli's creation. But Frank Morelli's dead, his life squeezed out by my hands. And Cassie has Layla.

But Ethan doesn't know any of this. How could he? I never told anyone about Cassie or my past. And now that past has come back to haunt me—to hurt Layla.

"It's complicated," I mutter, not ready to delve into that particular hell. "Just keep looking."

Ethan nods, though questions burn in his eyes. He turns back to his computer, and I force myself to stand again, gnashing my teeth against the streak of fire in my shoulder.

"What are you doing?" Ethan asks in alarm.

"Getting ready," I growl, scanning the too-bright basement for my gear. "We can't hide here forever."

I spot my go-bag in the corner, relieved Ethan had the foresight to grab it. I rummage through it, taking stock. Extra mags, a burner phone, a wad of cash. It's not much, but it's a start.

"Kaden, uh, Mr. Black, wait," Ethan says. "You can't just go charging out there. We need a plan."

I round on him, my patience fraying. "I have a plan. Find Layla, and put a bullet in anyone who gets in my way."

Ethan flinches but stands his ground. "And how exactly do you propose we do that? We have no leads and no idea where to even start looking. If we go in guns blazing, we could end up getting Layla killed."

As much as I hate to admit it, he's right. Cassie's smart; she's calculating. She'll be expecting me to come after her.

*She's my daughter.*

*She shot her own father in cold blood.*

I slump back on the couch. Each core memory is a jagged shard slicing into my heart.

I remember the day Cassie was born, how tiny and perfect she was in my arms. Her little hand gripping my finger with a strength that belied her size. I remember her first steps, her first words. The way her face would light up when I came home, her little legs running to meet me at the door.

But then the memories turn dark, twisted. The day I came home to find the house ransacked and blood on the floor. Cassie's room empty, her favorite stuffed rabbit abandoned on the bed. The frantic search, the police reports, the dead ends. The realization that my past sins had been visited upon my twelve-year-old daughter.

And what I turned myself into so I could find her.

It never occurred to me that Cassie would do something similar to survive. I can't reconcile the sweet, innocent girl I knew with the cold-eyed woman who put a bullet in my shoulder. What did Morelli do to her? What horrors did she endure to become this depraved reflection of herself?

The way Cassie smiled after she shot me, the pleasure she took in demanding Layla's life in return for mine, emboldens the voice in my head: *You failed her. You couldn't protect her. And now look what she's become.*

Cassie's bullet tore through my flesh like it meant nothing. But ... she didn't aim to kill.

"Mr. Black?"

Ethan's voice pulls me back.

"What?" I snap, harsher than I intend.

He winces but presses on. "I think I may have found something."

I'm on my feet, ignoring the stabbing pain in my right side, and walk over to Ethan's makeshift workstation. "What is it?"

"I've been trying to trace the source of the outside surveillance footage from Pulse Dynamic's building. Whoever hijacked the feed in the server room did a damn good job of covering their tracks." Ethan furrows his brow and leans closer to the screen. "But every connection leaves a trace, no matter how faint."

"Some kind of event was going on," I say, fragments of images coming together in my head as I try to recall what led up to Layla and me being cornered in the server room.

"Powerful people were there to conduct black market trades. Morelli was there, and his Mafia family always ensures their Ghost Leader doesn't leave a trace when he's present."

"So it's official. Morelli has her," Ethan concludes in a soft voice.

"No."

My denial draws his head up.

"Morelli's dead. I killed him."

Ethan's eyes widen behind his glasses. "Holy shit. Then who has her?"

I resist the urge to bow my head and allow the sheer weight of my circumstances to physically overwhelm me. "His ... successor."

Ethan turns his laptop to face me. "I've been trying to trace the digital trail. It's not much, but there's a faint signal, a sort of electronic echo."

I lean forward, ignoring the pull of my stitches.

"It's like a digital signature," Ethan explains. "Unique to the device that captured the footage—"

"I know what it is."

"Right. Of course." Ethan clears his throat. "A similar signature is bouncing off servers across the city. It's heavily encrypted, but the pattern is the same."

Hope, dangerous and fragile, blooms in my chest. "And?"

"I think I can trace it to a physical location. I'm running a decryption algorithm now."

The minutes drag by as Ethan spins the laptop to face him again, his eyes locked on the screen as he types. I pace the small room, my mind competing with itself on what could be the worst possibility, each one more grim than the last. What if Cassie's already gone underground? What if she's killed Layla? What if—

"Got it!" Ethan exclaims, his face awash in the blue glow of the screen. "The signal's coming from a place called the Siren's Call. It's a high-end nightclub downtown."

I freeze, the name sending a chill down my spine. *The Siren's Call.* I know it well. Most of Greycliff's residents believe it to be the number one way to enjoy nightlife around here, if one has deep pockets. Otherwise, they choose the only other option, a cheap dive bar nearby. But the popular nightclub is just a glitzy facade for the dark deeds that happen behind its hidden doors.

I never thought I'd have to set foot in that place again.

"Are you sure?" I ask, my voice unintentionally rough.

Ethan eyes me, alerted by my tone, and licks his lips before responding. "The, uh, encryption on the signal matches the surveillance footage from Pulse Dynamics, so ... yes?"

Unbidden, the most difficult memory of Layla surfaces. She's splayed across her bed, naked, her knees falling to the side as she exposes herself to me. Her breath skims over my skin, a fleeting warmth that pulled me from the hollow where I usually reside. Layla's golden blond hair, cascading over her shoulders, brushes against her nipples along with my fingers, and for a heartbeat, I'm anchored.

I tasted salt and skin, and it's a brand I've now marked a hundred times in memory. She was pressed against her mattress, her pussy arching for me, and I lost myself in the scent of coconut, sea salt, and *her,* in a way that it now clings to me.

My hands roamed, mapping every inch of her soft, bare

skin, every freckle and mole, claiming her with a fever I could barely temper in time. She's everything—the reason I'm breathing, the only thing grounding me. When her lips parted, soft gasps escaping, it was like a fire licked through me.

Layla's mine, yet I can't touch her enough, hold her tightly enough, to make her stay.

Instead of fucking her that night, though I desperately wanted to, I pressed her against me, fingers trailing down her spine, holding her in a viselike grip that felt like it should be impossible to break. She wasn't just with me at that moment. She imprinted on my soul, became an anchor pulling me from the brink after a decade of being lost at sea.

An anchor that broke its chain.

As Layla sinks into the opaque water of my nightmares, Cassie, barely five years old, takes her place in my head, her tiny hands clasped in mine as we walk along the misty Greycliff shoreline. It was a crisp autumn day, the kind where the air smells of burning leaves and cinnamon. Cassie danced ahead of me on the trail, her dark pigtails bouncing with each step. She wore a bright red coat, a spot of vivid color against the burnt tones of fall.

"Daddy, look!" she exclaims, pointing at a distant shape in the fog. "Is that a sea monster?"

I squint, making out the crumbling silhouette of the abandoned lighthouse on the peninsula. "No, Cassie-girl. That's just an old lighthouse."

Her blue eyes, mirrors of my own, widen with curiosity. "What's a lighthouse?"

I crouch down to her level, pulling her close. "It's a special building with a big light on top. It helps guide ships safely to shore when it's dark or foggy. But that one doesn't work anymore."

Cassie considers this. "Do you think I could give it my night-light in my room? I don't need it. I'm not scared of the dark anymore."

A lump forms in my throat at the memory, at the innocence in her voice. "I'm sure the lighthouse would appreciate that, Cass. But it's a little too big for your night-light."

She giggles, the sound pure and sweet. "Can we go see it up close sometime?"

I nod, tugging on one pigtail. "Sure thing, kiddo. We'll make an adventure out of it."

But we never did. I never took her to the lighthouse, never showed her the winding staircase or the view from the top. And now, that little girl is gone, replaced by a stranger who wants to hurt the woman I...

I shake my head, forcing the remembrance back.

Ethan taps the desk, his eyes scanning the screen. "There's something else here. Blueprints of the Siren's Call. And they're extensive."

I head over, leaning heavily on the desk. The blueprints show far more than the club's public areas. Subterranean levels snake beneath the building in a labyrinth of hidden rooms and passages.

"What the hell is all this?" Ethan mutters, zooming in.

I squint at the screen, the chill that had trickled down my spine reversing its course and spiraling back up. Ethan scrolls through the blueprints, each level revealing hidden interrogation rooms, soundproofed luxury chambers, rooms with no windows, rooms with nothing but mirrors, BDSM elements, a state-of-the-art surveillance hub... It's a fucking anthill of depravity.

Ethan's face pales. "If Layla's in there..."

He doesn't need to finish the thought. The dread settles in my gut like a lead weight. There are some things worse than death. But then something else catches my eye. A small notation in the corner of the blueprint, easily missed.

"What's that?" I ask, leaning closer.

Ethan follows my movement. "Looks like a server ID. Hold on."

Suddenly, Ethan's laptop emits a high-pitched whine. The screen flickers, and a face fills the display.

My blood runs cold.

"Hello, Daddy," Cassie purrs, her eyes—*my* eyes—gleaming with licentious joy. "Ready to play?"

# 3
## LAYLA

Cassie's fingers are like spider legs across my bruised cheek, her touch a mockery of tenderness.

She steps back, orbiting around me while I'm seated in the middle of my luxurious prison, my bare legs curled under me and my wrists freshly zip-tied. It's freezing, and my nipples are peaked under my tangle of hair, but I lost my modesty a while ago.

Cassie leans down until I'm staring into the inky-blue pools of her eyes. "Did Daddy also share how he likes to break pretty things? How he savors the sound of bones snapping beneath his hands?"

I squeeze my eyes shut, willing myself to stay present, not to get lost in Cassie's dark truth. "Why are you doing this? What do you want from me?"

She pulls back, studying me with a tilt of her head. "I want you to understand. To feel what I felt. To know the exquisite agony of being unmade and reforged in the image of a monster."

I search her face, trying to find a glimmer of the broken girl beneath this hellish creature. The cool air of the room feels heavy in my lungs.

"Cassie, I know what it feels like to feel betrayed by someone you trusted. But this—what you're doing—it won't change the past. It won't heal your pain."

Cassie's lip curls. "Healing is for the weak. I've embraced my scars and turned them into armor."

She turns away from me and paces the small room, her heels snapping like jaws against the floor. I watch her fluid movements closely, aware that at any moment, she could pivot and slap me senseless. Cassie is always impeccably dressed in long black gowns, short black cocktail dresses, or tight black bodysuits when she visits me. Her hair, the same color, is always down, cascading in waves nearly to her waist. The only color to her is her eyes—and the slash of red lipstick, brighter and cheerier than blood, yet somehow more sinister.

"What did he promise you?" she asks suddenly, turning to face me again. "How did he convince you that you were special?"

Cassie's words strike deep, unearthing memories I've fought to bury. Kaden lying beside me, his presence a comforting shield against the terrible world I'd found myself in. His touch was both commanding and gentle. He cared; I know he did. When he cooked me breakfast as the sun rose, the room filling with the aroma of sizzling bacon and freshly brewed coffee, I pictured it lasting forever.

I frown.

Is that what I thought? That on the other side of this, we'd make a home together, chat over coffee in the kitchen, and cuddle in front of the fire at night? Some of his last words to me were: *This isn't some sort of romantic adventure. I'm a killer, same as the men who broke in tonight to kill you. I was initially hired to murder you.*

"Kaden promised nothing," I finally reply. "I never needed him to."

Cassie's smile falls.

"You're a good liar," she acknowledges quietly. "But not good enough. I know exactly the kind of promises men like my father make. The kind that drips with honey and leaves you tasting your own blood at the end."

She reaches out, tracing a sharp nail along the curve of my jaw. I recoil but force myself to maintain eye contact.

"Did he whisper sweet nothings in your ear as he took you apart piece by piece? Did he make you feel cherished, adored, like the center of his twisted universe?" Cassie's voice is low and taunting. "I bet he did. Just like he did with my mother. Just like he did with every other woman foolish enough to fall for his charms."

Cassie's words should bite deeper than they do, but something in her tone makes me pause. There's an undertone of... curiosity? No. This is hungrier. Like she's probing for confirmation of a theory she's crafted about her father, not the truth of him.

"Tell me about these other women," I say carefully.

Her perfectly shaped brows lift. "Trying to be better than your competition?"

"No. Trying to understand."

"Understand what? How my father seduced and destroyed every woman he touched?" Her lip curls. "Or are you special? Different because of your spooky eyes? The one who'll *save* him?"

I don't respond. Any sort of reaction feels like stepping into a trap.

Cassie's hand returns to my face, this time gripping my jaw. "You want to understand? Fine. Let's start with my mother. Dear, sweet Angie Shaw, the war correspondent who thought she could tame the dangerous man. Sound familiar?"

She forces my chin up, her nails digging into my cheeks and reopening the scratches there. "He drew her in with that tortured look of his, didn't he? Made her feel safe even while setting off every warning bell. Protected her, cherished her, until she was drunk on his darkness."

"But Angie walked away," I say through gritted teeth. "She made her choice."

"Oh, you think that's what happened?" Cassie's laugh is sharp enough to draw more blood from my cheek. "You think she just *left*? Moved on to her war stories and forgot all about us?"

She releases my jaw, roughly pushing my head to the side, and straightens, smoothing nonexistent wrinkles from her skintight outfit. "Would you like to hear her voice?"

It takes a minute to process what she just said. "What?"

Cassie glides to an elegant side table and picks up her phone. Her black fingernail hovers over the screen. "Daddy kept all her messages. The ones she left after she realized what kind of man he truly was. After she started seeing danger in every corner of our house."

"I don't—"

A woman's voice fills the room, tinny and frightened:

*"Kaden, they're following me. Ever since that story I filed about the cartel... God, I think they know about Cassie. Please, I need—"*

Cassie cuts off the recording. "She thought running would save her. Just like you thought staying would save you."

The weight of implication suffocates me in the same way the pillowcase over my head did. "What happened to her?"

"What do you think?" Cassie's smile is all teeth. "The same thing that happens to everyone who gets too close to him. They snap. Or they disappear." She taps her phone. "Would you like to hear how she sounded at the end?"

I choke back a sob. "Why are you making me listen to this?"

"Because you need to understand what he is. What loving him does to people." She crouches in front of me, her blue eyes steady on mine.

Normally, people don't know how to stay focused on me, their gaze darting between my blue and brown eye. Not her.

"And," Cassie continues, "because I want you to help me show him what he really is."

My heart clenches at the unrestrained ache in her words, the unhealed wounds festering beneath her icy exterior, yet she gives me no time to reason with her.

Cassie's breath is cool against my face, smelling of mint and expensive wine. "Did you know he used to record me, too? Reading bedtime stories, singing little songs. He was obsessed with preserving every moment."

She tilts her head, studying me like a mortician

assessing the next corpse they must embalm. "The mighty Scythe, brought low by sentiment. All those recordings, gathering dust while I screamed in the dark. While Morelli made me record *different* kinds of messages."

I try again. "He searched for you. Kaden never stopped—"

"Looking?" Cassie's voice drops to a whisper. "Or replacing me?"

Before I can process her meaning, she stands and strides to the room's corner. A red light blinks in the shadows—a camera I hadn't noticed before. She plucks something from beside it and returns, holding up a small recorder.

"Let's play a game," she says, her lips curving. "A little father-daughter project. Since you're so *good* at taking my place."

"I was *never* your replacement."

"You live in the lighthouse he used to run past every morning, where I was *buried alive* while everyone walked overhead, searching the horizon for me instead of below ground." Each word is a precise cut. "Did he cook you breakfast there? Stand at that countertop and pretend he was still whole? Tell me, when he touched you, did you taste the guilt on his tongue?"

I lift my chin. "I won't help you hurt him."

Cassie's smile is a ragged wound. "No? Then perhaps we should send him something else. The sounds of his new love being unmade, just like his first." She leans in close, her eyes glittering. "Trust me, those screams will haunt him far longer than any sentiment could."

"I won't scream for you either." The words come out

stronger than I feel. "You can hurt me, torture me, but I won't give you what you want."

"Such loyalty." Cassie traces her fingers down my throat, a ghost of pressure that promises violence. "I had that once. The desperate need to protect him, to keep his love." Her touch turns cruel, nails piercing through my skin. "But protecting him is what ruined me. And now it's going to break you."

She releases me and moves to a sleek laptop on a nearby table. "Do you really think I need your cooperation?"

With a few keystrokes, my voice fills the room in fragments of conversations with Kaden; intimate moments pieced together into something twisted and wrong.

*"You think you mean something to me? ... Not even close.*

*"I'd rather drown than let you save me. I don't want you.*

*"Weak... just like the rest.*

*"I feel nothing for you—nothing.*

*"You bring blood, you bring death ... and for what? Nothing I want.*

*"Everything you touch ... just turns to darkness.*

*"Why would I want ... someone like you?*

*"You don't even know me.*

*"I'm not yours, and I never will be."*

My blood runs cold as I hear myself say things I never did, the words parsed together to form cruel sentences, then warped into terrible meanings. To get through it, I grasp onto the one thread of silver weaving through my horror: Cassie wouldn't be doing all this if Kaden were dead.

"Kaden will never believe it," I rasp through the thick emotion in my throat.

"Technology is remarkable," Cassie muses, too caught

up in her games to notice the gears turning in my head. "But you're right. These amateur edits are nothing compared to what I could create with some fresh material."

She turns the laptop so I can see the screen. Multiple windows show different angles of the Siren's Call—the elegant lounge upstairs, the private rooms. In one feed, masked men drag something heavy wrapped in plastic.

"My father's methods were crude. Effective, but crude." Cassie's voice takes on an instructor's tone. "Morelli, though, he taught me that true torture is art. It requires creativity. Vision." She gestures to the feeds. "And the right stage."

The door to my prison opens, and two men drag in a body wrapped in plastic. They dump it in front of me with a wet thud.

"No..."

The denial escapes me before I can stop it, covered in guttural dread.

*Kaden.*

"Don't worry, this one's already dead." Cassie nudges the plastic bundle with her toe. "But the next one ... well, that depends on you."

She crouches and unzips the plastic. The smell hits me first—decay and metal. Then I see the eerily familiar face, frozen in a silent scream.

"Remember Debbie Weber?" Cassie asks conversationally. "From your coding team at Pulse?"

The room spins. Debbie. Sweet, quiet Debbie who helped me debug my first major project. Who always remembered my coffee order when she went to fetch some for the group.

"She disappeared two weeks ago," Cassie says. "Guess she got too curious about certain projects."

Cassie zips the bag closed. "Would you like to know what we did to her first? Or should I show you? After all, you'll need to know your lines for the recording we're going to send to Daddy."

Debbie's postmortem features contort in pure agony. I want to scream the way she should be able to, horror and rage building until it's unbearable, but I swallow it down. I can't give Cassie the satisfaction.

*She's Kaden's daughter*, my inner voice whispers, reminding me that if there's still humanity in him, there must be remnants in her. It took me time and a healthy amount of determination to find the fading spark inside Kaden, struggling to hold on while he allowed the poison of vengeance to seep into his veins, blackening his soul. But it was there. I'd been able to grasp it and pull it back to the surface, that small ember of hope, to show him there is still reason to care.

I can do it with Cassie. I *must* find it in Cassie, or else I'll see the same fate as Debbie. Worse, so will Kaden.

"You think you're so terrible," I say to Cassie. "You're proud of it. But you're not."

Cassie's eyes flash with temper before she schools it behind her cool facade. "No, darling. I'm what terror creates."

She stands and gestures to the men. They haul Debbie's body away, leaving a smear of blood on the floor.

"Poor Ethan," Cassie suddenly says, her back to me as she wipes her hands on a silk handkerchief. "Always pining after you from his little cubicle. Trying so hard to be the hero." She looks at me over her shoulder. Her lips curve. "Did you know he still comes to work? Sits there pretending everything's normal while searching for you on his breaks? It's almost sweet."

Ice fills my veins. "Leave him out of this."

"Why? Because he's innocent?" She laughs. "So was Debbie. So was I."

Cassie moves to a polished brass bar cart and pours herself a drink of pricey, golden champagne. "Tell me, how do you think he'll sound when we make him scream? Will he call for you like you're going to call for Daddy?"

She lifts the crystal flute to to her lips and smirks over the rim. "Or would you rather spare him that pain?"

Cassie sashays over to me, hooking my jaw and prying my mouth open despite my struggles. She forces my head back until my neck strains, then pours the entire glass of champagne down my throat until I'm choking.

The bubbles burn as I splutter and gasp, champagne dribbling down my chin. Cassie releases me with a disgusted sigh, and I slump forward, coughing violently.

"What do you think Ethan will do when the investigators show how you used his access codes?" Cassie asks while trailing a finger around the rim of the empty flute. "When they find evidence you manipulated his credentials to access the servers after hours?"

Setting the glass down, Cassie returns to her laptop, pulling up logs. "It would destroy him, wouldn't it? Ethan's dreams of redemption after that college prank, shattered by trusting you. It's your choice, Layla. Either you confess to corporate espionage and pin it on poor Ethan..." She taps a few keys, and another window pops up, lines of damning code next to Ethan's employee ID. "Or you can record a very special message for Daddy dearest."

My mind races to uncover a solution. I can't let Cassie hurt Ethan. But I also can't give her what she wants—a confession implicating both of us in crimes we didn't do.

As if reading my thoughts, Cassie taps a few keys and another window pops up, showing lines of code. "See this? With a few alterations, I can make it look like Ethan's been embezzling funds and selling company secrets. His life would be ruined. And it would be all your fault."

I glare at her, my hands balled into fists despite the zip ties cutting into my skin.

"What'll it be, Layla?"

I sneer at her, imbuing all my frustration into that single tic in the corner of my mouth. "Neither."

Unaffected, Cassie shrugs. "Suit yourself."

She heads toward me with a vicious smile.

# 4
## KADEN

The screams pour from Ethan's laptop speakers, each one dragging a fresh razor down my spine.

*"Please..."* Layla's voice breaks on a sob. *"I can't—"*

The sound of something wet and sharp cuts her off. Her next scream holds a different kind of agony.

My fist goes through the screen, silencing the audio but not the echoes inside my skull. Glass bites into my knuckles, blood trickling onto the shattered display.

"That's not—those screams are fake, right?" Ethan's voice shakes behind me. "Someone's messing with my system right now, making us hear—"

"My daughter's doing this."

The confession tastes like charcoal.

"Your *what* now?" Ethan chokes. Papers scatter as he stumbles back. "Hold up. You have a kid? An evil tech genius kid? Because she came through some seriously encrypted channels and—" He stops, his face draining of color. "Oh

God. There are two of you. Two murderous, terrifying ... wait, how old is she?"

I yank the hard drive from the ruined laptop, my shoulder screaming in protest, but the pain is distant, meaningless.

"Twenty-two. And she learned from someone worse than me."

"Worse than—" Ethan's nervous laugh dies as another audio file starts playing from his phone now that his laptop is destroyed. Layla's whimpers fill the playroom.

I'm across the room before he can blink, yanking his phone from his pocket and crushing it under my boot.

"She's in our systems," Ethan whispers. "All of them. Like a ghost in the machine."

"Then we become ghosts, too." I move to Ethan's makeshift desk, finding the children's craft corner and unrolling a sheet of blank paper. I pluck a black crayon from a cup of them, muscle memory from another life taking over. "Tell me everything you remember about the Siren's Call's layout when you were studying the blueprints on your computer. Every exit, every service entrance."

"Service entrance?" Ethan rubs his face in thought. "Uh, there's one in back, near the kitchens. I dropped off code for their point-of-sale systems last month. Had to dodge the seafood delivery guys."

His eyes keep darting to his smashed phone like he's waiting for it to resurrect and scream again.

I press the crayon harder against the paper, letting the sharp strokes anchor me against Layla's fresh cries still ricocheting through my skull. The building takes shape under my hands—three stories of stone and glass wrapped in

Greycliff's maritime Gothic aesthetic. But I'm more interested in what lies beneath. Old buildings like this always have secrets rotting in their bones.

"What do you remember?" I demand again. "Where were the stairs located? Elevators?"

The crayon snaps in my grip.

"Just the freight elevator for deliveries. But..." Ethan's glasses fog from the hot flush of his cheeks as he leans over my shoulder. "Wait. When I was comparing the blueprints to the city records, the sub-levels should go way deeper. I remember thinking it was weird when I put them up side by side. The basement level we can access is only using, like, half the square footage."

A sound pierces the air. High and electronic, like feedback from dead speakers. We both freeze as Layla's voice filters through, but this time it's different. Intimate.

"*Tell me how he touched you,*" Cassie's voice demands.

Layla's answering whimper sends an iceberg into my veins.

"*Did his hands shake? When he wrapped them around your throat, did you feel how badly he wanted to squeeze?*"

I rear up and head to my gear bag, pulling out the burner phone responsible and throwing it against the wall. It lands between a child's stick-figure drawing of her complete family before raining down in plastic shards. The sound cuts off as abruptly as it started, leaving us in silence thick enough to choke on. But I know there will be more. Cassie's playing us like a symphony, each scream and sob a note designed to drive me closer to the edge.

"Jesus," Ethan breathes. "That's seriously your kid torturing Layla? Because she sounds like she's gunning for

Supervillain of the Year and—" He stumbles back when I turn to face him. "Right. Sorry. Not helping. I just—I'm really worried about Layla."

I force my attention back to the paper, adding details in quick, savage strokes from a red crayon this time. "The original building was a bank. Pre-Prohibition. Which means…"

"Secret tunnels?" Ethan perks up. "Like for smuggling booze?"

"Like for moving money. And now probably moving other things." I sketch in the likely routes, the paths I would use if I were setting up a criminal empire. "Cassie wouldn't waste time monitoring standard entrances. She's waiting for us to find the real way in."

"So her name is Cassie. And it's definitely a trap."

"Yes."

"And we're going in anyway."

"Yes."

Ethan slumps into the tiny chair, his knees hovering near his ears. "Cool. Cool, cool, cool. Just wanted to make sure we're on the same suicidal page here." He pushes his glasses up, smearing the sweat on his face. "Should I ask why Cassie's doing this? The whole torture-via-surround-sound thing?"

I drop the remnants of the red crayon from inside my fist. The lines on the paper have gone jagged, the potential secret tunnels looking more like slashes from a butcher knife.

"She wants me to suffer." My statement comes out low and hoarse, scraped raw, though I haven't been shouting. "And she knows the best way to do that is to make Layla suffer in my place."

Ethan goes still. "That's messed up."

I turn away, but not before catching the shift in his expression. The hint of sympathy, of pity. It burns like acid on my skin. I haven't done anything to deserve it. Not after the things I've done. The things that led Cassie to this point.

"You're carrying extra gear," I note, watching Ethan open a backpack beside him and pull out a tablet. "Destroy it."

"But what if—" He catches my look and sighs, flicking a switch on the side of the tablet. "I'm keeping the tablet, but I'll make sure it's on silent. If Cassie's in the system, maybe I can..." His fingers drum against the device. "Maybe I can track her signal or at least figure out which servers she's using."

I turn back to the crude map, memorizing the likely tunnel routes. "You think you can out-code my daughter?"

"I think..." Ethan's throat bobs. "I think Layla needs every advantage we can give her."

The honest concern in his voice hits harder than it should. I've spent years building walls, learning to shut out everything but vengeance. But Ethan's humanity keeps finding cracks, seeping through like water around stone.

"Tell me about the security systems," I say, changing the subject. "What did you notice when you had it up on your laptop?"

"Standard stuff on the surface. Cameras, motion sensors, key card readers." He pushes his glasses up again, a nervous tic I'm starting to recognize. "But there were blind spots. Big ones. Like they wanted to look secure without actually watching certain areas."

"Makes sense for a front operation." I trace one of the

theoretical tunnel routes. "They'd need ways to move product without documentation."

"Product?" Ethan's voice cracks. "You mean people? Are they—" He looks green. "Never mind. I don't want to know."

A phone starts ringing somewhere upstairs. We both tense, but it's just a standard landline. Still, Ethan's hands shake as he slips the tablet back into his pack.

"The basement level that's actually on the books," he explains, his voice tight but steady, "it's got these thick walls here and here." He points at sections of my map. "Way thicker than they need to be. Could be old vault spaces from the bank days, or..."

"Or places to hide doors that aren't supposed to exist." I nod. "Good catch."

He blinks at the praise, then frowns. "But Cassie will be expecting us to find those. She knows you'd look for hidden entrances."

"She's not just expecting it. She's counting on it." I start gathering my minimal gear, wincing when I forget about my shoulder and haul a strap over it. "That's why we're not going to use them."

"We're not?"

"No." I check my weapons, making sure everything's secure. "We're going through the front door."

"The ... what?" Ethan scrambles to his feet. "But that's insane. They'll see us coming."

"Exactly." I meet his eyes. "Sometimes the best way to spring a trap is to walk right into it—just not in the way they expect."

Understanding dawns on his face, followed quickly by horror. "Oh God. What are you planning?"

"Nothing complicated." I head for the stairs. "We're going to give my daughter exactly what she wants: a show."

"A show," he echoes weakly, hurrying to keep up. "Great. Because your family's definition of entertainment seems really healthy and not at all terrifying."

I pause at the bottom of the stairs, the weight of what we're about to do settling like spent gunpowder in my chest. "Ethan. You don't have to come."

"Yeah, I do." He straightens, steel entering his voice despite the fear in his eyes. "Layla's my friend. And friends don't let friends get tortured by psycho tech genius crime families alone."

I don't respond, but I let him see my slight nod of acknowledgment before I start up the stairs.

Behind us, the crayon map lies abandoned on the floor, its red lines looking more and more like blood spatter in the basement light.

# 5
## LAYLA

The lighter's flame dances closer to my skin. Cassie holds it with the same delicate precision she uses on her keyboards, studying how the heat makes my muscles twitch. My wrists are raw meat against the zip ties, but the pain helps. It keeps me anchored when the rest of me wants to drift away.

"You understand why I have to do this?"

Her voice is almost gentle. Blood from her last session still dries tacky between my shoulder blades, where she carved something in delicate strokes.

The wounds are precise, surgical almost, mapped across my skin like a constellation of Cassie's rage. She's been methodical, each cut and burn placed where Kaden will see them first when he finds me. If he finds me.

My arms bear the brunt of her handiwork. Long, thin slices crisscross from wrist to elbow, a macabre latticework that weeps crimson tears. Cassie has carved her initials into the tender flesh of my inner forearm, signing her masterpiece.

The burns are concentrated on my shoulders and collarbones, angry red welts in the shape of a clockface, scorching a trail of them across my skin, a mocking perversion of Kaden's tattoos.

She's left my face untouched, save for a single cut bisecting my left eyebrow. A precision strike, mirroring the scar that mars Kaden's own brow.

"He needs to hear what he left behind."

Cassie rises, the cool wind of her departure nearly causing me to weep in gratitude, and adjusts a dial on her remote. My recorded voice fills the suite through hidden speakers. The sound makes my stomach turn—not because of the agony captured in those moments, but because of how carefully she's edited them. Layered them. Built them into something worse than the truth.

I try to swallow, but it's like my throat is lined with broken seashells.

She perches on the leather armrest beside my prone form on the floor, close enough that I can smell her perfume, sweetly at odds with the dried blood under her manicured talons. My blood.

I force my head up despite the way it makes the room spin.

"You're admirable, you know." She studies me with eyes like arctic water. "You lasted pretty long. Trying to stay quiet for him, it's sweet. Misguided, but sweet."

The monitors lining one wall after she revealed them by opening a hidden panel paint us in electronic twilight. Security feeds, thermal imaging, enough screens to build a digital maze of the Siren's Call's secrets. I focus on them instead of the way my nerves keep misfiring, phantom echoes of what she's done.

I knew there was a reason I never wanted to go to this nightclub. And I'm relieved she hasn't moved me out of Greycliff. Maybe I still have a chance.

Easier than thinking about what comes next. About whether I can stay silent this time.

An alert chimes. Soft, almost musical.

Cassie goes still.

"Well." She sets the lighter aside with ceremonial care. "Right on schedule."

The main screen comes alive, and my heart stops. Not because of the security feed's grainy footage of Siren's Call's rain-slick courtyard. Not because of the armed figures moving into position, their weapons catching moonlight.

Because of the way Kaden moves through them. Like every step is a promise written in blood.

My heart stutters back to life, an aching, desperate rhythm that matches Kaden's relentless stride. He's here. He's alive. The relief is so sharp it steals my breath, a searing, bittersweet ache that lodges behind my breastbone and all the fresh cuts.

I drink in every detail of him like a woman dying of thirst. The way his broad shoulders fill out his black tactical gear, the coiled grace of his movements, lethal and precise. His raven hair is slick with rain, plastered to his forehead in jagged points that only emphasize the stark planes of his mask.

But it's his eyes that undo me. Those piercing neon eyes of his mask that seem to stare straight through the camera and into my battered soul.

"Look how handsome he is." Cassie's fingers hover over the image, not quite touching. "The way he flows between the shadows. I used to dream about it. How he'd move when he finally came for me." Her laughter holds glass edges. "Watched every security feed I could hack, studying him. Learning him. The way his shoulders set before violence. How that mask of his would hide every micro-expression most people miss when he's not wearing it."

On the screen, Kaden passes the first group of guards placed strategically around the courtyard and hidden by concrete and greenery. Their guns come up.

Cassie's voice drops to a whisper. "I could give the kill order. Right here. Right now. Unless you have something to give me."

The lighter's flame returns, close enough that my skin prickles with remembered pain. "What? What is it that you want from me?"

"Tell me how it felt," Cassie says in an almost childlike lilt. "The first time you saw what he really is. When the mask cracked and the monster showed through."

The memory floods back. Not of the killing spree inside my home, but of after. Of watching him wash brain matter from his sleeve and how his voice stayed perfectly level, even when describing exactly how he'd unmade the men who threatened me as I washed their blood from my living room floor. What he did to Dawson down in Pulse's server rooms...

"He didn't break character." The truth tastes like copper as I voice it. "That's what unnerved me. There was no mask. No monster. Just ... him."

Cassie picks up her phone from the side table, taps it a

few times, then murmurs into it. The guards' weapons waver. Lower.

"Him," Cassie repeats after she finishes with the person on the other end of the phone. Something vulnerable flashes across her face. "Yes. That's ... yes."

Kaden stands in the center of the courtyard, surrounded by her men. Their weapons gleam in the rain-scattered light from the club's high-end fixtures. I track his movement across the screen without her having to force me because I can't look away. I'm both relieved that he's here and terrified that he's come.

"Here's how this is going to work."

I don't realize Cassie's slithered closer until she traces one of the fresher burns on my shoulder, and I bite down on a cry. "You tell me which guard gets to go home. Or they all empty their magazines into the Father of the Year in the center there."

"Playing God doesn't suit you."

My voice comes out drawn but steady. The AI prototype I discovered weeks ago could play God with thousands of lives. This is just one more impossible choice.

She ignores me.

"Do you see the one on the left?" Cassie asks. She leans close. "That's Carlos. He has a daughter. She's bright. Creative. Wants to study engineering, but Daddy's salary is the only thing keeping her in school. Imagine her learning how her father died. Imagine that weight."

The guards raise their weapons while they stay hidden behind the manicured bushes and trees lining the walkway to the nightclub. Kaden's maybe twenty feet away.

"Choose," Cassie whispers. "His daughter's pain or yours?"

My throat closes. These men aren't innocent. They chose this life, chose to work for someone like Morelli, like Cassie. But their children didn't choose this.

My pulse roars in my ears. Carlos's daughter will grow up without a father, or Kaden bleeds out on rain-slick pavement. It's the same kind of choice I'm realizing Cassie forces on everyone—whose pain matters more?

The weight of lives I'll never meet presses down. Carlos checks his weapon, professional, practiced. A man who knows his job. A father who took blood money to give his daughter a better life.

I close my eyes. Open them. "The right guard. Take the right guard."

"You mean David?" She taps the screen where the guard to the right of Carlos crouches. "He has terminal cancer. About a year to live without treatment. His insurance lapsed, so he took this job because Morelli had a soft spot for cancer patients. Anyway, David has a daughter, too. Tammy's only eight." Her smile curves sharp. "You sure you want to pick David?"

I focus on the screens, filtering out her damning words and memorizing positions, calculating angles. The same analytical mind that spotted the patterns in that AI system now works to keep Kaden alive. Because that's what this is really about—the code I discovered, the one that could turn Cassie's Mafia operation into an automated nightmare. One that could predict and manipulate human behavior on a scale that would make her untouchable.

Cassie could be lying about these backstories, but she's

taking too much joy reciting their backgrounds. From what I've gleaned, this is exactly the kind of thing that gets her off.

My heart hammers against my ribs. On screen, David shifts his weight and checks his sector. A man with nothing left to lose but time.

"Yes." The concession scrapes my throat raw. "I pick David."

Her laughter spills out of her mouth like liquid mercury.

"I was hoping you'd say that." She lifts her phone. "David, advance and engage our enemy target."

David rises, weapon trained. Kaden remains statue-still, but I spot the micro-adjustments in his stance. The way his weight shifts as he registers the threat in his periphery.

"Tammy made him a get-well card yesterday," Cassie says while I force my attention to stay on the screen. "Covered in glitter. Used her allowance to buy the fancy paper."

I can't breathe. Can't think. The world narrows to the security feed, to the death warrant I've signed.

Kaden remains motionless, a dark sentinel in the heart of the courtyard. Rain sluices down his mask, his gear, but he doesn't twitch. Doesn't react. Not until David steps within range.

It happens in a blink, a blur of motion too fast for the camera to capture cleanly. Kaden moves, and then David is on the ground, his weapon skittering away across the slick cobblestones.

Kaden wrenches David's arms behind his back, a brutal hold that must be agony because David's mouth is wrenched open in a silent scream. The crack of bone follows, then the wet sound of a crushed throat. He drops without a sound, and I taste copper where I've bitten through my lip.

"Beautiful." Cassie's voice holds something like reverence. "The efficiency. The control." She lifts the phone again. "All units engage. Let's see how many more children we can orphan tonight."

I tear my gaze away from the carnage on the screen to the mutant posed beside me, a smile on her lips and a toxic glint in her eye. An innocent little girl turned into Morelli's impeccably cruel doll. I can barely make Cassie out through the welling tears, but I don't have to. I've learned enough.

Some monsters are just made.

Others are carefully, lovingly crafted.

# 6

## KADEN

Warm blood slides down my arms as I take my first step into the foyer of Siren's Call. The movement costs me. My right leg drags slightly, as evidenced by the ambush in the courtyard outside and all the men I had to take out to even make it to the doors.

They were expecting me. That much is obvious.

"Mr. Black—Scythe—are you good? All clear?" Ethan's voice crackles through my earpiece, his natural state of panic evident despite his safe distance.

I risk a single glance over my shoulder to add a visual while I answer him. "They won't be a problem anymore."

Despite the automatic weapons trained on me, these guards had too much faith that such machinery would shield them from a man with a decade-old grudge. I'd been outnumbered greater and outgunned worse many times before. The first two fell before they could even raise their rifles, throats opened in crimson smiles. Spinning low, I hamstrung the third, my knife finding the femoral artery as he crumpled. Only then did I resort to the two pistols from my thigh holsters.

Time slowed as I entered the hyper-focused flow state that activates in moments like these. My arms moved of their own accord, my wounded shoulder forgotten, lining up shot after shot with lethal precision.

*Pop. Pop-pop. Pop.*

Four guards crumpled with neat bullet holes centered between their eyes.

As the remaining eight scattered for cover, I lunged forward, rolling behind a stone pillar. Chunks of concrete sprayed as they peppered my position with blind fire. Waiting for the telltale click of empty magazines, I vaulted over the pillar's remains and closed the distance.

That's not to say they didn't get some shots in. Grunting, I force my wounded leg to bear more weight and head deeper inside.

The foyer is cavernous, all gleaming obsidian and gilded accents. A stark contrast to the rusted, salt-sprayed exterior of the building. And eerily silent now, the gunfire echo fading into memory.

I scan for movement, for the telltale twitch of finger on trigger, but only my reflection looks back at me from the polished black walls. Dozens of Kadens, all bloodstained and wary.

"Talk me through this," I say into the mic in my mask.

"Sure thing," Ethan says in my ear. "There should be a path directly ahead to the dance floor. You'll cut through there and find the private stairs to the VIP suites."

I hum my acknowledgment and creep forward, using a pistol to part the black velvet curtains directly in front of me.

When nothing darts out and shoots to kill, I slink through the fabric and into the main area.

The dance floor's empty—likely cleared for my arrival—but the strobes continue to pulse against the black lacquered floor, painting everything in stuttering shades of blue and red.

Adding to the sensory overload is a sudden blast of music, the bass pounding against my bones. I don't jump in surprise at the intrusion, but it drowns out any chance of detecting enemies. I stick close to the edges, scanning in every direction.

It's much too deserted.

"Ethan, where's the staircase?" I growl into the mic.

Static crackles in my ear, Ethan's voice breaking up. "Should be … northeast corner … signal's getting…"

The line goes dead. I tap my earpiece. "Ethan? Do you copy?"

Silence.

A cold dread settles in my gut. They're jamming the signal. Cutting me off.

I quicken my pace. Every instinct screams this is a trap, that I'm being herded, but I have no choice. Layla's here somewhere, and I'll be damned if I leave without her. The flashing lights throw jagged shadows across the walls, morphing them into phantom assailants with each strobe.

"Ethan, I need eyes," I say into the mic.

Nothing.

The music swells, distorted notes clawing at my eardrums. I rip out the useless earpiece, accepting that I'll be doing the rest alone.

Gritting my teeth against the pain lancing through my

leg and joining in with my shoulder, I press onward, pistols at the ready. The stairs should be just ahead, according to Ethan's last transmission.

Just as the northeast corner comes into view, the music cuts out abruptly, plunging the dance floor into a silence as jarring as the previous cacophony.

I pause, every muscle tensed, expecting an ambush. But the only sound is the soft scuff of my boots against the lacquered floor as I approach the ornate double doors sealing the stairway to the VIP suites' gilded carvings of mermaids. Once I push through the doors, soft, ambient lighting emanates from recessed sconces shaped like seashells, casting an eerie blue-green glow across the curving, black-carpeted staircase. Each step downward is a battle against the fire in my thigh and the ache in my shoulder, but I clench my jaw, forcing the pain into a distant corner of my mind.

The second my boot hits the first landing, I scan the dimness for movement. Nothing. Just closed doors leading to unknown rooms. Suites for Greycliff's elite and their visitors to indulge away from prying eyes.

My focus doubles back when I spot the last door on the left standing ajar. I stare at it while lowering my guns. An invitation or a trap?

Probably both.

During my killing spree to get to this point, I didn't think of Cassie. I couldn't. But here, standing on the precipice of witnessing who she's become and what she might've done to Layla, my feet turn to lead. On a silent inhale, I step toward the open door, my heart just another weight to contend with. My fingers tighten against the triggers of each pistol ever so slightly.

*I can't kill her.*

Even the thought shortens my breath. When I broke into the Siren's Call, I had one motivation, a single-minded goal: *Save Layla.*

The how of it, however...

*Save her.*

I shake myself out of it, keeping to the present. My grip tightens on the guns when I take that final step through the doorway, and my world narrows into a single point of focus.

The private suite drowns in shadows and electronic blue light from a wall of screens, broken only by rain-streaked neon bleeding through the windows. The light catches on wet patches across the floor that, at first glance, appear to be water.

Not water. Blood.

Then I see her.

Layla kneels in the center of the room, naked as the moment she was torn from my arms and brought here. The blood has dried in delicate patterns across her skin, like someone wanted me to admire their work. Her chest rises and falls in shallow bursts, but her eyes—when they find mine, the naked relief in them tears something loose in my chest.

"Kaden."

Her voice breaks on my name.

Before I can respond, another voice cuts through the space.

"Dad."

The title stops me cold. A glacial stillness takes hold,

freezing everything but my focus as Cassie's face seeps out of the shadows behind Layla, one hand tangled in Layla's hair. My daughter. My failure. She's beautiful in the way broken things can be beautiful, all sharp edges and jagged grace. The neon catches in her ebony waves, painting her in shifting shades of white and blue, making her look both younger and older than her years.

Cassie pulls until Layla's head is forced upward and her chin juts out. "I made her scream for you."

That sentence holds a familiarity that flays me open. Each word carefully chosen and precisely placed. Like the cuts decorating Layla's skin.

"Recorded every note. But you know what the best part was?" Cassie tightens her hold, and I watch Layla's cheek muscles spasm against whatever pain she's suppressing. "She tried so hard to stay quiet. To protect you. Just like I used to."

The parallel hits like a physical blow.

"Let her go."

The order comes out like a plea, stripped of everything but need.

"Layla's never hurt you. This is between us."

Layla stays perfectly still under Cassie's grip, but her eyes never leave mine. A steadiness cuts through the blood and fear—the same strength that's kept her alive through whatever hell the past days have brought.

"You want to hear something funny?" Cassie continues, her voice dropping to a whisper. "She wouldn't crack. Not really. No matter what I did."

Her hand slides to Layla's throat, cupping the front until her thumb and forefinger dig under Layla's jaw. "It's like she thought being yours would protect her. Like belonging to you meant anything."

One twitch of my finger could end this, but the pistols feel like dead weights. The cost ... Fuck, the cost.

My daughter stands in front of me, where every breath she takes is a miracle. The *thing* she's become wears my failures like a second skin.

And so, I shed the thing I've become. One gun clatters to the floor as I release my grip on it. Cassie tracks the weapon's fall with eyes of ice. Raising my free hand, I remove the mask of the Scythe and let her see the man. Her father.

"Please," I implore. "Talk to me. I'm here."

"Talk?" Cassie's voice cracks. "Like when I was seven and you explained why Mommy wasn't coming home? Or when I was twelve and Papa Morelli explained why you stopped looking?"

I close my eyes against her reference to Frank Morelli—*Papa*—unable to hide the sifting agony under my lids.

"He lied to you. I *never* stopped—"

"Or how about this." Cassie forges on. "Let's really get to know each other, all three of us. Happy little family. Oh, speaking of families, how many do you think you tore apart by becoming the Scythe?"

The silence after her question is as tangible as razor blades.

"Or would you prefer I call more of my men up here so we can watch them tear apart Layla?"

"Seventeen," I finally say. The admission falls like a stone.

"Did becoming the Scythe help you forget? All those

contracts, all that blood money… was it easier than remembering you had a daughter?"

Her question falters as she looks down at Layla. "He's so good at math. Always was. Even keeps count of his sins."

"Cassie, you can't possibly believe I would become this version of myself if I gave up searching for you."

Cassie's fingers sink deeper into Layla's scalp. Layla's nostrils start to flare.

"Want to know my count, Daddy? Want to know how many I've killed?"

Something beeps. Soft, almost subliminal. A flash of text scrolls across one of the screens behind Cassie by her elbow.

Ethan.

Through the monitors behind her, I catch glimpses of his work: security cameras going dark in sequence, emergency exits unlocking, backup systems failing. He's isolating this floor, ensuring Cassie's men can't reach us even if she calls for them. More importantly, he's making sure we'll have a way out once this ends.

I steel myself. *Keep stalling. I can still get both of them out of here.*

"None," I answer Cassie. "You haven't killed anyone. Because you knew exactly where I was. You just wanted me to suffer first."

"Ding, ding, ding!" Her laugh could shatter the window. "Give the big, scary Scythe a prize. But you're only half right." She jerks Layla's head up until it's painful. "I didn't kill anyone because Papa Morelli taught me something better. Want to see?"

My hand still holding a pistol clenches around the warmed metal.

*I can't. I won't. I can't. I must.*

Cassie releases Layla with a shove. Layla grimaces and wheezes but keeps her gaze locked on mine, like I'm offering her solace.

But Cassie grabs the back of Layla's head again, jerks it back, and graces Layla's neck with a knife this time.

"I'm going to kill her because you love her." Cassie's voice breaks on every word. "Because you looked at her and saw something worth saving. Worth protecting. Worth—"

Layla moves.

Her head snaps back, catching Cassie in the nose. The knife slides across skin but misses her artery as Cassie staggers. I'm already in motion, crossing the space between us like death given form.

But Cassie's faster than I remember. The gun I'd let fall to the floor appears in her hand like magic, leveled at Layla's head.

"Choose," she snarls through bloody teeth. "Shoot *me* and watch me die, or drop your weapon and watch *her* die."

I stop short, my pistol raised and aimed at Cassie's heart. The impossible choice robs the air from my lungs. Shoot my own daughter, or let the woman who's woken me from a deep, hollow sleep die before my eyes. Layla, who's suffered so much already, who's given me a reason to hope again. I can't lose her. I won't survive it.

But Cassie...

Layla remains still under Cassie's hold, a gun pressed to her temple. But her beautiful, mismatched eyes never waver from mine, and in them, I see her unspoken plea to do what needs to be done. Even now, even with her life on the line, she's trying to be strong for me.

My heart implodes in my chest. Cassie's finger tightens on the trigger, her eyes alight with a manic desperation. She's trembling, tears streaming down her blood-smeared cheeks, but her aim stays true.

This murderous version of her mixes with the little girl who used to fall asleep in my arms. The child who trusted me to keep the monsters at bay, never knowing we would become ones ourselves. Shooting her would be like putting a bullet through my own heart.

And that's when the idea comes.

I turn my gun, pushing the muzzle against my chest, right above my heart.

Cassie's gaze narrows as she follows the movement.

"I choose neither," I say, my voice steady despite the tremor at the base of my throat.

Shock flickers across her face before it hardens into a sneer. "Do you think I won't pull the trigger and make her die on your corpse?"

"I know you will."

I take a step forward, the gun pressing harder against my chest to hide my trembling grip. "And I know why. Because I failed you, Cassandra. In every way a father can fail his daughter. I wasn't there to protect you."

Her hand shakes, the muzzle of her gun wavering against Layla's temple. "You don't get to do this. To make this about you."

"But it is about me. It always has been. My failures, my sins, my inability to save the ones I love most." I chance a glance at Layla, apology and regret bleeding from my stare. "I thought becoming the Scythe would help me find you, would give me the power to bring you home. But all it did was turn me into the very thing I was trying to destroy."

"Shut up." Her fingers flex around the gun. Layla's rapid breaths syncopate with my pounding heart. "You don't get to—you can't just..."

"I can," I say softly, my own voice rough with unshed tears. "Because it's the truth. I let vengeance consume me, let it twist me into someone I didn't recognize. Someone who couldn't see past his own pain." I take another step, the gun digging into my chest until I feel it rubbing against bone. "But I see you now, Cassie. I see my little girl, hurting and lost. And I am so, so sorry."

A single tear slips down her cheek, catching on a scar at the corner of her mouth. A scar I should have prevented.

"It's too late," she whispers, but there's a waver in her voice, a hairline fracture in her cold facade. "You can't fix this with pretty words."

"I know." I hold her gaze steady, letting her see the sincerity, the bone-deep remorse. "I let them take you. I let them hurt you in ways no child should ever be hurt."

Tears stream freely down Cassie's face now, landing on the top of Layla's head and soaking through the dirtied blond strands. It kills me not to look at her, not to include her in this and reassure her somehow, but I have to stay on Cassie. *She has to drop the gun.*

"I hate you," she whispers.

"And I'll never forgive myself. But Cassie, this path you're on, this darkness you've embraced ... it won't heal the wounds inside you. Trust me, I know."

Cassie's face contorts, tears and blood smearing

together as a sob wracks through her tall, slight frame. *Fuck, she's grown so much...*

I'm so wrapped up in the heartbreak of her that I miss her eyes darkening, the storm building behind the blue.

"Papa showed me the truth. That love is a lie, a weakness to be toyed with." She presses the muzzle harder into Layla's temple, making Layla sob. "He taught me how to turn it into a weapon."

It takes all my willpower to fight the urge to lunge for the gun. One wrong move and someone's blood will paint the walls. And I don't want anyone here to bleed.

"Cassie, listen to me. Whatever Morelli told you, whatever he did, it was wrong. He poisoned everything good and pure inside you."

"No!" she shrieks, the sound bouncing off the walls. "He made me strong. He showed me my true potential." Cassie then flicks her attention to Layla, a cruel smile curling her lips. "Just like I'll show you."

Denial wrenches from my throat at the same time Cassie shifts the gun and slams the butt of it against Layla's head.

Layla crumples to the floor, her body going limp after the pistol connects with her skull. A ragged shout tears from my throat as I surge forward, desperate to reach her.

But Cassie moves like a viper, all lightning speed and venomous grace. She becomes the apprentice other criminals whisper about, the ones who fear both her intelligence and viciousness. The one who Morelli groomed himself.

She sidesteps my charge and brings her knee up into my stomach, driving the air from my chest. I stumble, wheezing, but manage to catch her wrist as she aims the gun at my head and tries to shoot. We grapple for control, our faces inches apart. Her eyes blaze with a feral intensity, the madness of a caged animal finally set free.

"Cassie, please," I rasp, my fingers digging into her skin. "Don't do this."

She snarls, baring bloodstained teeth. With a burst of strength, she wrenches her arm free and reverses our positions, slamming me back against the wall. Stars explode across my vision as my head cracks against the concrete because I let her. I can't retaliate the way I normally would. I won't.

"You still don't get it, do you?" she hisses, pressing the gun under my chin. "I'm not your little girl anymore."

"Cassandra Black." I try again, my voice strained. "That's who you are. Who you'll always be."

She digs the gun barrel deeper into my flesh. The pain radiating from the back of my skull wars with the ache in my chest, both physical and emotional.

Cassie laughs then. "Black? Like the family we never were?"

Her free hand comes up to grip my jaw, her sharpened nails biting through stubble and into flesh. "You really are pathetic, clinging to this fantasy that you can save me, like there's anything left to save."

I swallow against the pressure on my throat, against the truth in her words. "There's always something left to save."

My fatal mistake comes before I can stop it. I let my eyes wander, allowing them to land on Layla's unconscious form on the floor, blood trickling from the gash on her temple and staining her hair crimson.

Cassie notices it, her expression transforming into cold fury before a humorless laugh escapes her lips. "Oh, Dad. Convincing yourself that you're the hero trying to save the princess when you're the story's villain. But this isn't your little girl's fairy tale. Layla isn't your light to guide you home. This is a nightmare, and I'm not letting you wake up."

I force myself to face the hatred and betrayal blazing in those ice-blue eyes that once looked at me with such love and trust. "Cassie, I—"

But before I can finish, she moves with a speed that defies logic. In a blur of black and crimson, she slams the butt of the gun against my head, and an explosion of pain blooms behind my eyes.

I tilt sideways, the room swaying as I fight to stay on my feet. Cassie takes advantage of my disorientation, driving her knee into my groin and making me double over in a painful whoosh of remaining oxygen.

Gasping, I buckle, my vision swimming. Through the haze of agony, I see Cassie step over my body, her heels clicking against marble as she approaches Layla's unmoving body.

Cassie looms over Layla, her form wavering and splitting into multiples. The gun dangles loosely from her fingers. She crouches down, bringing her face level with Layla's.

"I win, Daddy," she says as she trails a finger down Layla's cheek.

*This isn't a game to me,* I thought I could say, but I can't move my lips.

I try to reach for her, for them both, but my vision is failing.

Paralyzed by the insidious pull of unconsciousness, I blink once, twice, helpless as Cassie hovers over Layla.

Then everything goes dark.

# 7
## LAYLA

Returning to consciousness is like drowning in reverse, each forced breath a new way to suffer. Each heartbeat is a hammer to my skull. Something cold presses against one cheek—the floor—except for one spot that feels wrong. Warm and wet.

Moving sends lightning bolts through my closed lids, so I force my muscles to relax while trying to piece together where I am and what happened.

Sound comes next, distorted like I'm underwater. A steady hum somewhere to my left. My own threadbare breathing. But there's another sound, barely there. Another set of exhales, slow and uneven.

I'm not alone.

The effort to open my eyes costs more than it should. The world blurs, then sharpens in pieces. Dark wood panels. Brass fixtures gone green with artistic age. A massive desk that looks like it was carved from shipwrecks. Details from before I blacked out, when this was just another opulent torture chamber in Cassie's private quarters.

*Cassie. Kaden's daughter. The Siren's Call suite.*

*Kaden.*

*KADEN.*

The irregular breathing comes again, closer than I thought. I force my head to turn, fighting the wave of nausea brought on by the movement.

My heart stops.

Kaden lies crumpled on the floor beside me, his face turned away. Still. So still.

Any tactical gear he wore is gone. The feared Scythe is as naked as I've ever seen him—maskless in a black T-shirt, cargo pants, and bare feet.

I dig my nails into the carpet, dragging myself onto my elbows despite the extreme desire to lie down and go back to sleep. Blood oozes down the side of my face, hot and sticky, from where Cassie's blow sent me crashing to the floor. The room tilts and spins as I stagger to my feet, nearly losing my balance.

But I can't stop. Not when Kaden lies there so still, his chest barely rising with each shallow breath.

I half stumble, half shuffle to him, not trusting my legs to hold me up. Glass crunches under my bare feet from the shattered decanter that must have toppled during Kaden and Cassie's confrontation, but I hardly feel the sting. All I can focus on is reaching him.

His name escapes my lips in a hoarse whisper, my voice foreign to my own ears. Frankly, I'm shocked I've retained the ability to use it after days upon days of screaming.

"Kaden," I rasp again, collapsing to my knees beside him and ignoring the jolt it sends through my weary body.

But it's all I can do. With my hands still tied behind my back, I can't touch him. I'm stopped from feeling for injuries and checking for a pulse. And because of that, a quiet, keening wheeze soaks my lips, along with tears that should've dried up weeks ago.

Lowering my head, I rest the side of my face against his chest and hear a steady heartbeat. My shoulders sag, and I sob, staying there, soaking up his warmth and proof of life.

Time stretches, marked only by the thud of Kaden's heart against my ear and the tattered symphony of our breathing. But then, in a burst of movement too quick for my damaged reflexes, Kaden surges to life.

His eyes snap open, wild and feverish, pupils blown wide. I have enough time to lift my head and softly call out his name again before he surges forward, seizing me by the shoulders and slamming me onto my back, my tied hands crushed under the press of my body weight. Air whooshes from my mouth as he pins me with his body, one dirtied, bloodied hand clamping around my throat.

Kaden snarls above me, his eyes empty, all traces of the man I trust consumed by the instinctual killer within. His fingers tighten, seconds from crushing my trachea, and a vicious thrill slithers through me.

Because even like this—feral, brutal, reduced to his basest nature—he's magnificent. Strands of his raven hair fall across his brow, and beads of sweat glisten above the taut lines of his face. His full lips are pulled back in a vicious snarl, revealing the glint of white teeth. The scar slicing through his brow to his cheek has turned a mesmerizing purple-white.

A traitorous part of me wants to lean into his violence, to let it consume me until I forget the nightmare we're trapped in.

He's a fallen angel, a dark, avenging spirit, and at last, I have my escape. I'm ready to succumb.

I can't. I shouldn't. Because if I go, I'm leaving Kaden alone, and he's been so stripped of life for so long.

"Kaden," I command in a tight, strangled voice. "It's me. It's Layla."

His fingers flex around my throat, digging into the mottled canvas of healing bruises and fresh contusions on my skin. The pressure builds until gray fuzz rings my vision.

Then awareness crashes over his expression between one labored breath and the next. His hand retreats from my neck as if scalded, leaving me coughing on flakes of dried blood and built-up saliva.

"Wraithling?" He chokes out my pet name. "Jesus, I could have—"

"I'm okay," I reassure him quickly, even as I cough, my abused windpipe protesting the words. "I've gone through worse."

Kaden rises to his knees, one on either side of my hips. His eyes widen as he takes in the sight of me splayed underneath him. I can only imagine what he sees.

A patchwork of particolored bruises in sickening shades of purple and yellow, angry red lacerations crisscrossing my skin, dried blood peeling off in rust-colored patches.

Cracks of anguish break through his stone expression as

he reaches out, his hands hovering over the injuries to my chest as if he's afraid to touch me and cause more damage.

"Layla." His voice shatters on my name. "What has she done to you?"

"Nothing I couldn't survive." I taste the tang of blood on my tongue as I respond. "I'm still here, Kaden. I-I didn't break."

The golden lamplight casts harsh rays across the planes of his face, accentuating the hollows of his cheeks and dark circles under his eyes. Those coldwater eyes shine before he blinks the emotion away.

It hurts to look at him, too, so I shift my weight and wince, my hands tingling with lack of blood flow.

Kaden notices. His brows come down, a line forming between them like a mark between heartache and fury. "Can you roll to your side?"

Nodding stiffly, I roll with the help of my legs and a hiss between my clenched teeth.

He seeks out the plastic restraints on my wrists, and I can't help but shiver at his touch, his rare tenderness.

With a low grunt, Kaden manages to slip his fingers beneath the zip tie, his short nails scraping against my raw skin. He works at the plastic with single-minded determination, his brows keeping low.

After several agonizing moments, the pressure around my wrists suddenly releases with a soft snap. I fall onto my back and bring my arms forward with a grateful sob, my biceps protesting the unfamiliar motion. Pins and needles shoot under my skin, circulation returning in a painful rush.

"Th-Thank you."

It takes so much effort to say it through the swell of relief.

"Your gratitude is nothing I deserve," he murmurs as he shifts his weight off me, his breath stalling as he lifts his injured leg.

I shake my head, denying the subtext that this is his fault, not trusting myself to speak past the lump in my throat. Instead, I watch as Kaden remains on his knees and shrugs out of his T-shirt, gripping the collar and peeling it up and over his head in one smooth motion. A lifetime of conditioning allows him to power through the discomfort.

I can't help but stare, transfixed by the shift of his muscles beneath his olive skin. His sculpted chest is a work of art, all hard planes and ridges, decorated with scars and tattoos. A dangling square of gauze barely holds on at his shoulder, revealing the puckered, starburst wound he received from Cassie's bullet. There's another thin, precise line curving around his ribs, too clean to be anything but a knife. And a jagged gash across his right pectoral, angry, red, and recent. But what calls to me the most is the smattering of dark hair trailing down from his navel and disappearing into the waistband of his pants.

I'm prevented from losing any remaining saliva I have left by drooling when Kaden holds the shirt out to me, his expression unreadable, save for his eyes holding on to mine.

"Here," he says, his voice rough. "Put this on."

Rising into a pained sit, I reach for the offered garment with a trembling hand, my fingers brushing against his. The contact is electric, improper in this environment yet refusing to leave. I clutch the shirt to my chest, the fabric still warm from his body heat.

Averting my gaze, I slip my arms into the sleeves, ignoring the scream of my newly freed muscles at the movement. The collar catches on a gash across my cheekbone, and I wince, a small sound escaping through my teeth.

Kaden's hands are there in an instant, his touch gentle as he helps guide the shirt over my head until it pools at my thighs.

"Thank you," I whisper once more.

I'm not just thanking him for the shirt, and he knows it.

His jaw clenches, and he gives a curt nod instead of denying the gratitude this time, his eyes raking over me and cataloging every remaining visible injury.

I pull the sleeves as low as they can go and wrap my arms around myself, savoring the sensation of being clothed and shielded from the voyeuristic gazes of Cassie's men.

It wasn't always Cassie who visited this room. Sometimes she'd send others to shove a water bottle against my lips, tilting it so most of it streamed down my chin instead of going in my mouth. A few would leer, quipping that soon it would be their cum dribbling down my face when they finished fucking my mouth.

It never happened. I'm grateful for not having to endure such indignity, but to be *grateful* to anyone in this situation messes with my mind, with what is good versus what's terrible. I'm experiencing shades of gray I never thought possible.

Kaden doesn't look away, watching every thought play across my face. Not once does he break his stare despite the clear effort it's taking to control his expression.

"I'm getting you out of here," he vows.

He pushes to his feet with a grunt and prowls around

the suite, his weight distributed unevenly to avoid aggravating his injuries. The corded muscles of his back ripple beneath his skin, and I swallow.

Leave it to Kaden to quench my thirst when I've been nothing but parched for days. I don't miss the chance to drink him in.

His keen gaze sweeps over every inch of the space, searching for any weakness, any chance at escape.

The walls are a rich, dark wood, polished to a high shine that reflects the light from the antique lamps and sconces. Intricate carvings of sirens and sea monsters dance along the edges of his fingers as he tests for hidden catches or loose panels but comes up empty.

I want to tell him I've shuffled around this room what seems like hundreds of times, and though I didn't have the freedom of my hands, it didn't take long to become certain Cassie wouldn't leave me in a room with an escape hatch. But after an eternity of staring at nothing but this suite or Cassie's cold face or sneering men, watching Kaden's defensive skills and the grace with which he moves is nothing short of a gift.

He moves to the windows next, floor-to-ceiling panes of glass that offer a breathtaking view of the town's skyline. The lights of Greycliff twinkle like fallen stars against the inky black of the night sky, and the distant sound of waves crashing against the cliffs is a mocking reminder of the freedom that lies just out of reach. Kaden tests the locks, the hinges, even the glass itself, but it's all reinforced and impenetrable.

Frustration emanates from him in palpable waves as he stalks to the far side of the room. But then he pauses, his posture going rigid. I follow his gaze to see what caught his attention. A door, nearly hidden in the intricately carved wall paneling.

He glances back at me.

I answer the question in his eyes. "The bathroom."

Quickly, I break our connection, staring at the carpeting beneath my feet. On occasion, I was dragged into that decadent en suite, shoved into the shower, and sprayed down like an animal with ice water. Other times, I was pushed onto the toilet and told to relieve myself on command. At first, it was difficult, the humiliation so much that my bladder refused to comply. But it didn't take long to overcome once necessity overtook dignity.

Kaden studies my face for a long moment, reading the unspoken trauma behind my features. His jaw clenches, a muscle ticking beneath the surface before he takes a deliberate step toward me.

"Wraithling," he says softly, his velvet baritone caressing my name. "Come here."

My throat constricts, but slowly, I get to my feet.

His large, calloused hand engulfs mine as he leads me to the bathroom.

I know what's behind that door. The bathroom's luxury feels like another form of mockery now. Veined marble in deep greens and golds that I've studied through tears, memorizing patterns while fighting to keep my composure during "supervised visits." The massive soaking tub dominates one wall, its brass faucets shaped like siren heads, their patina matching the oxidized sconces. The shower spans an entire wall behind heavy glass etched with scenes of storms and shipwrecks. Fitting since that's where Cassie's men held me under the spray until I couldn't breathe. Even the heated floor was cruel, its warmth seeping into my bare feet while I waited for the shivering to stop.

Everything in there speaks of wealth and comfort, but all I can envision is another room where Cassie turned luxury into a weapon.

"Layla," Kaden prods gently beside me. "It's all right now."

He squeezes my hand while he swings the door open.

The shower draws my eye first—all those multiple rainfall showerheads pelted me like frozen bullets. But...

Kaden turns the faucet until steam curls invitingly from the fogged panes.

He draws me closer, his touch impossibly gentle for hands that render so much violence. "The water's warm. And you're shaking."

"I don't know if I can..."

My voice pitches, the admission burning my throat.

His fingers thread through mine, steady despite the bruises and cuts on them.

"You're safe with me."

With infinite care, he helps me shed his shirt, his touch lingering on each new expanse of skin revealed. I tremble, though not from cold, as his fingertips graze the curve of my shoulder and the swell of my breast.

He sheds his own pants efficiently, uncaring of his own nudity. I can't help but take another drink. His body is incredible, my dark warrior god made into flesh.

Kaden guides me into the spray, his hands never leaving me.

I stop when my head is under the warm water, the water

sluicing over my skin, turning pink as it swirls down the drain as the grime and blood wash away.

Kaden reaches for a bottle of shampoo—an incongruously delicate glass flacon I was never allowed to touch—and pools a measure into his palm. With tender fingers, he works the lather through my matted hair, careful of the tangles and tender spots on my scalp. I lean into his chest, my eyes fluttering closed as a sigh escapes my lips. The scent of sandalwood and amber envelops us, chasing away the lingering odors of blood and hurt and fear.

He guides my head back under the spray, his hand cupping my neck to shield the soap from my eyes as he rinses my hair clean. I keep my eyes closed, focusing only on the sensation of him against me and the heat of the water comforting us both.

When he's satisfied my hair is rinsed clean, Kaden reaches for a washcloth and a bar of creamy soap. He works up a rich lather before smoothing the cloth over my skin in long, soothing strokes. It's so needed that I ignore the sting of soap against my cuts.

Starting at my shoulders, he drags the cloth across my collarbones and down over the swells of my breasts. I shiver as he circles each nipple, the rough fabric a delicious contrast to his gentle touch. He continues down my stomach, tracing the ridges of my abused ribs and the hollow of my navel.

I hold my breath as he sinks to his knees before me, the washcloth skating over the V of my hips and the tops of my thighs.

Logical Me knows he's not doing this for pleasure, that Kaden just wants to soothe and wash away what trauma he can, but when he looks up at me through a veil of wet lashes, his blue eyes molten, all I want is him. The tenderness in his touch ignites something deeper than our circumstances, something that makes me forget where I am.

His fingers still against my thigh.

"Wraithling."

My name comes out as both a warning and a question wrapped in need.

# 8

## LAYLA

"Please." I thread my fingers through Kaden's wet hair as he kneels before me in the shower. "It's been so long. Make me feel something else. Something that's just us."

He presses his forehead against my pelvis, breathing hard. "This isn't why I—"

"I know."

And I do. He wanted to wash away cruelty and nothing more. "But I need you."

His grip tightens, but his forehead still rests against me like I'm something precious.

"You deserve better than this," he says as water pools at his collarbone. "Better than a desperate fuck in a gilded cage."

"I deserve you," I tell him, my voice unwavering despite the slight tremor in my fingers when I lay them on his shoulders. "I deserve this moment with you, no matter where we are."

Slowly, deliberately, he turns his head and presses a searing kiss to the inside of my thigh.

In response, I guide his hand between my legs and push his fingers between my folds, wet for him well before we entered the shower's rainfall.

With a groan, Kaden takes control, delving deeper. I whimper at the first electric touch against my aching clit, my head falling back.

He strokes me with devastating precision, winding me tighter and tighter at the base of my spine.

"Fuck," he curses, his breath hot against my skin. "I'm not supposed to want this right now."

My fingers tighten in his hair as his mouth replaces his fingers, his tongue flicking over my sensitive flesh with maddening skill. Pleasure coils tighter, my thighs trembling against his shoulders.

"You're allowed to want," I manage to gasp out. "I want it too. I want you."

He groans, and the vibration nearly undoes me. My knees threaten to buckle, but his strong hands grasp my hips, holding me upright as he devours me.

"Kaden, please..." I'm so close, my voice a desperate whine. I'm vaguely aware that we shouldn't linger, that danger still lurks beyond the false sanctuary of steam and tile. But I'm lost in paradise and don't want to find my way home.

"That's it," he coaxes as I writhe against his fingers, his lips, his tongue. "Let me feel you come."

I shatter with a broken moan, my inner muscles clenching on emptiness when he removes his fingers.

I'm just about to mourn the loss when he surges to his

feet. I melt against him, reveling in his taste, his scent, the sleek slide of his wet skin against mine. His hands map the contours of my body, igniting pleasure in their wake.

I gasp as he lifts me effortlessly, pinning me against the cool marble wall while the drowning sailors of sinking ships look on and the sirens scream in victory.

My legs wrap around his waist, drawing him closer until his hard length is notched at my entrance.

"Kaden," I say through my pants, "your leg. You shouldn't lift me—"

Kaden nips and sucks down the column of my throat, lingering over my racing pulse. "You think I want to feel anything less than the agony you carry? Let me take the pain. Your body might protest, but mine begs for the burden."

Water sluices down the small spaces between us as he presses his forehead against mine.

"I need you," he rasps, echoing my earlier words. "I've never needed anything the way I need you."

In answer, I roll my hips, taking him inside me inch by delicious inch. We groan in unison at the exquisite way he splits me open.

"Layla." My name is a sibilant brand on his tongue. "Are you sure?"

"I'm sure," I tell him, my fingers digging into his shoulders.

Something flashes in Kaden's eyes then—something fierce and feral and utterly centered on me. He begins to move, driving into me with deep, powerful strokes that send sparks skittering down my nerve endings.

With our bodies slick from the shower and our shared

need, Kaden claims my mouth in another scorching kiss that leaves me happily drowning like those sailors.

His tongue delves deep, demanding entrance that I grant eagerly. He tastes of desperation and desire, of things long denied finally being seized.

My wet heat slides along his rigid length, eliciting a throaty groan from deep in his chest. His hands tighten on my thighs, digging into my flesh hard enough to leave marks. More reminders that this is real, that we're together despite everything conspiring to keep us apart.

"Please," I beg against his lips.

A fractured moan escapes my throat as he fills me to the hilt, our bodies joined as closely as two people can be. He stills, giving me a moment to adjust to his considerable size. His forehead finds mine again, our thready breaths mingling in the scant space between our lips.

"Layla," he rumbles, his voice strained with the effort of holding back. "You feel ... fuck, you're perfect."

I answer him with another roll of my hips, urging him even deeper. He curses, low and harsh, his control snapping.

"Forgive me for what I'm about to do to you," he says hoarsely. "I want to treat you like glass, but there's nothing soft left in me. The Scythe took me over a long time ago—" His eyes rake over my bruised body curled around him. "And he doesn't know how to be gentle."

He begins to move then, pounding into me with a sudden, primal ferocity that chokes my breath. The slap of wet skin against skin echoes obscenely in the marble shower, punctuated by my increasingly desperate cries.

Kaden sets a brutal pace, his hips snapping forward relentlessly as he drives himself deeper, harder, faster. It's almost too much, the line between a good ache and a bad ache—those shades of gray—blurring until I can't tell one from the other. But I don't want him to stop. I never want him to stop.

The cool tiles at my back contrast deliciously with his body's fiery heat and the spray's blanketing warmth.

Steam billows around us, adding to the dreamlike quality as we lose ourselves in sensation—the slick slide of skin, the sting of nails dragging over goosebumped flesh, and the sparks traveling along my nerves.

The room I hated so much and now love.

I hold on, nails scoring angry red lines down the flexing muscles of his back as I encourage him with wordless cries and pleas for more, harder, faster.

The whirlpool low in my belly circles tighter with every thrust, every brush of his dick against my aching clit.

"Yes," I keen, my head thrown back against the wall as I give myself over to the exquisite agony of his possession.

The sharp sting of water against fresh wounds is soothed by his hips, slowing the slide against my sensitive flesh until I'm keening, my head thrashing against the wall. Then a powerful thrust hits that perfect spot inside me, stoking the flames.

He snarls, baring his teeth against my throat before biting down hard enough to mark. I cry out, my body bowing into his touch, silently begging for more. Always more. He gives it to me without hesitation, one hand releasing my thigh to palm my breast roughly. He rolls my nipple between his fingers, tugging just shy of too hard.

"You're mine," he rasps, punctuating each word with a

sharp thrust that makes me see stars. "No matter what happens next, you will always be mine."

Tears prick my eyes, the salt mingling with the rivulets of water streaming down my face. "I'm yours. My heart is yours."

Something raw and broken twists his features at my declaration, and his rhythm falters for a beat before redoubling in intensity. He kisses me again, devouring me like a man starved. I match him with equal fervor and pour every ounce of my love, my lust, into the clash of our mouths.

"That's it, Wraithling," he praises. "Let me feel you come apart on my cock."

"Kaden," I pant, my body straining against invisible bonds. "I'm going to ... I can't..."

"Let go, Layla," he commands. "I'll catch you. I will always fucking catch you."

With a crushing sob, I come apart in his arms, my inner muscles clamping down on him like a vise.

That's all the encouragement he needs. As the shower rains down on us, Kaden follows me over the edge with a guttural shout, shuddering as he spills himself deep inside me.

We stay locked together as we come down, our hearts gradually slowing from their frantic gallop. Kaden peppers gentle kisses across my face, my neck, my shoulders.

"I thought I lost you," he says against my clavicle.

The water trickles to a stop as Kaden guides us away from its warmth. He sets me down gently, his hands lingering on my waist as if reluctant to let go. Just as reluctant, I trace the paths of water droplets on his chest, sliding down to where scars and cuts crisscross his skin.

Kaden's thumb brushes my cheekbone, drawing my head up. Our breaths mingle in the steamy air, forming gossamer threads of three unspoken words, the scariest ones of all.

*I love you.*

I said them to Kaden before I was taken, pressing the meaning into his lips before being torn away from him. He didn't say them back, and I don't think it was because our time was cut short. Even now, after everything we've shared, after the reverence he showed my body, those words remain locked behind his walls.

I understand. Love is a liability he can't afford. But understanding doesn't stop the ache.

Those words sit heavy on my tongue again, but I force them back. This isn't the time, not with his lost daughter's rage waiting beyond these walls.

"We should dry off," Kaden says, his hand falling from my cheek.

I nod, reluctant to break the spell he's cast but aware of its fragility. As we step out, I commit every detail to memory—the slick tiles beneath my feet, the way Kaden's hair clings to his forehead, and the lingering warmth of his skin against mine. I'll hold on to it when the horrors start again, when I'm desperate for something good amid all this agony, because I'm certain Cassie's not finished with us.

Kaden wraps a plush towel around my shoulders before securing another at his hips.

I pull the soft cotton around my body, seeking its comfort now that I'm not wrapped around Kaden, but the moment of respite shatters as my eyes land on the floor where Kaden's pile of clothes should be. I scan the bathroom in a panic while the steam clears—like they might've just wandered off to another room by themselves—before landing on Kaden. His gaze has also sharpened, not on the area where his clothes should be, but beside the vanity where two silk robes are strategically placed—one red, one black.

"Kaden…"

His jaw clenches as he stares at the robes. "I know."

Someone was here while we were lost in each other. This moment was stolen from me, just like so much else. Nausea rises in my throat at the thought of unseen eyes on my bare skin, of my vulnerability on display.

I flinch when Kaden's hand lands on my shoulder, hating myself for the reaction even as I lean into his touch, craving his steadiness.

"Layla," he says, turning me to face him. "We'll figure this out. I won't let her hurt you."

*Her.* His daughter. The reminder that Cassie has orchestrated this nightmare sends a fresh shudder coursing through me. I can't imagine the additional layer of horror Kaden must be feeling to have his own flesh and blood violating his privacy, his intimacy.

But he pushes it down, his focus solely on me as he rubs soothing circles on my back. "Our choice is to put them on or stay in the towels."

"Don't forget the third option," I say, trying for a joke, though my voice shakes. "We can always stay naked. It's nothing they haven't seen before."

My joke falls flat.

With grim determination, Kaden moves closer to examine the robes. He lifts the smaller red one first, checking seams, pockets, anywhere something could be hidden for the purpose of hurting me.

Only when he's certain it's safe does he help me into it, the silk cool and slippery against my skin. The exquisite fabric is no doubt expensive, but it feels like a mockery of comfort, my gilded cage closing in.

Kaden ties his robe with efficient motions, his eyes never leaving me as I fumble with my own belt, my fingers clumsy and trembling. He steps closer, gently brushing my hands aside to secure the knot himself. The simple act of care splinters something in me, and I sag against him, burying my face in his chest.

His arms come around me instantly, strong and solid.

"I've got you," he murmurs into my hair. "I'm not going anywhere."

I want to believe him, but fear claws at my insides, diabolical whispers filling my head. Nowhere is safe. She's always watching, always one step ahead. How can we fight an enemy that knows our every move? An enemy whom Kaden *loves* with every fiber of his being?

As if sensing my spiraling thoughts, Kaden cups my face, tilting my head up to meet his gaze.

"One second at a time, Wraithling. That's all we can do. We survive this second, then the next. Together."

*Together.* The word is a lifeline.

Clinging to Kaden's promise, I take a deep breath and nod. Hand in hand, we step out of the bathroom to face whatever fresh hell awaits me.

Only to stop short at the scene laid out in front of us.

# 9
## LAYLA

The suite has been transformed. Where before it was a sort of luxury-chic torture chamber, it now resembles a perverse parody of a romantic date.

A table set for two sits in the center of the room, draped in a crisp white tablecloth and adorned with gleaming silver and delicate china. Crystal wineglasses catch the light from dozens of flickering candles scattered throughout the space.

A rolling cart sits beside the table, bearing covered dishes that waft tantalizing aromas that my stomach will tear through my skin to access.

But the romantic veneer is tainted, perverted. The candles are a deep, arterial red, their wax dripping like blood down the sides. The wine in the glasses is such a dark burgundy it's nearly black. And the china, upon closer inspection, is adorned not with the typical floral patterns but with writhing, tortured figures.

I gulp at the sight.

This isn't a gesture of care or apology. It's a thinly veiled threat.

Kaden's hand tightens around mine as he surveys the room, his posture rigid and eyes sharp. Tension wafts from him, every muscle primed and ready to strike.

He's in full soldier mode now, hyperaware and assessing each new element in our surroundings.

Kaden's gaze lands on the bed and narrows. I follow his line of sight, and my breath catches.

The covers are turned down invitingly, rose petals scattered across the silk sheets. But strewn among the petals are glossy photographs. From this distance, I can't make out the images, but a sense of foreboding streaks down my spine.

Kaden releases my hand to approach the bed. He lifts one of the photos, examining it closely, and his already severe expression hardens further. Wordlessly, he hands it to me as I come up beside him.

It's a surveillance shot of me. I'm walking down Main Street, my hair whipping in the wind and a distracted expression on my face. Based on my outfit, it was taken in the spring long before Kaden—or Cassie—entered my life. The realization that she's been watching and gathering information for so much longer than I thought sends a violent shiver through me.

With mounting dread, I pick up another photo. This one shows the Scythe and me in the forest, our first encounter, standing close and engaged in an intense conversation. My eyes are locked on his through the mask, my infallible attraction to him written all over my face and captured in high definition.

Kaden snatches up another photo, pressing so hard, the

pads of his fingers turn white. It shows me pinned against the railing at the top of the lighthouse, Kaden's hand around my throat, just before he pushed his fingers inside me. The angle is taken from the beach below, capturing the exact instant my body curved into his touch rather than away from the threat of falling.

Cassie had witnessed my surrender to him and seen how quickly I gave myself over to the man who was supposed to be my killer.

Kaden's fingers dig into the photo's edges. He'd been so certain of his control that night, forcing my submission while holding me over the railing. Yet Cassie also documented his first taste of weakness for me.

Another photo reveals the moment Kaden saved me from being hit by a car in the fog before I knew him as the Scythe. His powerful frame yanks me back, our bodies colliding with the pavement. Even through the mist, you can see the instant connection between us—my fingers clutching his arm, my startled gaze meeting his scarred face for the first time.

I glance at one more photo, one of Reaper sitting on my bedroom's windowsill at the lighthouse keeper's cottage, staring directly down the lens of the camera where she must've spotted Cassie hiding and snapping photos a few yards away. I put my hands to my mouth and turn my back, readying to be sick.

Until I hear Kaden's breaths coming out hard and fast, his composure fracturing with every exhale.

I whirl back around, momentarily forgetting my nausea at his palpable anguish. "Kaden? What is it?"

He's lifted another photo from the rumpled sheets, and

this one is different. Older. The edges are worn, the colors slightly faded. In it, a much younger Kaden smiles at the camera, his features carefree. Perched on his shoulders is a little girl, no more than four or five years old, her tiny hands fisted in his dark hair as she throws her head back in gleeful laughter.

Pain lances through me at the pure joy captured in this single snapshot—a father and daughter in a moment of unbridled happiness, unaware of the horrific fate waiting in the wings.

More photos are scattered across the sheets, a bread-crumb trail of memories. Each one he touches seems to rip open a new wound—Kaden teaching Cassie to ride a bike, the two of them covered in flour while baking, and Cassie asleep on Kaden's chest, his hand protectively cradling her head even in slumber.

My heart cracks for the little girl smiling up at her daddy with such unbridled trust and adoration, for the man who had that precious love ripped away. I can't begin to imagine the despair and self-loathing that must be carving him up inside to know that same little girl is now the architect of our suffering.

Kaden screws his eyes shut against the onslaught.

I lay a tentative hand on his arm, feeling the tremors running through him. "Kaden..."

"She was my everything." His voice is scraped raw. "And I failed her."

"You didn't fail her," I say fiercely. "What happened to Cassie is not your fault."

A harsh laugh rips from his throat. "Isn't it?"

"The only assholes here are the ones who stole her from

you," I counter. "The ones who broke a little girl, something you would never, *ever* do."

"Daddy was always so careful with his little girl, wasn't he?"

The voice behind us is light, playful, and almost musical. We spin around to find Cassie lounging in the doorway, twirling one of Kaden's knives between her fingers with practiced ease. Her eyes gleam with manic energy as she surveys the scattered photos.

"All those rules about being gentle, being kind." She catches the knife by its tip. "Look how well that turned out." Her grin widens, sharp and wrong. "*I'm* the one who breaks things now. Want to see how good I've gotten at it?"

# 10

## KADEN

Cassie clicks her tongue, gesturing to the ostentatious dining setup. "Sit. Both of you."

She's traded her skintight bodycon dress for a long black gown. She's beautiful either way, but seeing Cassie appear so elegant yet remain so ugly inside renders my heart still.

To avoid any further confrontation, I guide Layla to her chair, keeping my body between her and my daughter.

"Isn't this cozy?" Cassie circles behind us once we're seated, trailing her fingers across our shoulders. "The three of us together. One big happy family."

She stops behind Layla's chair, hands coming to rest on her shoulders. I tense, but Cassie just leans down to whisper in Layla's ear, "Did Daddy tell you about our Sunday dinners? How he'd cook my favorite meals?" Her fingers flex against Layla's pulse points. "Now I get to play hostess."

You two must be starving after all that ... reconnecting." Her grin stretches wider. "I heard every delicious moment.

The way you begged for each other." She gestures to our wineglasses. "Drink up. The night's still young."

Layla's eyes meet mine across the table, wide and fearful. The sight of it fills me with a helpless rage that threatens to boil over, but I force it down, knowing that any outburst will only play into Cassie's hands.

"What do you want, sweetheart?" I ask Cassie, my voice low and controlled.

Cassie laughs, a thready, silvery sound. "What do I want? You should know better than to ask such a silly question."

Layla flinches away from Cassie's touch, her hand unsteady as she reaches for her wine.

Cassie's fingers glide away from Layla's shoulders. "Good girl."

She moves to the domed dishes on the neighboring cart, and I feel a sense of trepidation settle in the pit of my stomach. Knowing Cassie, this is no ordinary meal. Every bite, every sip, is likely to be laced with some new form of torment.

As if on cue, one of Cassie's men steps into the suite and removes the silver domes. The aroma of roasted meat and fragrant spices fills the air, but the sight of the food turns my stomach. Each dish is artfully arranged, but there's something grotesque about the presentation. It's as if the chef has taken perverse pleasure in creating a gluttonous feast for two when Layla's been starved for days.

Cassie licks gravy from her finger, studying Layla.

"Drink," she commands, all playfulness evaporating. "I went through a lot of trouble to pick the perfect vintage."

The threat sharpens between us. I want to reach across

the table and snatch the glass from Layla's fingers, but Cassie's watching me like a feline tracking another trespassing predator.

"Don't worry," she croons to Layla. "If I wanted either of you dead, I wouldn't waste good wine doing it. Harris, darling, won't you serve our guests?"

Cassie's honey-sweet voice drips with false affection.

Harris lifts a plate, then approaches Layla. Her eyes stay on mine, a silent plea in their depths. My cheek muscles ache as I slam my teeth together and watch this man spoon out small amounts of each dish onto her plate.

"More," Cassie commands. "She's far too thin. We can't have her wasting away, can we?"

I grind my teeth as Harris doubles the portions. Layla's plate is heaped with food she has no appetite for.

Cassie bends forward, her elbows on the table and her chin resting on her interlaced fingers, watching Layla intensely.

I offer a distraction while curling my hands into fists under the table. "Why don't you tell us about your plans, sweetheart? This can't just be about playing house."

Cassie's eyes *clink* against mine as we connect, and they narrow as she assesses me.

"Tell me, Daddy," Cassie says, her tone deceptively light. "How does it feel to be back in the bosom of your family? To have both your girls here with you, right where they belong?"

I'm coming to understand what Cassie wants, though she circles it like a circus ringleader cracking whips at her wild animals. That is, if that circus were half decayed and her animals recently clawed themselves out of fresh graves.

I don't look at Layla when I say, "Layla's not my girl, Cassie. She never was. You are."

Cassie's grin falters, a flicker of something dangerous crossing her lips before she smooths it away.

I hold Cassie's gaze, watching the gears turn behind those calculating eyes, so much like my own. She's searching for a crack, a weakness to exploit, but I won't give her one.

"Is that so?" Cassie muses, tapping a red fingernail against her lower lip. "Then I suppose you won't mind standing by as I peel away every last shred of her sanity, piece by agonizing piece. She got my face pretty good with that headbutt earlier. I had to double the amount of my concealer."

I force a chuckle, the sound grating against my throat. "Is that what this is about, Cassie? You want me to prove my love for you by letting you hurt someone else?"

Cassie's lips twist into a snarl as she straightens. "You're as much a demon as me, Daddy. You just hide it better than most."

The fabric of her dress whispers against her legs as she stalks around the table.

"Both of you, eat." She gestures to the feast. "I want to see you enjoy every bite."

I cut into the rib eye Harris placed in front of me while going through all the different scenarios to get Layla out of this place, all of them forcing my hand.

Across the table, Layla picks at her food, each movement cautious and measured.

"You know what's funny?" Cassie leans over Layla's shoulder and traces the rim of Layla's wineglass. "All those girls down the hall cry for their daddies, too. Just like I used to." Her features turn vicious. "But their fathers aren't here to save them. Not like you, Daddy."

The fork bends in my grip. "What girls?"

"My collection. Daughters whose fathers failed them." She props her hands on her hips. "Want to meet them? Or would you rather watch what I do to your little kitten here next?"

The choice hits me like a physical blow. Protect Layla, or save innocent girls from my daughter's madness.

"You don't have to do this," I say, fighting to keep my voice steady.

"Oh, but I do." Cassie snaps her fingers, and two more men enter, one carrying a briefcase. "Time to mark what's yours, Daddy. Just like Papa Morelli did me."

I don't think. One second, I'm bending a metal fork in my hand, and the next, I'm tossing the table aside, dishes and food scattering as the table slams sideways. Before she can blink in surprise, I grab Layla's wrist and pull her out of her seat and behind me and stare down my daughter, though any ferociousness I feel isn't directed at Cassie.

Her men prowl closer, guns raised and directed at my forehead.

"*What* did he do to you?" I demand.

Cassie steps back, her crimson lips curving into a smile equal parts bitter and triumphant. She lifts her hands to the thin straps of her gown, letting them slide off her shoulders. The fabric pools at her waist, revealing the intricate tattoo that spans her upper chest and cradles her breasts.

It's grotesque, a tangled collection of scales and thorns

that combine to create the sharp maw of a dragon, gaping open to devour the heart that beats in Cassie's chest.

"Cass..." My voice isn't my own. I can't tear my eyes away from what mars her skin.

"He did this to me on my sixteenth birthday," Cassie says, tracing the edges of the tattoo with a perfectly manicured fingernail. "Held me down while this was carved into my skin, so I'd never forget who I belonged to."

My blood runs cold, rage and revulsion at war within the red.

Layla makes a small, distressed sound behind me, and I feel her press closer, her slight frame trembling against my back. Cassie's attention snaps to her, carnivorous.

"Don't worry, kitten. I have something special planned for you," she says as she pulls her straps back up.

"Cassie, please," I try, fighting to keep my voice steady. "If you want to punish someone, punish me."

Cassie laughs. "I intend to. But first, you're going to watch as I mark your little pet. Just like Papa made me watch when he took his other girls."

She snaps her fingers again, and one of her men lowers his gun and steps forward, the briefcase in his opposite hand. He sets it on the velvet couch and opens it, revealing a gleaming tattoo gun and an array of inks and needles.

My heart pounds in my ears as Cassie selects the gun and loads it with black ink. She tests the needle against her finger, a bead of blood welling up against her porcelain skin.

I lunge for the closest man and the gun he's aiming, but another of her goons intercepts me, twisting my arms behind me. He doesn't think to compromise my legs, though.

In one fluid movement, I hook one of his ankles and force us both sideways until we topple to the ground. Layla takes advantage of the distraction and runs for the nearest lamp, brandishing it before cracking it on top of the guy's head, laying him out like a stuffed beanbag under me.

Cassie *tsks*, wagging the tattoo gun in admonishment, and I freeze.

"Now, now. Behave, or I'll make this hurt more than it has to."

"Stop this," I snarl at her, grimacing as I come to a stand and step in front of Layla, who's heaving as she drops the remnants of porcelain in her hand. "I failed you, and I'll regret that until the day I die. But I won't fail Layla, too. I'll die before I let you touch her."

Cassie's eyes shine with fury, and for one terrible second, I think she might just get rid of the complication and kill me, but then her expression smooths into an icy calm that's somehow even more terrifying.

Three more men storm inside the suite, dressed in impeccable all-black suits, and head straight for me. I square up, my fists not my first choice for a weapon but effective nonetheless, until Cassie orders, "Hold her," lazily gesturing at Layla with the tattoo gun.

Two of them seize Layla's arms, dragging her forward despite her desperate struggles. One side of her robe falls open, revealing everything she's endured up until this point, no part of her skin as flawless as it once was.

I roar and lunge, but *fuck*, something was in the food. The wine. The room tilts, though I'm aiming straight.

One guy sees his opening and restrains my hands behind my back. I thrash, but his grip is unbreakable as whatever drug Cassie thought up absorbs into my bloodstream. "What did you do? What did you give me?"

"Relax, it's not poison this time." Cassie waltzes to Layla, who's positioned flat on the bed, rose petals and photos scattering as she fights the men holding her down. "Though I still haven't gotten a thank-you for shooting you up with an antidote before exiting that fun event where I got my prize."

She trails the tattoo gun along Layla's exposed collarbone. Layla becomes still and flinches, a whimper escaping her lips.

"Shh, it's okay, kitten," Cassie croons, brushing Layla's hair aside to expose the graceful curve of her neck. "I'm going to make you so pretty for Daddy."

She nods to Harris, who lingers near the briefcase and now steps forward. He tilts Layla's chin up with clinical precision. Layla's eyes are wide and glassy as they look for me.

"I'm here. I'm here. I'm not leaving you," I say to her, even as my legs start to give out.

Cassie hums in approval as she studies Layla's throat, the tattoo gun buzzing to life in Harris's hand.

The needle descends, and Layla cries out as it punctures her delicate skin. A single black line starts at her throat, as precise as the cut of a scalpel. Cassie watches Harris work with rabid fascination, the needle dragging across Layla's skin in precise, elegant lines.

"See how the ink splits into these delicate little branches?" Cassie says, tracing a finger along the fresh lines, uncaring of smearing the blood and ink. "Like veins ... or fracture lines. So fragile. So easy to destroy."

Layla retches, tears spilling down her cheeks as she tries in vain to pull away.

I strain against the men holding me back, the drug turning my limbs to lead. "Cassie, stop this. I'm begging you."

"Begging?" She laughs, a jarring sound. "The great Kaden Black, the Scythe, is begging? If only your enemies could see you now."

She turns her focus back to Layla, head tilting as she examines Harris's progress. The design is taking shape—a series of thin, branching lines that spread like a web from the hollow of Layla's throat. Beautiful in its simplicity. Horrifying in its implication.

"Do you know what this is, Daddy?" Cassie asks, almost conversationally. "It's a map. The exact guide for how and where to slit her throat."

Adrenaline floods my veins. I will *end* the man behind me and all the others in this room before another minute passes.

"I've seen it done a few times," Cassie continues. "Messy work, but I was inspired by the artistry of it. Harris used to be a tattoo artist, you see. Before he came to us. And now sweet Layla will wear it always. A pretty little guide for spilling her blood."

Layla makes a choked sound, fresh tears spilling over. I feel something fracture inside my chest.

And I finally break.

"You're a monster," I rasp. "A fucking monster wearing my daughter's face."

Cassie just laughs again, fingers trailing down Layla's arm. "Oh, Daddy. You have no idea."

She leans down, her lips brushing Layla's as she stage-whispers, "When Harris is done, this will be a collar you can never take off. An eternal reminder etched into your beautiful body. That you belong to him ... and he belongs to me."

"Eyes on me, Wraithling," I murmur, refusing to fall to my knees from the drug. "Just look at me."

Layla latches onto my stare, even as she shakes and weeps under the gun.

"We know the truth, don't we, kitten?" Cassie says, severing our connection as she smooths back Layla's damp hair with a mockingly tender touch. "My father's love comes with a death sentence."

# 11

## LAYLA

My fingers trace the new ink etched into my throat, a map of my own execution drawn by the daughter of the man who'd destroy worlds to protect me. The swollen lines burn beneath my touch.

"Don't."

I flinch as Kaden brushes my hand aside, his calloused one surprisingly delicate as he examines Cassie's handiwork. I lie tangled in silk sheets, my body aching. Kaden sits beside me, his weight dipping the mattress.

"Hold still," he murmurs.

The damp cloth in his hand is cool against the inflamed flesh, a temporary balm to the violation I can feel all the way to my bones. I haven't moved from the bed, too shocked to so much as sit up after Cassie flounced out of the room, taking her horrible men with her. She didn't say when she would come back, but she never has. Cassie just ... appears.

Kaden's clinical and assessing touch contains an undercurrent of possessiveness in the way his thumb lingers on my pulse point, as if reassuring himself that I'm still here, still breathing.

"I will burn every one of those assholes alive," he says, his gaze locked on my neck. "Without hesitation."

I should be horrified by his words, by the casual brutality of his conviction. But a part of me, the part irrevocably changed by what I've endured, approves. That would do the same for him, consequences be damned.

"I know," I murmur, reaching out to brush a strand of hair from his forehead. I linger on the jagged scar that curves under his brow, a reminder of the battles he's fought and the demons he carries.

He leans into my touch, his eyes fluttering closed for a moment.

"Cassie..." His voice is rough with an emotion I can't quite name. "What happened to her ... what Morelli did..."

I wait, my heart in my throat, as he struggles to find the words.

But he trails off, his gaze distant and haunted.

"Why did she do this to me?" I whisper.

I can tell my question slices through him, cold and cruel. But there's something else beneath, an undercurrent of rage that I was stolen from him. I want to assure him that Cassie may have branded my skin, but Kaden has claimed my soul.

"This doesn't change anything," I say fiercely. "I'm yours."

Black flares in his gaze, fierce and feral. He bows his head until his lips touch the side of my neck.

"Mine," he growls before kissing the hot, angry skin.

The word is a vow, a promise sealed in ink and blood. A

shudder ripples through me at the declaration, his lips on my skin.

I tangle my fingers in his hair, holding him close as his lips trail along the edges of the tattoo, each brush a searing brand. But the desperate edge to his voice, the rawness, speaks of the scars Cassie left on his soul this day. I know the memories are tearing at him, the weight of the past threatening to drag him under.

I tug gently, urging him up until I can see his face. His eyes are storm-tossed, a tempest of rage and anguish.

"Kaden," I whisper, my thumbs brushing his cheekbones. "Talk to me."

He exhales a sound that's almost a growl. "She's not the little girl I remember. That Cassie is gone. I don't know if there's anything left to save. What she's done to you ... if anyone else did this, *anyone*, I would've given them a slow, violent death. I'd want them to suffer. I would've let you watch me tear them open to get your justice. Cassie has made it impossible for me to save her, yet I can't kill her to save you."

I swallow past the permanent lump in my throat. Kaden's feelings for his daughter and me are tearing him apart, but I'm not as conflicted. Cassie has tortured me, played numerous mind games, and enjoyed putting me on display for her men. She allowed their threats of rape and assault so I'd stay terrified and complacent, no matter how many knives she sharpened against my skin. I never knew the twelve-year-old whose younger years are frozen in time and scattered around me, covered in rose petals and blood. Yet I never knew love growing up the way she did with Kaden. Cassie *knows* what real love feels like. She must remember her time with her dad. Doesn't she miss it? How can she truly believe Kaden abandoned her for all these years?

"You're right," I say. "She's not that little girl anymore. She's grown now, and she's made her choices."

"What about the choices taken from her?" he counters.

"You can't blame yourself for that." I stroke my fingers through his hair.

"Wraithling, you're ten years too late," he says with a quiet rasp.

My heart clenches at the anguish in his words and the fear that Cassie is gone forever.

We stay like this for a long moment, me running my fingers through his hair, him kissing away the pain, drawing strength from each other.

Reluctantly, I tug on his hair, gently pulling him back so I can see his face. "We need to get out of here. *Please.* After that, we can figure out what to do about Cassie."

The thought of her return churns every organ inside my body, all of them shriveling with remembered agony. The sound of her laughter still rings in my ears.

Kaden works his jaw, his attention snapping to the wall panel that hides a bank of computer screens. He replies under his breath so surveillance won't catch his voice. "Ethan. He's on the outside. He'll be working to shut down the network and initiate a blackout so we can escape."

Kaden frowns, as if reluctant to admit the next part. "It was our plan B."

I blink, surprised, but manage to keep my reply at the same low octave as his. "Ethan's still involved? With you? You two are working together?"

Guilt twists like a knife at the center of my heart. When I confessed to Ethan about the illegal AI all employees at Pulse Dynamics were inadvertently creating, I didn't expect him to want to stay by my side when I broke into the building and tried to destroy Project Oracle. Ethan was determined to remain in communication with me, but all of that went away when Dawson found me, drugged and stripped me, and...

I clear my throat, forcing myself away from what happened next, and focus on the loss of the smartwatch Ethan and I used to keep in touch.

So many terrible consequences occurred after Dawson took that watch. Kaden broke in and violently killed Dawson. Then he sought his vengeance on Morelli, killing him next. Cassie revealed herself soon after, shooting Kaden and incapacitating him enough to kidnap me.

During all that, Ethan was cut off—or was he? Could he still hear everything on the watch Dawson tossed aside? Is that how Kaden got out of the server room? Did Ethan...?

Kaden predicts every panicked thought. "The idiot saved me. He pulled me out, hid me in a basement, and patched me up. Did you truly believe that boy would leave you to be kidnapped by the Mafia?"

"Patched you up? The same Ethan who nearly passed out when I accidentally stapled my thumb?"

The memory of Ethan's pale face and shaking hands that day in the office feels like it belongs to another lifetime.

"People adapt." Kaden's thumb traces the edge of my tattoo.

I lower my eyes in understanding. This unwanted tattoo is now a part of me, whether I survive long enough to remove it or not. I haven't asked Kaden to describe it to me or take me to a mirror. It doesn't matter what the design is. It's a reflection of this place, this torture, and it's as dark and unwelcome as hell would be.

"He's still out there," Kaden says, eyes fixed on the wall panel. "And he knows what he's doing."

"What if she hurts him?" I say, the fear for my friend making my voice rise an octave. "What if she uses him to get to us?"

Kaden cups one side of my face, turning me to look at him. With his features so shadowed, his scars seem deeper, his eyes harder. But something else is there too—a carefully banked fire.

"Right now, just believe in me." His words carry the weight of every kill, every calculated move that led him to this point. "I will get you out of here, and Ethan will be safe."

I clutch at his hand holding my face, letting his conviction anchor me. "Ok—"

A sound pierces through the momentary peace we found in each other's arms. A scream, high and agonized, bleeds through the walls.

I jolt upright, my heart pounding against my ribs. Kaden tenses, his grip on me tightening reflexively.

"Fuck," he murmurs.

The scream comes again. It's a sound of pure, unadulterated agony, the kind that can only be wrung from a human throat by the most unspeakable horrors. I've never heard anything like it in all my time here, and the unfamiliarity of it makes my blood run cold.

"What is that?" I whisper.

Kaden's on his feet in an instant, stalking toward the door. I scramble after him, my legs tangling in my loosened robe and bundled sheets.

"Kaden, wait!" I hiss as he presses his ear to the door.

For all we know, a gun is pointed directly at his temple on the other side.

He pauses and looks back at me.

"I can't just sit here and listen to that," he says. "Not when I know what she's capable of."

I swallow hard, my stomach churning at the thought of what Cassie might be doing to elicit such horrible screams. But I force myself to take a deep breath, to think past the terror that threatens to overwhelm me.

"If we try anything, we'll just make it worse." My voice shakes despite my effort to keep it steady. "For both of us."

Kaden's hand tightens on the doorknob, the tendons in his forearm standing out in sharp relief. For a moment, I think he might wrench the door open anyway, consequences be damned. But then he exhales in a harsh sound that seems to billow around the room.

I close the distance, my bare feet soundless on the plush carpeting. I reach up, wrapping my hands around his neck. Kaden's skin is hot to the touch, as if fury is burning him from the inside out.

I press my face against his chest, bared within the V of his robe, trying to ground us both. Movement catches my eye. The scattered photos on the bed shift as the sheets settle from my frazzled exit, and one slides free and drifts to the ground.

It's not Cassie and Kaden. The girl in this photo is a stranger, maybe in her twenties, with long dark hair and terrified eyes. She's bound to a gold-embellished antique chair, and tears stream down her face. Behind her stands a man I don't recognize, his expression haunted as he watches whatever's happening outside the frame.

My hands fall from Kaden's neck. "There are more."

He turns, following my gaze to where other photos have spilled across the sheets. We stride to the foot of the bed as one, studying the other photos we missed when we were so focused on ourselves and Cassie.

Sifting through, I find ones showing different girls with different older men—fathers forced to witness their daughters' suffering. Some photos are clearly recent, others aged and worn. All of them document the same sick game Cassie's playing with us now, though she's never within the frame.

"She's been planning this," I whisper, the realization hitting me like a wave of salty, fish-scented water. "All this time, she's been collecting daughters. Testing them."

Kaden's hands clench at his sides as he stares at the evidence of Cassie's obsession. "Not testing. Conditioning."

Oh God. I want to throw up. "Conditioning for what?"

# 12
## LAYLA

Kaden picks up one of the older photos.

A man in a business suit stares at the camera, his expression a mix of despair and resignation. In his hand is a pair of pliers, poised over the delicate fingers of a young woman bound to a chair. Her face is a mask of white terror.

Another photo shows the same man, his features twisted in anguish as he closes the pliers over the girl's index finger. Her mouth is open in a silent scream, and in the background, I can see another girl, bound and gagged, her eyes wide with horror. That one has blond hair, like him. Striking green eyes, like him.

His daughter is watching him torture another girl.

I grab a bunch of photos, then rifle through them with shaking hands. The early shots show fathers forced to watch as their daughters are subjected to unspeakable torments— burned, beaten, cut. Their faces are studies in helpless agony, the kind of pain that goes beyond the physical.

A chilling pattern emerges the deeper I delve. The same

fathers appear again and again, but their roles begin to shift. No longer just helpless victims ... they become active participants in the torture.

One sequence shows a father, his face gaunt and haunted, holding a glowing branding iron. In the next photo, he's pressing it against the bare skin of a sobbing girl, his own daughter visible in the background, her face a mix of relief and revulsion.

Another series depicts a man wielding a whip, his hands shaking as he brings it down across the back of a screaming young woman. The progression is sickening. By the final photo, his face is an impassive mask, the whip striking with cruel precision.

Photo after photo tells the same story: Fathers forced to make impossible choices, to inflict pain on others in order to spare their own daughters from worse torments.

I look at Kaden, unable to prevent the horror from leeching the blood from my face. Cassie's not just collecting daughters—she's breaking their fathers, reshaping them into ghouls of her own creation.

"She's turning them into weapons," I say. "The fathers. She's conditioning them to do anything, hurt anyone, to keep their daughters safe."

A muscle ticks in his cheek. "Once she breaks them, she owns them. They'll be loyal to her, to the Syndicate, because she holds their daughters' lives in her hands."

The scream comes again, muffled by the walls but no less agonizing. I flinch, the photos fluttering from my fingers.

"The men she constantly has with her," I breathe, the

realization hitting me like a punch to the gut. "Do you think...?"

Kaden's eyes meet mine, a maelstrom of rage and anguish swirling in their depths. "Morelli gave her these men as playthings, and given her brilliance, she turned them into her personal servants."

I think back on Harris, the man who gave me the tattoo currently throbbing at my neck. All the men who came in here were leering and throwing around threats but never acting on them.

"What kind of men is she finding?" I ask, more to myself than Kaden.

"Ones who will do anything for their daughters."

Kaden lowers his chin and rubs his weary eyes with a fist.

"Yes, but *who* are they?" My vision unfocuses as I ponder this. "Cassie likes to talk to me when she—well. When she's in here visiting. I've come to learn she doesn't do anything without reason. She wouldn't just be collecting random men who have kids. She'd be doing her research."

Kaden grabs my hand, his thumb brushing over my knuckles. "Cassie wants us to know she's building an army of men loyal to her not out of greed or fear but out of love. The most dangerous kind of devotion."

"The AI I tried to destroy." My spine goes ramrod straight from the implication. With an army of broken fathers at her command, men in positions of power and influence, Cassie could reshape the very fabric of society. CEOs, politicians, judges...

"By controlling key players in the economy, they could

help implement the AI's influence over markets, elections, and God knows what else."

And at the center of it all, Cassie herself, a queen of shattered glass, ruling over a kingdom built on the bones of innocence.

I'm cold, almost numb, but I force myself to ask the question that haunts me. "Kaden, if she's using me..."

My voice cracks, the rest of the sentence sticking in my throat, but I don't need to finish my thought.

Kaden's eyes snap to mine. His squeezes my hand to the point that it hurts, then pulls me into his chest, his startling warmth seeping into me and keeping the chill at bay.

"I would tear apart both heaven and hell to protect you. I don't give a shit that these men started off innocent. I will burn each of these fathers alive the very second I have an opening. And I swear to you, on everything I have left, that I will not let her destroy me."

He tips my chin up, his eyes boring into mine. I reach up, my fingers tracing the hard line of his jaw.

"I know," I say. "I know because I would do the same for you."

Something flares in his eyes, hot and bright. His arms tighten around me, drawing me closer until our breaths mingle. "You are my fucking universe."

I surge onto my tiptoes, capturing his mouth in a bruising kiss. He groans, crushing me to his chest. I pour everything into that kiss—my fear, my love, my desperate need for him. He meets me with equal fervor, his tongue sweeping into my mouth, claiming me, consuming me.

I cling to him, my lighthouse in this storm of madness.

Another scream rips through the air, closer this time. Another girl we can't save.

The pain and exhaustion finally catch up with me, and my body sways where I stand. Kaden notices immediately.

"When did you last sleep, Wraithling?"

His voice carries an edge I recognize. He's realizing how much Cassie's "visits" have deprived me of basic needs.

The photos still litter the bed, evidence of other women's suffering that I can't bear to sleep among. As I reach to clear them, my hands shake with fatigue.

Kaden's hands, strong and sure, close over mine, stilling their trembling. With a gracefulness that belies the fury simmering beneath his skin, he guides me to sit on the edge of the bed, then gathers the pictures himself.

He stacks them in his hands, his jawline so pronounced I fear his teeth might crack from the pressure. Every line of his body is taut with barely contained rage, a predator poised to strike in a depleted, controlled environment. He prowls to one corner and tosses them in a small trash can so hard, it nearly tips over. But when Kaden turns back to me, his expression softens, the typhoon in his eyes calming to a soft rain.

"Let's get you to bed," he murmurs. "It's not ideal, but you've got to sleep. I'll watch over you."

He eases me back onto the pillows, drawing the covers over my abused body.

I wince as the fabric brushes against the raw wounds on my skin, a whimper escaping through my teeth.

Kaden stills. For a moment, I think he might put his fist through a wall. Or worse, tear the door off its hinges to hunt down every man who hurt me and tear them apart with his bare hands.

But I'm aware that he won't. Because the real perpetrator, the one responsible, is the very woman he can't hurt.

Kaden takes a deep breath, then perches on the edge of the bed, his hip pressing against mine. He runs his fingers through my hair, carefully untangling the damp snarls.

"Close your eyes," he murmurs, pressing a kiss to my forehead. "I won't let any harm come to you while you dream."

I want to argue, to insist that he needs rest too, but my eyelids are already drooping, my body surrendering to the exhaustion that drags at me. What helps is the steady pressure of Kaden's hand in mine, an unspoken promise that he'll still be here when I wake.

His thumb traces soothing circles while sleep tugs at me, its insistent fingers dragging me under despite the adrenaline still pumping through my veins.

But as I hover on the edge of consciousness, the noises next door begin to change.

The dull thud of fists meeting flesh takes on a frenzied cadence, each impact landing with sickening irregularity.

A voice rises above the cacophony, female and achingly familiar. Cassie.

Her words are indistinct, lost to the barrier of brick and plaster, but there's no mistaking the fury that laces each syllable. It's the auditory embodiment of a gathering storm, dark and seething and poised to obliterate everything in its path.

"What's going on?" I ask Kaden.

Cassie's voice pitches higher, the words coming faster now, a staccato burst of vitriol.

Kaden replies without tearing his attention off the locked door. "I believe she just saw me tucking you into bed."

The blows next door reach a crescendo, each one punctuated by a gurgling male scream. I burrow deeper into the covers, pressing my face into the pillow as if I can block out the horror unfolding on the other side of the wall.

Kaden shifts beside me, resting his free hand on my back. Even through the fabric of my shirt, I can feel the heat of his touch and the pounding pulse that thrums through his body.

"Breathe, Layla," he murmurs, his voice a low rumble that vibrates through his hand and into me. "Focus on my voice, on my touch. Let everything else fade away."

Another scream rips through the air, this one high and thin and filled with a despair so profound that it makes me moan into the pillow. It's the sound of someone being unmade, of a soul being split into a thousand pieces.

And through it all, Cassie's laughter weaves like a discordant melody, and she follows me all the way into oblivion.

# 13
## KADEN

I don't sleep. Instead, I stare at the door, eyes burning despite the weight of exhaustion pressing down.

Layla thrashes in her sleep beside me, her hair spilling across the pillow. She whimpers, caught in the throes of a nightmare, and my chest constricts. I move from my perch on the bed and lie down next to her, gathering her in my arms and chasing away the demons that haunt her.

Cassie has ceased her torture next door, as even monsters need to sleep. But the memory of her malicious laughter bounces around my skull, coupled with her jealous vitriol.

What I did with Layla, tucking her into bed and soothing her to sleep, wasn't done with the intention of sending Cassie into a rage. Only in hindsight did I realize that watching such a thing would've been too much for my wayward daughter to handle.

Cameras are set up all around this suite—lenses in ceiling corners and listening devices under lampshades. My daughter has this room covered. No doubt that's how she noticed me caring for Layla and treating her like a porcelain doll when I helped her to bed.

Cassie lashed out—not at Layla or me but at strangers in the adjacent suite.

So many observations hit me at once. I couldn't fall asleep even if I wanted to. Cassie has a signature, even if she doesn't know it. She locks us all in luxurious suites, surrounded by indulgence yet deprived of it at the same time. Before my arrival, Cassie had Layla bound, naked, and curled up on the expensive carpet as she tortured her.

*Tortured.*

My Wraithling at the mercy of my daughter. I can trace the map of pain Cassie left on Layla's body. Each cut, scratch, and burn escalated in damage as more time went by and I hadn't come yet. Layla's pain was all for me. To punish, I suppose, and flay my heart open.

It worked.

However, Cassie doesn't know how easily I can compartmentalize. I can put on my assassin's mind like a second skin. Layla's suffering kills me inside, but it doesn't affect the Scythe.

I scan the room as him, running through each interaction with Cassie so far. I detach from emotion as I analyze Cassie's behavior, searching for patterns and pressure points. She's re-creating the traumas of her past, using this suite as a stage to act out her twisted fantasies. The lavish decor, the cameras, and the psychological torment are all designed to make us feel as helpless and abandoned as she once did.

I can start with the photos, the ones I sifted into a pile

and tossed in the trash—but not before I noticed a glaring error on Cassie's part.

She meant for these pictures to horrify us, and it worked. Yet when the Scythe glances at the photos scattered across the bed showing the twisted and grotesque forms of men and women, their faces contorted in pain and fear, he notices no images of young girls. Only adults.

Despite her clear intention to punish fathers and daughters, likely echoing her own suffering at Morelli's hands, she didn't take girls her age when she went through this horror.

Therefore, she has a line that she won't cross. She doesn't want to hurt children.

My darling, evil girl still clings to a piece of morality.

The father in me holds on to that, using it as a beacon of hope that I can get through to her.

The Scythe knows better and wants to figure out how to make it a weakness and use it against her.

I stroke Layla's hair, my touch light so as not to wake her. She needs the rest, needs to gather her strength for the trials ahead. Because I know Cassie won't stop. She'll keep pushing, keep prodding at our weaknesses until she finds the one that ends us. I press a kiss to Layla's forehead, breathing in her scent. Even now, with exhaustion and fear clinging to her skin, she's intoxicating. My Wraithling, my love. I'll burn the world down before I let anyone take her from me.

Layla stirs, her brow furrowing as another nightmare takes hold. I stroke the side of her face with my thumb, murmuring sweet nothings. Even in slumber, she leans into my hand, seeking comfort. The trust she places in me, after everything I've done, is both humbling and worrying.

I don't deserve her. But I'll be damned if I let Cassie destroy the one pure thing in my life.

Carefully, I extract myself from Layla's embrace. The suite is eerily quiet, the only sound the soft hum of the computers behind the hidden wall panel. I'm determined to find the button to open it, but not yet. Not when so many cameras are on me. Ideally, Ethan is in there somewhere, working his magic. If he can find a way to disable Cassie's cameras and the electronic lock on the door, maybe I can come up with a plan that doesn't involve torture and death. I'll get Layla out of here as soon as the green lights in the cameras I've spotted go off.

Until then, I pace the room, my mind churning. I start to pull open drawers to give myself something to do. Expecting most of them to be empty, I'm pleasantly surprised when one of them in an antique armoire holds two black sweat sets, one in my size and one in Layla's.

It's a gift horse, to be sure, but I'd rather look it in the mouth than wander around naked under a black silk robe while my daughter figures out ways to mutilate me. I collect the cashmere sets and put them in the bathroom for later when Layla rouses.

When my continued pacing brings me to the trash bin, I pick up one of the pictures, studying the agonized face of a middle-aged man, his eyes wide and glassy and his mouth wrenched open. I recognize the look. I've seen it on my own victims in the moments before I ended their lives.

And I worry that the only way I can get through to Cassie is to be the Scythe, the cold-blooded killer, just like her. I close my eyes, taking a deep breath. I can feel the Scythe digging at the edges of my mind, begging to be let loose. It would be so easy to give in, to let him take control. He knows how to deal with Cassie and speak her language of blood and pain.

He whispers in my ear, telling me that he can save Layla and beat Cassie at her own game. All I have to do is let him out.

I stop in front of the window, staring out at the morning fog in the rising dawn. Cassie knows she has me trapped between my love for Layla and my duty as a father. She'll use that against me, just as she's using Layla's love for me.

If I cross this line, if I fully embrace the Scythe and go off tormenting some poor soul at Cassie's behest, I risk losing that. Losing her.

My attention drifts to her sleeping form, so small and fragile amid the opulent sheets. I want to gather Layla in my arms and keep her there. But I can't protect her forever. Sooner or later, Cassie will force my hand, and Layla won't be here when that time comes.

I'll get her out.

For Layla's chance of having a future free from the Blacks, I will do what I must. Even if it means that she escapes and I stay behind.

The more I think about those photos of broken fathers, the more I see Cassie's fatal flaw—she expects everyone to choose violence. It's what Morelli taught her, what I reinforced by becoming the Scythe.

But as I watch Layla sleep, I remember how she reached for me even after witnessing my darkest acts. How her touch gentles me when everything in me screams for blood.

The Scythe whispers that love is weakness. But watching my daughter torture others to re-create her pain, I realize she's still that little girl searching for her father's embrace.

Maybe the way to break her isn't through more violence. It's by showing her what Morelli could never understand, that real power lies in choosing tenderness when you're capable of cruelty.

I cross the room and climb back into bed, tracing the tattoo on Layla's throat. My daughter designed this to mark ownership and to prove love always leads to pain.

It's time to show her she's wrong.

Gently, I rouse Layla from her fitful slumber. She blinks up at me, confusion and fear warring in her bicolored gaze.

"Kaden? What's going on?"

"Shh, Wraithling. Just follow my lead."

I pull her into my arms, cradling her against my chest as I carry her to the bathroom. The tile is cold against my bare feet. I set Layla down on the marble counter, keeping my hands on her waist to steady her and stepping between her spread legs, her satin robe fluttering open to accept me.

She searches my face, trying to read my intentions. I let the mask of the Scythe fall away, revealing the man beneath. The man who would do anything for her.

"Do you trust me?" I whisper, my lips brushing the shell of her ear.

She doesn't hesitate. "Yes."

"Then help me show Cassie that forcing someone's submission will never be as powerful as earning it."

I capture Layla's lips in a hard kiss. She responds instantly, her arms twining around my neck as she parts her lips to grant me entrance. I plunder her mouth, claiming her and branding her as mine.

My hands roam her body, skimming over the satin. I want to rip it off, to feel Layla's bare skin. But not yet. This is about devotion. There are no cameras in the bathroom. Cassie can't see us in this intimate act, but she'll undoubtedly hear us.

I worship Layla with gentle touches and reverent kisses, finding every sore and ache peppering her skin and showing her with my mouth what my words could never adequately express.

That she is cherished. That she is loved beyond reason. Beyond madness.

Let Cassie hear. Let her witness. Let it gnaw at her, fester in her malignant soul until she can't stand it anymore.

For now, though, my focus is solely on Layla—on bringing her pleasure and chasing away the shadows that cling to her. I trail my lips down the column of her throat, my tongue flicking out to taste her new tattoo.

She arches into me, a breathy moan escaping her lips.

"Kaden..."

The way she says my name makes me so hard, I'm relieved I'm not wearing pants. I allow my own robe to puddle to the floor, then use my hands to slide hers off her shoulders, only the loose knot of the tie at her hips remaining.

She shivers under my touch, goose bumps rising in the wake of my fingertips.

"You're so beautiful," I murmur against her collarbone before trailing kisses lower. "Let me show you how much I adore you."

I take my time exploring her body, worshipping every inch with reverent hands and lips, conscious of her wounds.

I trace the curve of her breasts, teasing her nipples with flicks of my tongue until they peak into rosy buds. Layla gasps and arches into my touch, her fingers tangling in my hair.

Slowly, I work my way down her taut, bruised stomach, dragging open-mouthed kisses along heated flesh. When I reach the apex of her thighs, Layla holds her breath in anticipation. I hook her legs over my shoulders and breathe her in, intoxicated by her heady scent.

"Kaden, please..."

I stop. "Am I hurting you?"

"No. Not even a little. But should we be doing...?"

"Trust me, Wraithling. Remember?"

I pull any reply from her lips by parting her glistening folds with my tongue. She cries out at the first long lick, hips canting to meet my mouth. I lap at her essence, savoring her sweetness as I circle her sensitive bud. Layla writhes against me, reduced to husky moans and gasps.

Slipping two fingers inside her tight heat, I stroke her inner walls, curling to hit that secret spot that makes her see stars. I can feel her clenching around my digits as I bring her higher.

"That's it," I encourage between licks. "Let go for me."

A few more thrusts of my fingers and flicks of my tongue send her over the edge. Layla releases a keening cry, her thighs trembling on my shoulders. I don't stop working her through the waves of her release until she's boneless and sated.

Lifting my head, I take in the flush of her skin, the rapid rise and fall of her chest. Slowly, I kiss my way back up her body until I reach her lips.

"I will get you out of here," I profess against her mouth. "No matter what happens, never doubt that."

I reclaim her lips in a deep, consuming kiss, letting it say everything I can't put into words—my devotion, my need, my promise to always fight for her.

When we finally break apart, I rest my forehead against hers and sheathe myself inside her with one smooth thrust. We both groan at the exquisite sensation, fitting together like two halves of a whole.

I set a slow, deep rhythm, savoring each drag of my hardness against her tight heat. Layla matches me stroke for stroke, rolling her hips to take me impossibly deeper, whimpering and arching into me, her body begging for more even as she hurts. And still, we move, lost in each other despite the pain.

"I can't ... I can't hold on..." Layla whispers between pants.

"Don't."

I capture her lips again as I increase the tempo of my thrusts, swallowing her moans of pleasure. Layla hooks her ankles behind my back, breathing my name while her nails dig crescents into my shoulders. The slight sting only heightens my pleasure.

Releasing her hips, I brace one hand against the mirror behind her. The other finds the apex of her thighs, my thumb circling her sensitive pearl in time with my deep strokes. Layla moans, her head falling back as I work her closer to the edge.

I angle my hips to hit that secret spot within her. Her walls clench around my length as she lets go, milking my own release from me. Burying my face in the crook of her neck, I muffle my groan of ecstasy against the reddened flesh of her new tattoo.

We stay locked together as we catch our breath, pulses gradually slowing. I'm savoring the feel of her in my arms, safe and sated. For this stolen moment, the rest of the world falls away. No Cassie, no threats, just us.

Let my deranged daughter see our "weaknesses"—the tenderness, the trust, the depths of our devotion. By the time I'm done, Cassie will realize that love, real love, isn't fragile strings to be snipped one by one.

It's an unbreakable tether, soul to soul. And I'll use that to strangle the madness right out of her.

Reluctantly, I slip free of Layla's heat and help her off the counter on unsteady legs. I keep an arm around her waist as I lead us to the pile of folded clothes I set in here earlier.

If she's surprised at the sudden appearance of clothing, Layla doesn't show it. Likely because her days have been full of rude awakenings, so she'll take what small perks she can get.

Layla leans into me as I help her slip on the black cashmere sweatpants and hoodie. The fabric swallows her petite frame, but it's a relief to see her clothed and protected, even in this small way. I quickly pull on my own matching set before guiding her back into the bedroom.

As soon as we cross the threshold, a slow clap echoes through the room. Cassie's face fills the wall of monitors that have appeared now that the wall panel is open, an annoyed smirk on her lips.

"Bravo," she drawls. "What a touching display of affection. I didn't realize Stockholm syndrome could develop so quickly."

I feel Layla stiffen beside me, but I keep my expression neutral.

"I'm not her captor, Cassandra." I use her full name like a reprimand. "Layla came to me willingly, knowing exactly what I am. Unlike you, I don't need to force submission."

Cassie's eyes flare at the subtle jab. "Love is a lie men like you tell to justify their sins. You abandoned me. Just like you'll abandon her."

"I never abandoned you, Cassie. I will keep saying that to you until I'm blue in the face. Until you can *hear* me. Morelli—"

"DON'T SAY HIS NAME!" she shrieks, slamming her fist against something off-screen. The image shudders. "You have no idea what he did to me. What I suffered while you played house with your little whore."

I swallow hard, emotion threatening to choke me. "I tore apart every man who stood in the way of finding you. To save you from that fucker's clutches. I'm so sorry, Cassie. But do not mistake my failings as a father for a lack of love. If I could go back, if I could trade places with you, I would. In a heartbeat. I would endure every torment, every degradation, if it meant sparing you even a moment of pain."

Cassie's eyelashes flicker—a glimmer of my true daughter, but it's quickly consumed by the flames of her wrath.

"You think fucking this whore will make me see you differently?" She scoffs, but there's an undercurrent of uncertainty. "Physical pleasure is fleeting. It doesn't prove anything."

"Doesn't it? Tell me, when was the last time you touched someone with genuine affection? Not to hurt or control, but simply to show care?"

I see the conflict in her eyes, the war between the frightened child who wants to believe and the hardened woman shaped by cruelty.

Then she disappears.

The screens split into multiple feeds, each one showing a different room in what I assume is another suite in the club. Bound and gagged figures writhe on beds and floors, their naked bodies decorated with bruises and burns. Men and women, all in various states of agony.

Cassie's singsong tone cuts through the miserable scene. "You showed me your love. Now let me show you mine."

# 14
## LAYLA

The wall of screens is bright with human suffering. Cassie is making us watch, but instead of focusing on the women's faces and how much they hurt, I force myself to mentally list the details and try to note anything that could help us.

I'm not tied up anymore, curled into a fetal position and waiting for the next beating. I can finally be useful and start using my mind now that Kaden is supporting me through this wretched hell. My eyes drift from frame to frame while Cassie gleefully narrates each father's descent into monstrosity by torturing other men's daughters. In one feed, a man methodically breaks fingers while his own daughter watches. In another, someone applies a branding iron with mechanical precision. The scenes blur together until my vision swims and my stomach twists, but something keeps drawing my attention to the bottom right monitor. Not obviously different, but wrong enough to make my tech-oriented mind itch.

"Monitor number four took the longest," Cassie says through the speakers, distracting me from peering closer. "Father and daughter clung to their trust in each other as if their unwavering loyalty would force me to let them go." She laughs under her breath. "Isn't that sweet?"

It hurts to swallow when I look where she directed. A woman, maybe a few years younger than me, is held by another man, a knife to her throat. The man, likely her father, stands over another woman bound on a lavish velvet couch, his hand shaking as he holds a scalpel.

"Wraithling." Kaden's voice cuts through the screams coming from the speakers and the blood-rush in my ears. "Don't watch."

But I can't look away. I feel like I owe it to them to remember what they went through so it fuels me to do what they couldn't: escape.

There's a flicker in the screen, like a skipping frame, and suddenly, crimson blooms across the woman's abdomen.

Kaden remains stoic and hard beside me. Witnessing violence isn't new to him, but his arm tightens around my shoulders. I squint at the screen where the flicker was, ignoring the bile rising in my throat as the scene plays out in nauseating detail.

There it is again.

A line of code, lasting barely a fraction of a second. My lips move silently, parsing the string of ones and zeros.

"Ethan," I breathe, hope sparking in my chest.

Kaden squeezes my shoulder. "What is it?"

I keep my voice low, praying Cassie's audio doesn't pick it up over the din of anguished pleas. "He's found a way into her system."

"Can he shut it down?" Kaden asks, his breath warm against my ear.

I shake my head minutely. "He's working on it. It's the most sophisticated I've ever seen. But this is his way of telling us to be ready."

On monitor #4, the woman's body goes limp, a final tear tracing down her ashen cheek. The father drops the scalpel, shaking so hard he can barely stand.

And the man holding his daughter slits her throat. She crumples to the ground at the same time her father's agonized wail overtakes all the other screams.

"And then there was one," Cassie purrs.

The monitors stutter, then die. Kaden pushes me behind him like they're about to explode. But all of them plunge into black screens save for the one on the bottom right. The monitor that made me want to look harder.

Of course, Cassie doesn't give me time to process just how small her snake-sized heart is before she moves on to her next atrocity.

The man has his back to the camera, and his shoulders are hunched. He hasn't moved since I first looked at the screen. No one else is in the suite decorated in shades of blue and gold with plush curtains and a four-poster bed. At first, I thought that was why this particular screen grabbed me— this man is alone when all the other monitors had at least two people in the frame. But no, that's not it. I'm sure his greatest fear is just waiting off-screen and will appear for Cassie's entertainment soon.

The man lifts his head, his attention snapping to the door, and that's when I figure out what drew my suspicion in the first place.

There's no audio.

Then he turns.

His lanky frame twists reluctantly, his messy brown hair and nervous tics unmistakable.

"Ethan," I whisper in sharp disbelief.

"She fucking caught him," Kaden rasps. "But he just sent us a message. Cassie can't be that fast—"

"It was a recording." I say what both of us are thinking with painful clarity. "And a trap."

Ethan looks directly at the camera, our gazes locking through the lens. He pushes his glasses up the bridge of his nose, a gesture so familiar it makes my heart ache.

I shake my head in denial, unable to tear my eyes away from the screen.

Ethan is saying something, his lips moving rapidly, but we can't hear him. He gestures to something off-camera, his movements frantic.

And then Cassie steps into the frame.

"Oh God." My hand flies to my mouth.

She's wearing her preferred leather catsuit that clings to her lithe frame, her raven hair pulled back in a sleek ponytail. She circles Ethan like a shark, her fingers trailing across his shoulders.

Ethan grimaces at her touch, but he doesn't move away. His eyes dart to the camera again, pleading.

Cassie knows Ethan is my weakness, the one person other than Kaden I would do anything to protect. And now she has him.

A strangled sound escapes my lips. My legs give out, and Kaden's arm is the only thing that keeps me from falling to the floor.

"We need to get to him," I say, clinging to Kaden's forearm. "We need to get out of here and *get to him*."

My voice rises to a shriek, and I tear from Kaden's hold and race to the door.

"Layla—" Kaden says, but nothing he does will be of any use unless he *breaks* this *goddamn* door.

"She can't kill him." I press my hands against the door, then start pounding on it. "She can't kill him! *Let me out! Let me out, goddammit!*"

"Wraithling, please." Kaden's hands come down on my shoulders, pulling me away.

"I told you I'd find your pressure points, kitten," Cassie says, her voice suddenly filling the room. "And look, isn't this the perfect one?"

I spin to the monitors with heaving breaths.

Cassie's smile is all sharp edges as she leans in close to Ethan, her lips moving with words we can't hear. He tries to jerk away, but she digs her nails into his cheeks, forcing him to look at her.

My heart pounds against my ribs as I watch helplessly, my mind racing to find a way out of this godforsaken place.

Ethan's gaze flicks to the camera again, and this time, I spot the desperation in his eyes, the silent plea for us to understand. He's trying to tell me something, but what?

Cassie follows his line of sight. Her lips curve into a smirk as she steps behind Ethan and drapes her arms over his shoulders in a mockery of an embrace.

Ethan shudders, his Adam's apple bobbing. "Layla, don't—"

Cassie clamps a hand over his mouth. "Shh. It's not your turn to speak."

Rage boils under my skin at the way she touches him, the possessive gleam in her eyes. But it's the pure fear in Ethan's face that kills me and the knowledge that he's suffering because of my choices.

"Cassandra Grace *Black*," Kaden snaps. The threat of the impending doom in his tone even makes me stiff with apprehension.

He steps around me and prowls toward the monitors, his hands curled into pissed-off fists. "Get the *fuck* away from that boy and air your disagreements with me. No one else."

Cassie reaches into the holster at her hip in answer and pulls out a gleaming knife, pressing the point under Ethan's chin. He goes perfectly still, save for the rapid rise and fall of his chest.

"It's quite simple, really." Cassie's tone is conversational as if she's not holding a blade to my best friend's neck. "You have a choice, kitten. Either you slice into Dad or I paint this room with your little hacker's blood."

My heart stops. I can't breathe, can't think.

Kaden grabs me and pulls me in tight.

"Cut into me yourself," he seethes. "Stop making others do your dirty work."

A slow, wicked smile spreads across her face. "By the way, it's Cassandra Morelli now."

I feel more than see Kaden's sharp intake of breath. His heartbeat thunders beneath my cheek.

"Morelli," he repeats, the name dripping with venom. "You are not his daughter, Cassandra. You are *mine*."

Kaden's fingers dig into my arms as if I'm the only thing keeping him tethered.

"That bastard stole you from me. Twisted you into this—"

"Bitch?" Cassie finishes for him. "No, Daddy dearest. He made me strong. Powerful. He had fucked-up ways of getting me there, but here I am."

"Morelli was a sadistic bastard who destroys everything he touches," Kaden growls. "But even he can't erase the truth of who you are, Cassie. Defiance is in your blood. My blood. You're stronger than his depraved manipulations."

If Cassie is affected by Kaden's declaration, we don't see it. She gives us her profile and traces the knife along Ethan's jawline, leaving a thin line of crimson in its wake. Ethan squeezes his eyes shut, a single tear escaping down his cheek.

"Cassie, please," I beg, my lower lip trembling.

She presses the knife harder against Ethan's throat, eliciting a choked gasp from him. "Now, kitten is going to prove her loyalty. To me. To the Morelli name."

Desperation and terror rip through me. I can't hurt Kaden. I won't. But Ethan ... oh God, my sweet, brilliant friend who only ever wanted to keep me safe. I can't let Ethan die.

"Clock's ticking, kitten. Either you make Daddy bleed or this room gets an instant makeover."

Kaden's hand finds mine, his fingers lacing through my own.

"Layla," he says softly. "It's okay. Do what you have to do."

I shake my head, then bury my face in his chest. "I can't. I won't."

He brings our joined hands closer to his heart. "You can,

and you will." Kaden uses his free hand to tip my chin up until our gazes meet. "I can take it, Wraithling. I promise."

A sob catches in my throat. I know what he's doing and why he's accepting Cassie's demands. My neck still throbs from the tattoo I received while being pinned down, and Kaden was forced to look on. I'd wager it was the first time in a very long time that Kaden felt helpless. To endure punishment, especially coming from me, is exactly the type of situation he feels he deserves because he couldn't save me. His own flesh and blood has locked us in this room of horrors, and he still can't save me.

But he is not the villain. Not in my story.

"Layla." Kaden stops my line of thought as if he can sense my direction. "You know what you have to do."

"You don't deserve this." I look back at him and into those coolblue eyes, finding the warm pools within. "I don't blame you for any of this, do you understand?"

Kaden's eyelids lower.

The sob I've been choking on finally climbs out. "Kaden, no. Even if I agree to this, there's nothing here. This room is stripped of anything I could use."

"That's the fun part!"

Cassie's unsettling cheer interrupts the moment.

"After all," she continues, "necessity is the mother of invention."

Not only do I have to hurt Kaden but I also have to find a makeshift weapon? Cassandra Grace Black, or whatever the hell her name is now, has backed me into a corner in the same way so many reluctant fathers were. And I feel the same way they did. I'm starting to *hate* her. To change who I am inside.

My gaze darts around the room, searching for anything I could use to inflict enough pain without causing lasting damage. The thought of harming Kaden makes me want to heave, but I can't let Ethan die.

"The mirror," Kaden says quietly, tilting his head toward the bathroom. "Break it."

Understanding dawns, cold and heavy in my gut.

Reluctantly, Kaden releases his hold on me so I can approach the bathroom. Once inside, I stand in front of the mirror. My reflection stares back—pale, bruised, and haunted.

Until I zero in on the neck tattoo.

Pitch-black vines and thorns snake across my neck, growing wider in the front and thinning out at the sides, just like a slashed throat. No leaves adorn the barren limbs, and the vines stretch out into fractured pathways, some tangling low over my throat. But knowing what I do now about Cassie's men and how she acquired most of them, Harris offered beauty where he could. Small black flowers along the thinner branches, using shading and lighting for wisps of fog, and the tiny wings of birds flitting among the thorns.

The inked skin is swollen and red at the edges and angry from not being cared for. The tattoo took endless hours of pain to become this creation. It also stole a piece of me I can never get back. I've always been different with my blue and brown eye, but this. *This* isn't something I was born with. This was placed on me, forced on me, and is a permanent mark of hate.

It's not just the tattoo but everything it represents—the

violation, the helplessness, and the sheer cruelty of what's been done to me and so many others.

My hands curl into fists at my sides, nails biting into my palms. The pain is a distant thing, drowned out by the roaring in my ears. I'm shaking, my whole body trembling with a rage so intense that I can't breathe.

With a scream that tears from the depths of my soul, I lash out, my fist connecting with the mirror in a blinding explosion of rage and glass. The surface shatters, radiating spiderwebbing cracks from the point of impact. Shards rain down, tinkling against the sink and floor like jagged diamonds.

I pluck the largest shard of glass from the spiderweb forming at the point of impact, ignoring the way it slices into my palm. Crimson drips down my wrist, staining the white porcelain sink.

Kaden appears in the doorway, his expression a mix of concern and grim understanding. He reaches for me, but I shake my head. As much as I long for his comfort and strength, I know I need to perform this next part on my own. He moves to the side so I can get through the doorway and stand in front of the monitors. Cassie is still there holding Ethan hostage, smiling. She's enjoying this, the sick bitch. Enjoying watching me suffer.

Kaden comes up behind me, pushing my hair to the side and kissing the nape of my neck before coming to the front. He gives me a single, solemn nod before reaching for the hem of his shirt and pulling it over his head.

I've seen his hard, sinuous power and his map of scars many times before, but this time, I'm adding to it.

This is wrong. It goes against everything I believe in, everything I am.

"That's it, kitten," Cassie croons from the speakers. "Save your friend over your lover. And I don't want a small scratch. I want you to dig in. Hurt him badly. I won't be content until he's on his knees."

I don't bother to look in her direction. Tears turn my vision hot. I whisper brokenly, "I don't want to do this."

Kaden's expression softens. He reaches out and tenderly brushes a strand of hair from my face, lingering on my cheek.

"You have to, Wraithling." His low voice is steady and strangely calming. "It's all right. I've endured far worse."

A choked sob escapes me. I know he has. I've mapped every one of his scars with delicate strokes in stolen moments of intimacy. Each one represents the unspeakable acts he's done. And still, he stands tall and proud.

"Look at me," Kaden commands.

I drag my gaze to his, desperate to drown myself in his fathomless blue depths. There's no fear there. Just something infinitely tender.

Something that looks a lot like love.

"You are not defined by the evil others do. This is not your choice," he says.

Fresh tears spill down my cheeks at his words. Even now, even as I prepare to cut into his flesh, he seeks to absolve me. To shoulder the burden of this heinous act.

I press my free hand over his heart, feeling the steady thrum beneath my palm. "I will never forgive myself for this."

"You will," he vows. "Because I already have."

Kaden covers my hand with his own, holding it fast against his chest. With his other hand, he reaches for the shard. His fingers close over mine, guiding the makeshift blade to hover over his skin.

"*Boring*," Cassie whines. "I had a better time catching Reaper and putting her and her rodents in a cage. Can we move on?"

I suck in a deep breath at her intended meaning.

"You're going after cat families now?" I ask, my voice not sounding like my own.

"There really is no line I won't cross," she replies. I can hear the dismissive shrug in her tone.

Rage and revulsion surge through my veins, warring with the agony of what I'm being forced to inflict.

With a trembling hand, I raise the shard, winking maliciously in the lamplight. Kaden doesn't flinch as I hold it high. He doesn't even look at it. He just stares into my eyes, injecting calm.

I bring the broken shard down with a small cry, slashing toward Kaden's bare chest. Time slows as the sharp edge glints with silver.

But before the keen edge can find its mark, Kaden's hand flashes out, quick as a striking viper. His fingers close around my wrist in an unbreakable grip, halting the shard's deadly descent a hairbreadth from his skin.

I gasp at the suddenness of his movement and the sheer strength in his grasp.

Kaden wrenches the shard from my hand and pivots, hurling it with lethal precision at the monitor displaying Cassie and Ethan. The screen explodes in a dazzling cascade of sparks, a few shards of glass raining down like razor-sharp confetti. The feed cuts out with a harsh crackle of static, plunging the room into sudden, oppressive silence.

I stare at the ruined monitor, chest heaving.

My hand goes to my mouth.

I say to Kaden through the cracks of my fingers, my voice a wet whisper, "What have you done?"

# 15
## KADEN

This is the first time I've heard Layla's voice go hoarse with betrayal, and I don't enjoy it.

I've heard that tone before, all the way from marks begging for their miserable lives to Layla writhing naked underneath me, upset that I took my fingers and tongue away at a crucial moment.

But never like this. Like I fucking failed her.

I stare at Layla, at the hurt etched into her pretty face. It's a terrible sight, and it cuts me deep, knowing I'm the one who put it there. Goddammit, I've never seen a more spectacular disaster in all my fucked-up life.

"You just killed Ethan!" she cries, pointing at the ruined monitor, sparks dancing at my feet.

"Wraithling." My voice comes out low, reminding her not to lose it right now.

"What did you do, Kaden? What did you fucking *do*? Cassie will be furious with us, and she'll take it out on

Ethan. And now I can't even see—I can't try to protect him. You've taken away the one thing we had—"

"Look at me," I order, but Layla just turns away, disgusted.

This woman will be the death of me. I crave her attention like my next breath, especially in this environment. It's desperate and essential. It drives me insane that she's turned her back on me.

Every instinct in me screams to close the distance between us. To claim her again, to remind her that she belongs to me in every way imaginable. But I hold back. Because as much as I want her, I don't want to hurt her more.

But having had enough of the silent treatment, I dart my hand out, catching her chin and forcing those beautiful tear-streaked eyes to meet mine. The icy touch of her skin sends an electric jolt through me that I relish—because it's real, because it's her, and she's alive.

I'm not one to comfort, but for Layla, I bend my fucking rules.

"I wasn't about to let you change," I murmur, forcing her chin up higher so she has no choice but to keep her stare steady on mine. "I've seen what this life does to people, and so have you. The choices we make, the lines we cross, it transforms us, hardens us. It turns us into something we never wanted to be."

My grip on her chin softens, my thumb grazing the delicate line of her jaw.

"When Cassie made you choose between hurting me or losing Ethan, I saw that same shade of darkness begin to consume you. So I couldn't let you do it."

Layla's brows come together, tears clinging to her lashes. "I didn't ask you to risk Ethan's life like that."

"I *will not* let you become like us. Like me. Like Cassie," I growl, the words tearing from my throat like the shards of glass splayed across the floor. "It would have broken something inside you to hurt me, even to save Ethan. And I couldn't bear to watch that happen."

Layla's lips part, a shaky breath escaping as she processes my words. "But Ethan... Cassie will..."

"She won't kill him," I assure her, my thumb brushing over her trembling bottom lip. "Not now, at least. She wanted us to watch, to see you relent. But now that the monitor's gone, she has no audience. It buys us time."

Layla's eyes flutter closed, a single tear trailing down her cheek. I catch it with my thumb, wiping it away with a gentleness that still feels foreign to me.

"If anyone knows my daughter best, it's me," I add. "Though she may argue otherwise."

Layla leans into my touch, her skin warm and inviting against my battle-scarred hand.

She whispers, "I don't know how to do this, how to survive this without losing myself."

I tilt her face up, our noses brushing as I bring us closer together. "You won't lose yourself. I won't let that happen. We'll find a way out of this, and when we do, I promise you'll still be the same stubborn, infuriating, beautiful woman who captured my black heart."

A watery laugh escapes her, and she nods, her nose brushing against mine.

"Okay," she breathes, her hands coming up to grip my wrists. "Okay. We'll find a way."

I lose the barest distance between our lips and capture hers in a kiss that says everything I can't vocalize. Layla releases my wrists and tangles her fingers in my hair as she pulls me as close as humanly possible, our bodies molding together like two halves from a severed whole. I'm crushing her body against mine as if I could absorb her light through sheer force of will.

After pulling away slightly, I stroke her hair before guiding her head to my chest. The beat of my heart syncs with hers as I wrap an arm around her waist possessively.

"What about Ethan?" she asks with such desperation, it makes me want to tear the world apart just to ease her pain.

"I have it under control," I assure her, and for the first time, I realize I mean it.

Not just for Layla's sake but for mine as well.

My daughter's next move will be to burst in here with Ethan, furious with us for not ceding to her control. And I will meet her madness with my darkness. It's high time I face her not as her father but as her equal.

With my free hand, I trail my fingers down Layla's arm, sending a shiver coursing through her body. Her breath hitches, and I find myself grinning at the effect I have on her.

It might be the last time I do.

I trace my fingers along the delicate curve of her neck, relishing the way her pulse quickens under my touch. She arches into me, a soft moan escaping her parted lips as I dip my head to press a kiss to the hollow of her throat.

Just as I reach up to massage the back of her neck to further soothe her, the door to the suite slams open with a resounding bang.

Layla tenses in my arms, both of our heads turning to find Cassie standing in the doorway with a deep frown on her bright red lips.

"You motherfuckers," she spits, dragging a bloodied and bruised Ethan into the room by the collar of his shirt.

A desperate sound comes from Layla. She tries to lurch forward, but I keep her locked within the safety of my embrace.

"It's okay, Layla," Ethan says through a split lip and broken teeth. "I'm okay."

A rock forms in my throat as Layla chokes back a sob.

This kid has been beaten to hell while facing down a psychopath, and his first instinct is to comfort my woman. My chest constricts, the foreign sensation of guilt eating away at my battered soul.

Cassie's eyes narrow dangerously as she takes in the sight of Layla and I, still wrapped in each other's arms despite the chaos she's unleashed. Her grip on Ethan's collar tightens, causing him to wince.

"Well, isn't this cozy," she says. "I go through all the trouble of arranging this little reunion, and you two are still making googly eyes at each other like a couple of lovesick swans. It's almost enough to make me gag."

She tosses Ethan to the floor, his body hitting the ground with a sickening thud. Layla tries to break free again, but I hold her fast.

"Cassie, please," Layla begs, her nails digging into my biceps. "You've made your point."

Cassie scoffs. "I'm nowhere near my point, kitten."

She crouches down next to Ethan, grabbing a fistful of his hair and yanking his head back. He groans in pain, his one good eye struggling to focus. Cassie must have gone berserk on Ethan the minute I smashed the monitor, and that ugly feeling of guilt in my stomach won't go away.

"I almost feel sorry for you," Cassie says to Ethan. "Caught in the middle of this family drama. But then I remember how eagerly you jumped in to protect poor Layla over there, and my sympathy for you just ... evaporates."

She releases his hair with a shove, rising to her feet and turning her attention back to us. "I have to admit, I'm impressed. I thought for sure my stunt with Ethan would be the final straw. That Layla would finally see you for the monster you are, choose Ethan, and turn her back on you for good."

Layla's jaw clenches, her eyes blazing with barely contained fury. "No matter what you do, I will never turn on him."

"Oh, *spare* me," Cassie groans. "Bonds are made to be broken, just like bones. Why don't you take a seat at the table, Ethan?"

When he doesn't move fast enough, Cassie kicks him in the ribs. The sight makes Layla jerk against me.

I adjust my grip, sliding my hand to her hip in a way that appears possessive but actually pins her in place. My daughter's eyes track the movement. Something ripples across her face—disgust? Envy?—before that broken-doll smile returns.

Ethan pushes himself up on shaky arms. Blood drips steadily from his nose, staining his torn shirt.

"Good boy," Cassie purrs.

I watch how she positions herself, with one hand still

gripping the hair at the back of his head and the other pressed between his shoulder blades.

Not the most efficient way to control someone. Morelli taught her strength when he should have taught her precision. Ethan stumbles but catches himself on the table's edge. Blood drips from his split lip onto the polished wood as Cassie forces him into the chair where Layla was forced to sit during our "romantic dinner."

"Hands on the table where Daddy can see them," she orders Ethan.

I continue to observe her technique with the Scythe's clinical detachment. Every move betrays Morelli's influence: all brutality and no finesse.

The way Cassie digs her nails into Ethan's wrist as she forces his hand flat against the wood, how she positions herself to loom over him rather than maintain proper supervision.

Cassie's fingers freeze over Ethan's hand. She tilts her head. "What was that, Daddy?"

"The angle's wrong," I explain, studying her grip with the same cold calculation I used on targets. "Morelli taught you to maximize pain. But pain without purpose is just ... messy."

Her eyes light up with manic curiosity. "And you'd know all about purpose, wouldn't you?" She shifts her grip, mimicking my tone. "Tell me then, what would you have taught your little girl?"

Layla's breath catches as she realizes what I'm doing— meeting Cassie's madness not as a father trying to save his daughter, but as someone who understands the artistry of breaking people.

"The wrist first," I say softly. "Control comes from immobilization."

Ethan raises his head, his good eye meeting mine, the betrayal in it cutting deeper than I expected. All that time we spent working together to find Layla, and now I'm teaching my psychotic daughter how to torture him properly.

Layla tips her head back, her lips parting.

"Kaden, don't."

Her tone carries more disappointment than fear.

The weight of their judgment should crush me. Instead, it crystallizes everything. They don't understand. To save them both, I need to become what I've always been. What made me the Scythe. What kept me alive while hunting for my daughter all those years.

"The wrist is boring," Cassie says, forcing Ethan's right hand flat against the polished wood.

Sweat beads on his forehead when he turns his attention back to her. His chest spasms with shallow breaths.

"I'll do what you want," he says, trying to reason with Cassie. "I'll help you, like you asked. I'll fix the AI, just don't —I *need* my fingers."

Layla gasps at the same time I stiffen. The stolen AI, the Oracle, has never been at the top of my priorities, but it was Layla's. She tried so hard to destroy it before it got into Morelli's hands. Instead, Morelli is dead and the Oracle's remnants are now in Cassie's hands, my daughter turned Mafia princess.

"Funny how quick you are to help now," Cassie says to Ethan, her eyes bright with that fractured intelligence that makes her dangerous. "When I asked you before—so nicely

—you said the code was too corrupt after Layla tinkered with it. That Oracle couldn't be salvaged." She traces the top of Ethan's finger almost tenderly. "Your code was clever," Cassie says, reaching Ethan's wrist and pressing into the tender underside. He presses his lips together, pushing fresh blood out of the cuts. "Routing through dead servers, mimicking old security protocols. But you got sloppy when you found the surveillance feeds. Too eager to help Daddy and his little kitten." She tilts her head. "All I had to do was follow your digital footprints right to that color-vomit basement. Though I have to admit"—Cassie's eyes glitter with that fractured light—"watching you try to fight back was almost cute. Like a mouse wiggling around in a trap."

Ethan tries to steady his breathing as blood drips down his chin. The betrayal in his eye when he looks at me deepens.

Cassie's lips curve. "So keep your noble refusal, Ethan. You're more useful as a lesson now."

Ethan pales. "Miss Black, *please...*"

My arms tighten around Layla, no longer just to keep her safe but to show Cassie exactly what I'm capable of when someone threatens what's mine. Time to let my daughter see that Morelli's education was remedial compared to what her real father could have taught her.

"The problem with Papa Morelli," I cut in just as Cassie is poised to wrench Ethan's index finger backward, "was that he relied too heavily on physical pain. Amateur stuff, really. Breaking fingers?" I let out a dark laugh. "I would have taught you how to break minds first. Bodies are just collateral damage."

Layla tries to rip out of my hold, but I continue, my eyes

locked on my daughter while dropping my arms from around Layla. "Want me to show you how it's done? How to really make someone suffer without leaving a single mark?"

The perfect predator's smile spreads across my face as I add, "After all, you got your talent for psychological warfare from somewhere. And it wasn't Morelli."

"You think you know better?" Cassie asks me, amused.

Challenge lights her eyes. That same manic gleam I've seen reflected back at me in the mirror after I finish my kills.

"Year one with Papa"—*crack*. Ethan howls—"is when I learned that screaming only makes it worse."

Ethan's index finger flops to the table, still attached, but the bone's fractured. He sobs, attempting to pull his arm out from Cassie's grip, but unable to.

I fear I'm at the point when I have to physically intervene. I don't want to lay hands on my daughter, but I have to stop this before Cassie pushes both Layla and Ethan beyond repair. But as I open my mouth, Cassie's head snaps up, her eyes locking with mine as she makes her next move.

*Crack*. Ethan's howl turns into a shriek. "Year two is when I started believing maybe he was right about my father not wanting me."

Layla sprints from behind me, throwing her arms around Ethan and sobbing her apologies in his ear.

"Aw," Cassie mocks as she watches Layla hug Ethan. After taking in the desperate scene, Cassie focuses on Ethan's ashen face, saying through a pretend frown, "Don't worry, baby. Only eight more years to go."

I brace my feet, noting Cassie's men filtering in. Five of her foot soldiers have positioned themselves around the suite to defend Cassie if need be. Their devotion to Frank

Morelli extends to her, and if it were any other universe, I'd be grateful my daughter had so much protection.

But what she endured to require these bodyguards...

I see it now, the cracks in her fragmented psyche. Morelli twisted her understanding of my love for her until it lost all meaning.

I briefly close my eyes and take a breath.

This is where I'm in my element—controlling and dominating others. It's what I do best, instilling fear while keeping them inexplicably drawn to me. It's beguiling. Addictive, even.

My eyes snap open just as Cassie prepares to snap Ethan's third finger.

I take a step forward. Cassie's men tense but don't engage.

"Morelli manipulated you through pain, Cassie," I say evenly, holding her wild gaze. "He systematically erased all evidence of my search for you and replaced it with his carefully crafted lies."

"Liar!" she shrieks, slamming Ethan's hand against the table. He cries out, Layla's sobs muffled against his neck.

"Deep down, a part of you knows the truth," I counter, taking another step. "A part of you remembers what it felt like to be loved unconditionally before Morelli poisoned your mind."

Cassie's nostrils flare, teetering on a knife's tip between her conditioning and the faint whisper of truth.

I fly across the room. Cassie doesn't even register my presence until my hand wraps around her slender wrist in an iron grip, halting her assault on Ethan.

"You're getting ahead of yourself, little one," I murmur.

I whip my head around and *tsk* when her men inch closer, weapons raised. "You boys know better than to piss me off. Aim those bullets at anyone in the room but yourself, and I'll kill your princess right here and now."

Layla lifts her head, her face going white with horror.

Cassie's eyes flare with indignation as she tries to yank her arm free from my hold, but her laugh belies her desire to escape.

"There he is! The real Kaden Black. Not the one who plays house with a bunch of kittens, but the one who'd snap his own daughter's neck."

My grip tightens on her wrist—not enough to hurt, but to command attention. "If I wanted you dead, you wouldn't be standing."

Her soldiers don't lower their weapons, but they don't advance either. They're waiting for her signal, which means...

"You orchestrated this." The realization hits as I study her face, that perfect blend of my calculation and Morelli's chaos. "Every move was designed to force my hand."

"Did you think I didn't notice?" Cassie says in answer. She tries to twist away again, but I hold firm. "How gentle you are with her? How you *protect* her?" The last word comes out like venom. "I had to know if you'd do it for me. If you'd become the Scythe to save your daughter." Her smile slices through me. "But you only break for her, don't you?"

My grip gentles on her wrist, but I don't release her. Not yet. "You're right. I would become an evil incarnate to protect what's mine." I lean closer, pitching my voice for her ears only. "But Cassie-girl, you've been mine since the day you were born."

She tries to jerk back, that triumphant smile faltering. "You're full of shit. You never—"

"I hunted Morelli through three continents." Each word carries the weight of ten years. "Left pieces of his organization scattered across twelve countries. The things I did to find you..." I pause to let her see the darkness in my eyes. "They would make even you shudder with revulsion."

Her foot soldiers shift uneasily.

"Let go of me," Cassie hisses through gritted teeth.

I ignore her demand. "You want to break Ethan, don't you? Really make him suffer."

Cassie stills, her curiosity piqued despite herself. "I'm listening."

I release her wrist and step back, circling the table and taking my time doing it. My path has been a dark one. I've killed. I've lied. I've deceived. But it's all been for her—Cassie. My daughter. My first obsession before Layla.

I'm not Second Lieutenant Kaden Black anymore. I haven't been for a very long time. At first sight of Cassie alive, I immediately flipped back to that man, the devoted father, the man who retired early so he could be there for his daughter as she first entered high school. It's taken me too long to realize that isn't who Cassie needed or wanted. Not anymore, because she's not the little girl I once knew. Not even close. Cassie wants the Scythe, the man whose skin I'm comfortable in, and I shouldn't have shed it in the first place. Not if I want to get through to her.

Ethan's labored breathing fills the room. He refuses to raise his head. Layla's muffled sobs make me clench my teeth, but I forge on.

"Physical pain is fleeting," I explain, my voice taking on a clinical detachment. "It's the anticipation, the fear of what's to come, that truly shatters a person's will. You want to get inside his head, make him question everything he thought he knew."

Cassie's eyes gleam with a twisted sort of fascination as she watches me, her anger momentarily forgotten. "And how do you suggest I do that?"

I pause behind Ethan's chair, my hands coming to rest on his trembling shoulders. He flinches at my touch. "Get the *fuck* off me."

"Exploit his weakness," I say, my fingers digging into Ethan's flesh. "Find the cracks in his armor and pry them open, one by one, until nothing is left but frayed, exposed nerves."

Layla glares at me through shining, bloodshot eyes. "Kaden, stop it."

I keep my eyes level on Cassie's even as my heart spasms at Layla's anguish in my periphery. "I've spent a decade looking for my daughter, and I've finally found you, Cass. I can't let you go this time, and I certainly can't hurt you. If I'm faced between Ethan and you ... I choose you."

Cassie's lips curve into a slow, wicked grin.

"*What?*" Layla's blue eye seems to go as dark as her brown one when I finally look her way. "You can't mean that. There has to be another way. I'll never forgive you for hurting Ethan. Do you understand me, *Scythe?* I will never. Forgive."

Turning back to Cassie, I nod toward Ethan. "He cares for Layla, that much is obvious."

Cassie's attention darts between Ethan, Layla, and me, intrigue mingling with delight. Her hand hovers near

Ethan's remaining fingers in his right hand, poised to inflict more pain if the whim strikes.

I watch her unflinchingly, silently daring her to make the next move—one that would shape not just this moment but our entire future.

Blood drips from Ethan's split lip onto the carpet, each droplet marking time like a morbid metronome. Layla's on her knees beside him, refusing to let go. I'm well aware she's ready to dive in front of Ethan and sacrifice herself depending on what comes next.

In fact, I'm counting on it.

# 16

## LAYLA

I've seen Kaden as the Scythe before. I've even desired the cold-hearted killer when he was covered in the viscera of his victims, his slash of white teeth when he callously smiled the only clean thing about him.

But it suddenly dawns on me that I've never seen the Scythe without his mask.

Until today.

His gunmetal veneer was unsettling in itself, a cold, expressionless thing that made it easy for the Scythe to intimidate and brutalize with consistent apathy. It never occurred to me that the Scythe's real face—*Kaden's* face—could mirror the mask so effortlessly.

His eyes seem to glow just like the mask's narrow slits but infinitely shrewder. There's no flicker of humanity in their depths as he stands behind Ethan's drooping, seated form and rests his hands on Ethan's shoulders. Cassie bounces eagerly on her heels, a rabid hunger in her gaze that makes my stomach turn.

"The key is precision," Kaden says to Cassie, his voice a low, instructive murmur. "You want to cause maximum pain with minimal damage."

Kaden refuses to look my way despite my obvious efforts to glare, curse, and sob at him to stop. To reach the man behind these lethal eyes that no longer need a mask to kill. I'd even take his horrible, blank expression, just to understand when exactly I stopped being the woman he'd kill for and became the one he'd kill. With each crack of Ethan's bones, I hear it—the sound of Kaden choosing violence over love.

Kaden curls his fingers into Ethan's shoulders, digging into the pressure points there. Ethan's eyes widen, and a muffled groan escapes. He's about to pass out, and I honestly wish he would so he could be spared this torture.

While Ethan groans, Kaden explains to Cassie, "Here, you can immobilize the arms temporarily. Useful for subduing without leaving marks. You try."

Cassie slinks around the table until she's beside Kaden, then mimics his grip on Ethan. Ethan shouts in a nonexistent language as she applies pressure, droplets of sweat mixing with the blood on his face.

"Good," Kaden praises at the same time he swipes my hands away when I try to pry Cassie's off Ethan.

I'm still kneeling in front of Ethan and refusing to go anywhere—a mantra I keep reminding him whenever his one good eye manages to focus on me.

"Now, the neck. Carotid artery." Kaden brushes Ethan's throat with his knuckles, where Ethan's pulse jumps erratically. "Steady pressure here will cause loss of consciousness in seconds. A little longer, and they'll never wake up."

Cassie leans in to get an up-close look. "I like the sound of that."

"The goal isn't to kill," Kaden chides. "Not yet. Move lower."

His fingertips skim over Ethan's sweat-soaked chest, his T-shirt no longer resembling any shade of white. Kaden again bats my hands away when I try to rest them on Ethan's chest and stop Kaden's descent.

"Move," Kaden commands, his attention finally, *finally* settling on me.

I immediately wished it hadn't. I don't recognize the man staring down at me. The one who looks like he'd rather decapitate me than deal with my sad attempts to protect my friend.

"I'm not going anywhere," I say through the terror strangling my voice. "And I didn't think you were, either."

Kaden slides his gaze back to Cassie like I mean nothing to him.

"Intercostal nerves," he says, pointing between Ethan's ribs on one side. "Extremely sensitive. You can elicit all kinds of interesting reactions. Not only that, but precise strikes here can fracture the ribs, driving splinters into the lungs."

His voice is almost dreamy, like he's describing a particularly beautiful sunset rather than a brutal technique.

Kaden presses down, and Ethan convulses, a choked scream tearing from his throat.

I surge to my feet, slamming my palms against Kaden's shoulders again and again. "You fucking *bastard*, get off him! He's done nothing to you. *Nothing!*"

Kaden continues relentlessly, treating me like an annoying but harmless fly.

"Solar plexus. Celiac plexus. Lumbar plexus. So many vulnerable points," he says while Ethan makes strangled noises of pure agony.

Until I slap Kaden across the face.

The crack of my palm against Kaden's cheek shocks everyone into stillness. Even Cassie's eyes widen, her hand frozen mid-reach toward Ethan's solar plexus.

And Kaden ... Kaden slowly turns to face me, a red handprint blooming on his skin.

"Layla," he says, his voice deceptively soft. "That wasn't very smart."

I lift my chin, meeting his gaze head-on even as my hand throbs and my heart races. "I don't care."

Kaden studies me for a long moment. Then, without warning, he grabs my wrist and yanks me toward him, spinning me around so my back is pressed against his chest. His other hand comes up to grip my throat, applying just enough pressure to make breathing difficult.

"You still haven't learned, have you?" he murmurs. "Kaden's gone."

I claw at his hand, struggling to draw air into my lungs. "Please," I rasp out. "This isn't you—"

Kaden only secures his hold on me.

Tears sting my eyes, blurring my vision. I blink them away, refusing to let him see how much his words hurt. "No. I don't believe that. I can't."

His chest moves with an unhurried chuckle. "Believe what you want. It doesn't change the truth."

Kaden releases me abruptly, shoving me away from him. I stumble, barely catching myself on the edge of the table.

Cassie steps forward eagerly, her eyes darting between Kaden and me. "Can I try now? On her?"

Kaden looks at me, and for a split second, I think I see a glimmer of hesitation. But then it's gone, and he nods curtly. "Go ahead. Show me what you've learned."

Cassie grins, feral and vicious, and stalks toward me. I back away instinctively even though there's nowhere to run.

I stare at Kaden, my face bloodless. Every ounce of life I have left has pooled into my heart and is about to burst.

*He wouldn't do this to me.*

This has to be a tactic, a Hail Mary of manipulation so he can distract Cassie and find an opening where Ethan and I can escape. Right?

Kaden wouldn't *do* this.

But he does.

He idly stands by while Cassie latches onto my upper arms, finding the same pressure points Kaden demonstrated on Ethan. I cry out as pain lances through my arms, my muscles seizing and refusing to obey. She laughs, high and manic, reveling in my suffering.

Kaden comes closer, giving me the once-over while I stare at him through my watery vision.

"Very good," he says to Cassie without redirecting his gaze. "Now, watch how she responds to more subtle approaches."

He trails a single finger down the side of my neck, barely grazing my skin. Against my will, I shudder, goose bumps erupting in the wake of his touch. Kaden's eyes remain cold and assessing.

"The carotid bodies are highly sensitive," he explains to Cassie. "Even light stimulation elicits an increased heart rate, flushing, and tremors. All automatic reactions she can't control."

"Stop," I whisper.

As if to prove his point, he repeats the motion on the other side of my neck. I try to hold myself rigid but fail to suppress another full-body shiver. Humiliated tears prick at my eyes.

"Please, stop," I ask again, hating how weak I sound.

Kaden ignores my plea. His hands skim down to my collarbones, thumbs resting in the hollows of my throat.

"The suprasternal notch is another key point. Firm pressure here constricts the trachea and stimulates the vagus nerve. You can modulate her breathing, induce coughing or gagging. Take away her air."

He demonstrates, pressing down until I'm gasping desperately for breath, black spots swarming my vision. Cassie watches with rapt attention, memorizing every cruel detail.

"Now the torso." Kaden's palms slide over my ribs. He maps the sensitive spaces between them, and my skin crawls with revulsion even as unwanted heat blooms in his wake.

"The external obliques are also remarkably responsive," he continues, hands drifting lower. "Stimulating the cutaneous branches of the nerves here provokes uncontrollable muscle tension."

He strokes along my sides, and my abdominal muscles clench painfully. I try to twist away, but his grip is iron, his hands digging into the hollows of my hips.

"Stop, I can't..." A broken sob escapes me.

"You can," Kaden counters, staring hard into my eyes. "And you will."

Kaden relents after a few agonizing seconds that feel like an eternity. I sag forward while backing away. Cassie looks on, delighted at her new arsenal of ways to torture while Kaden steps back, appraising me like a prized possession he's about to bequeath to her.

"The most potent weapon, Cassie, isn't pain. It's love. Wield it like a blade. Find the soft spots, the vulnerabilities, and press until they bleed."

He circles behind me, fingers skimming across my shoulders and raising goose bumps in their wake. I shudder, not in revulsion but in treacherous longing, wishing it were like before.

Until Kaden whispers near my ear, "Layla's deepest fear is abandonment."

I go rigid.

Abruptly, he wrenches me around to face him, gripping my chin. I stare into his eyes, searching desperately for a hint of the man I fell for, the man who held me tenderly and promised I'd never be alone again.

But there's only the Scythe staring back—detached, ruthless, empty.

"Where are you?" I ask, searching his emotionless face.

He talks over my crestfallen plea.

"Your mother was never there for you, choosing random men over taking care of her child. Your father, while he was on this earth, never thought to have you in his life. Only when he was dead did he give you a run-down cottage with an abandoned lighthouse, like that would somehow make up for over two decades of his absence. Yet you live there. You moved into the very spot where he made his home without you. Is it so you could bond with him somehow? Find meaning to the reason you were even conceived?"

Agony lances through me, sharper than any physical blow. The words I've never spoken aloud, never shared with anyone, spill from Kaden's lips like a toxin.

I crumple, knees giving out, but Kaden catches me. Not to comfort but to force me upright.

"Which parent gave you the mutated gene for those eyes of yours?" he relentlessly continues. "Do you even know?"

I squeeze my eyes shut, hot tears leaking from the corners. He's exposing me, flaying me open for Cassie's voyeuristic delight.

"Because her father left when she was young and her mother never paid attention to her, Layla's always felt ... unworthy of love." Kaden's voice is soft, almost tender, a jarring contrast to the brutality of his words. "It's why she clings so desperately to anyone who shows her affection. Like me."

A harsh sob wrenches from my throat. I want to deny it, to scream that he's wrong, but the denial sticks in my throat. Because it's true, isn't it? I latched onto Kaden, let myself trust him and love him because I was starved for it. So desperate to feel wanted.

"Poor little kitten," Cassie says. "So pathetic and needy."

Finally, Kaden releases his hold.

"Do you see what I did here, Cass? I tore her down, turned her into a sobbing mess, and I didn't have to lay a hand on her to do it."

"Kaden..." I say, hugging my arms around myself.

He raises his eyes to mine again. "I told you, Layla. Kaden is gone."

Cassie grins. "She still doesn't get it, does she? She actually thought you loved her. Then again, so did I. You can be very convincing."

Kaden moves to Cassie's side. "I found your weaknesses, Layla. Your soft spots. And I used them against you."

"No." I shake my head in refusal. "What we had, it was real. I know it was."

He scoffs. "You only saw what I wanted you to see."

Cassie clucks her tongue at me in disappointment. "Come on, Daddy. I have some other guests for you to work your magic on." She loops her arm through Kaden's. "We can come back to these two wet blankets later."

They both turn to the door, Ethan watching them with a hooded, hateful stare and me barely able to remain standing.

But.

"You want to talk about weaknesses, Scythe?" I spit out when his back is turned. "Let's talk about how you couldn't protect your own daughter. How you let her get taken right from under your nose while you were out for a morning run."

That gets both Kaden's and Cassie's attention.

"You weren't some green recruit then. You were special forces trained. Yet—" I laugh, a harsh, unfamiliar sound. "You couldn't even secure your own home properly. What kind of father does that make you?"

Kaden's face remains impassive, but I catch it—that microscopic twitch. Cassie goes very still.

"You want to break me by exposing my abandonment

issues?" I continue, straightening my spine with pretend bravado. "Fine. But at least my father never promised to protect me. You did. You promised Cassie everything and then failed."

Cassie's eyes dart between us, that crazed gleam of hers sparking with something else. Something younger.

"Want to know what I think?" I press on, even as warning bells ring in my head to stop. "I think you trained yourself to become the Scythe because you couldn't face being Kaden Black anymore. The man who failed his daughter so completely that he became exactly the kind of man who took her— another Morelli."

Kaden angles his head like a gun being cocked to fire. My heart is a battering ram, begging me to backtrack before I get myself killed.

"He's doing it again right now," I say to Cassie while forcing myself to hold Kaden's murderous stare. "Becoming the very monster who broke you. Because that's what he does, isn't it? When he can't protect someone, he becomes what hurts them instead."

Kaden moves so fast I barely register it. His hand locks around my throat, but I don't stop. I can't.

"Go ahead," I rasp out. "Prove me right. Show your daughter exactly who you really are."

His fingers dig in just enough to make breathing difficult. "You think you know me so well?"

"I know enough." My voice scrapes past his iron hand. "I know you gave up everything to find her. Your home. Your life. Your humanity."

Something flashes in Kaden's eyes. Not the cold calculation from before, but something raw. Wounded.

*"Shut up!"*

Cassie slams her hand on the table beside Ethan, making him flinch. Her composure cracks, that perfect Morelli programming starting to splinter.

"Want to know what's really pathetic?" I say in a strangled voice to Kaden. "Not your torture techniques—those are exactly what I'd expect from the Scythe. It's watching you pretend they mean nothing to you."

His fingers flex around my neck in silent warning, but I hold on to consciousness. "You're teaching your daughter how to destroy people like it's some kind of sick bonding exercise. But every time she hurts Ethan, every time you make me beg, I see it in your eyes. You're dying inside watching Cassie become everything you spent ten years fighting against."

Cassie's manic energy falters, just for a moment.

"Go ahead," I challenge Kaden, who hasn't broken our stare off. "Show her more pressure points. Teach her every way to make someone suffer. You're trying to prove you can be just as repulsive, just as influential. But you can't, can you? Because unlike Morelli, you actually love her."

Kaden's hand loosens on my throat, but I almost wish he'd keep choking me. It would be easier than the way his thumb strokes over my pulse, knowing exactly what that touch does to me.

And reminding me exactly who I'm playing with.

"Tell them," he murmurs, his eyes holding mine. "Tell Cassie and Ethan how your heart's racing not because you're afraid but because you want me. Even now. Even after watching Cassie disfigure your best friend."

I press my lips shut, but my body betrays me, leaning into his touch.

"You understand my daughter now, don't you?" Kaden's other hand slides into my hair, and I hate how my eyes flutter closed. "Why she'd do anything for the monster who shaped her. Because you would too, wouldn't you, Wraithling? You'd burn everything down for me, just like she would for Morelli."

"I'm nothing like her," I say, but the words sound hollow, even to me.

"No?" He pulls until I feel a sting in my scalp. "Then why aren't you running? Why aren't you trying to save Ethan? Because deep down, you know exactly how Cassie feels. To be remade by someone's darkness until you crave it more than air."

Kaden's deadly hold on me doesn't waver, not once, but Cassie remains incredibly still behind him. Her eyes narrow as she studies the way his thumb strokes my neck.

"You can't even hurt her properly, can you?"

Cassie's question comes out soft, dangerous, and her focus on my throat never strays. "Look at how you're holding her."

From his chair, Ethan makes a miserable sound. Blood drips steadily from his split lip onto his ruined shirt, his mangled fingers curled protectively against his chest.

Kaden squeezes tighter, but there's something else in his pressure against my neck. Something that makes Cassie's expression twist with a new kind of fury.

She paces like a caged animal, that unpredictable energy of hers building. "No, no, this isn't right. You're still holding back, Daddy. I can see it."

Cassie stalks toward us, her movements jerky and agitated. She points an accusing finger at Kaden. "You're not doing it right. This is supposed to be a lesson, not erotic asphyxiation."

Kaden's jaw ticks, but he doesn't release his hold on me. "This is what I'm trying to teach you. Having someone submit to you, even when facing death, is the ultimate form of power over a person."

But through a blazing stare, Cassie sees everything—the history between Kaden and me, the depraved tenderness, and the desire Kaden's fought hard to resist, even when he's at his worst.

Cassie circles us like a shark scenting blood in the water. Her gaze rakes over me, dissecting every point of contact between Kaden's body and mine.

"Look at you," she sneers. "The great and terrible Scythe, undone by a pair of pretty eyes and a tight cunt. It's disgusting."

"You're seeing things that aren't there," Kaden says to her through tight lips.

But she's just getting started. Cassie leans in close as I struggle to breathe, as my neck burns. "He'll never truly be yours, you know. No matter how much you spread your legs, no matter how sweetly you beg. Because at the end of the day, blood is thicker than water. And I'm his blood."

Tears sting my eyes, blurring my vision. I blink them away furiously, refusing to let her see how deep she can cut.

Cassie straightens, the corners of her mouth twitching.

"But I'm a generous daughter. I'm willing to give Daddy a chance to prove his loyalty. To show me once and for all where his true allegiance lies. Let go of the kitten's collar, Dad."

She turns her attention to Ethan, who watches the exchange with mounting dread. His face is a mask of blood and bruises, his one open eye wide with fear.

"Kill him," Cassie says simply.

# 17
## LAYLA

My heart stops. The whole world narrows down to those two words. *Kill him.*

Cassie claps her hands together, the sound loud and jarring in the tense silence. "Okay, boys! Let's set the stage, shall we? I want everyone to see this."

At her command, her men spring into action. They drag Ethan from his chair, ignoring his grunts of pain as they shove him to the center of the room. They force him to his knees, one brute holding him in place with a meaty hand on his shoulder.

Cassie's men form a loose circle around Ethan, their eager faces lit by the golden lamplight in the suite.

Kaden's hand falls away from my throat. He looks at Cassie, then at Ethan. His expression is unreadable.

"No more excuses. No more delays," Cassie continues. "You want to prove you're with me? Then do it. Kill Ethan Rutledge, nerd extraordinaire."

Ethan makes a low, pained sound. He tries to straighten

his posture, to face his fate with some semblance of dignity, but his injuries make it impossible. He slumps under the foot soldier's hand in defeat.

I can't let this happen.

"Kaden, please." I grab his arm, forcing him to look at me. "Don't do this. You're not Morelli. You don't kill innocents. All Ethan has done is help us. He saved your life! You're better than this."

For a moment, just a moment, I see the doubt in his eyes. A semblance of the man I know is still in there somewhere, buried beneath the Scythe.

Then he blinks.

Nothing reflects back at me. No warmth, not recognition. Just emptiness.

Kaden pulls his arm from my grasp and steps away. Toward Ethan.

"No!" I lunge after him, but Cassie grabs me, yanking me back. Her nails cut into my arms as she holds me in place.

"Watch," she hisses in my ear. "Watch what he's willing to do for me."

My heart seizes in my chest. This can't be happening. After everything, Kaden can't seriously be considering...

"I made my choice long ago," Kaden says quietly. He looks at Cassie. "My loyalty has always been to my daughter."

Ethan's eyes lock with mine. A silent apology. A goodbye.

Cassie practically vibrates with anticipation.

"Do it, Daddy," she urges. "Let's be a real family again."

For one breathless, endless moment, Kaden goes utterly still.

And then he moves.

Kaden looms over Ethan, who stares up at him with resignation. He knows there's no escape. No mercy to be found.

"To think I thought we could be friends one day," Ethan says to Kaden with a lopsided, weary smile on his lips.

"I'm sorry," Kaden says quietly. And then his hands are around Ethan's throat.

Ethan's eyes bulge. His mouth opens in a silent scream as Kaden squeezes, cutting off his air. His feet kick weakly against the carpeting.

A scream builds in my throat, tearing, clawing its way out. An inhuman sound of grief and rage.

No. *No, no, no!*

I thrash against Cassie's hold, desperate to get to them, as Cassie's laughter dances against the roaring in my ears.

Ethan's struggles grow weaker, his face turning a sickly shade of purple. And still, Kaden doesn't let go.

Ethan's eyes roll back, his body going slack under Kaden's merciless grip. I scream until my voice gives out, tears soaking my face as I watch the light fade from my best friend's face.

Kaden holds on a few seconds longer, ensuring there's no flicker of life left. Then he releases Ethan and steps back, letting his lifeless form crumple to the ground.

I fall to my knees, Cassie's hold on me loosening as she stares at her father with a mixture of awe and satisfaction.

"You did it," she breathes. "You really did it."

Kaden doesn't respond. He just looks down at Ethan's body.

I crawl forward, moving between the men's legs and

ignoring their jeers about my ass and how it would be nice to ram me from behind, and reach for Ethan with shaking hands. His skin is still warm, but his chest isn't moving.

He's gone.

A wail builds in my throat, tearing free in a raw, animalistic keen of grief. I gather Ethan into my arms, cradling his head against my chest as I rock him back and forth.

"No, no, please no," I sob brokenly. "Come back. Please come back."

But there's no answer. No miraculous resurrection. Just my friend's heavy, empty shell growing cold in my embrace.

I lost him. I couldn't save him.

Tears drip off my chin, soaking into Ethan's blood-matted hair as I clutch him tighter. As if I can somehow pour my own life force into him or bring him back through sheer force of will.

But I can't. I'm powerless. Helpless.

Just like I was when my father left. When my mother chose her revolving door of boyfriends over me.

Everyone leaves me in the end. I'm never enough to make them stay. I wasn't enough to get Kaden to change. To choose me.

Kaden's words echo in my head, taunting me. My deepest fear laid bare. *Abandonment.*

I feel Kaden's gaze, heavy and assessing. Watching me shatter. Watching me drown in a despair of his making.

"Look at me."

His voice cuts through my sobs, unfeeling and commanding.

Slowly, I raise my head.

He stares back at me, his expression devoid of warmth.

But then, just for a moment, he lets me in. A brief flash of ... regret? Apology? I can't be sure. It's gone before I can decipher it.

Kaden turns to face Cassie fully. "There. It's done."

Cassie applauds, bouncing on her toes like a delighted child.

"Oh, Daddy, that was perfect! The way he just ... went purple. So deliciously brutal."

She skips over to Kaden, throwing her arms around his neck. Kaden stiffens at her first affectionate display but puts his arms around her. His eyes never leave mine over her shoulder.

"I knew you'd prove yourself," Cassie purrs, nuzzling into his neck. "Knew you'd show everyone here you could be part of the Morelli family."

The men surrounding us chuckle and jeer their agreement. They leer at me, still cradling Ethan's lifeless body, like vultures eyeing a fresh carcass.

"So what now, boss?" one of the burlier men asks Cassie. "We still got the broad to deal with." He jerks his chin at me.

Cassie untangles herself from Kaden, tapping a finger against her lips thoughtfully.

"Hmm, you're right. Can't have any loose ends, can we?" She grins, feral and sharp. "Though it would be a shame not to have a little more fun with her first."

The men chuckle, a low, menacing rumble that sends icy tendrils of dread down my spine. I clutch Ethan tighter as if his body could somehow shield me.

"No."

Kaden's voice is quiet, but it cuts through the room like

the crack of a whip. Everyone falls silent, all eyes snapping to him.

Cassie frowns. "No? But, Daddy, she's a witness. She knows all about the AI and my plans. We can't just let her—"

"I said." Kaden moves, putting himself between the rest of the room and me. "No."

Confusion flickers across Cassie's face, quickly replaced by petulance. "You don't get to give orders here. This is my show, remember? My empire."

Kaden smiles. It's a chilling thing, devoid of compassion or humor. "Is it now?"

It happens so fast, my brain can hardly process it.

Kaden moves like smoke made into flesh, there one instant and gone the next. The first guard doesn't even have time to cry out before Kaden's hand locks around his throat, a quick twist snapping his neck with brutal efficiency. He drops without a sound.

The others are slow to react, disbelief warring with rising panic as they realize the Scythe has turned on them. Two men shoot at Kaden, but he flows around their bullets like water and gets to them, striking pressure points and nerve clusters with surgical precision. They crumple to boneless heaps at his feet.

Cassie watches, her expression morphing from confusion to shock to a grudging sort of admiration as Kaden tears through her men like they're made of paper. There's a terrible grace to his movements, a deadly dance honed by years of training and an intimate knowledge of the human body's frailties.

A stolen knife materializes in his hand. He chooses it

over the many guns available. He slashes, parries, and thrusts, blood spattering the walls, the floor, himself.

Through it all, Kaden's face remains a mask of icy calm. His eyes blaze like blue lightning, the only outward sign of the life raging within him.

And I can't look away, even as a traitorous heat unfurls low in my belly. Because seeing him like this, unleashed and unfettered, stokes a hidden part of me. A part that craves his darkness and yearns to be consumed by it.

In mere moments, it's over. The last guard falls with a gurgling sigh, Kaden's knife buried to the hilt in his eye socket. Kaden stands amid the carnage, his chest heaving, blood dripping from his hands and face.

Kaden stalks toward me, slow and purposeful, a jaguar approaching a trembling doe. Crimson drips from his fingertips. There is no remorse in his eyes. Only ice and shadow and the promise of exquisite ruin.

He crouches before me. I'm still cradling Ethan's lifeless form, and the dichotomy is jarring—the gentle way I hold my friend juxtaposed against the savagery of Kaden's blood-soaked hands as they reach for me. His fingers, slick and warm, brush my cheek. Paint me in the viscera of his kills.

"Wraithling," he murmurs, his voice a bleak caress. I shudder, leaning into his touch despite myself. Despite the horror of what those hands just did.

"Resist me," Kaden commands softly.

Compelled by some base instinct, I don't obey. I meet his gaze and fall into fathomless depths. Drown in the inky promise of his darkness.

His thumb traces my lower lip, smearing it scarlet. "You watched me tear them apart. Felt their blood spray your skin. And still…" His other hand curls around my nape, pulling me closer. "Your pulse races. Your pupils dilate. I can smell your arousal, sweet and thick."

I tremble under his knowing gaze and his words, hating how right he is. Hating how much I crave his merciless touch even as I cradle the broken body he destroyed.

A broken sound escapes me, half sob, half moan.

"Don't be so devastated," Kaden croons loud enough for Cassie to hear, his fingers tangling in my hair. Gripping tight. A delicious sting.

Kaden leans in, his breath ghosting over my parted lips as he murmurs, "Because I never left you, and the boy is still alive."

# 18
## KADEN

The sheer relief in Layla's eyes is worth the violent killing of ten *more* men.

I know how this must look to her, seeing me like this. But I don't read fear or revulsion on her face. Only that sweet relief shines through unshed tears.

She understands.

This is what I had to become to keep her safe.

I push to my feet and turn to Cassie, who stands motionless a few feet away, her face a mask of shock under the blood spatter that hit her while I made a mess.

"Do you see now?" I ask her, my voice hoarse despite never using it while I fought. "I became this for you. And I'll stay this for you."

I could have ended Cassie's reign of terror within seconds of being dragged into this suite. Could have painted these walls red before Cassie even realized what was happening. But I needed to buy time. Time for Cassie to trust me, time to get Layla out of here, time to try to save my daughter.

My chest constricts at the memory of what I've put Layla through these past hours. The devastation etched into her delicate features as I turned on her, spewing venom and lies, each word a dagger to my own heart. I can still hear her anguished cries, her pleas for mercy, as I forced myself to ignore them, to return to the role of the ruthless, unfeeling Scythe.

And Ethan, the kid who'd become an unwitting ally of mine. His blood is on my hands, literally and figuratively. I can feel it, sticky and warm, mingling with the blood of Cassie's men. The sickening crunch of bone, the wet gurgle of his screams as I worked him over, all while Layla watched in abject horror. I had to make it real, had to sell the depraved depths I was willing to sink to. Even if it meant shattering the tentative trust Layla had placed in me.

But it was all for her. Every bruise, every scream, every wretched act.

Necessary evils to keep Layla breathing, to shield her from the true extent of my daughter's madness. I'd have endured a thousand more torments and shredded my soul beyond recognition, as long as it meant sparing Layla from suffering the same fate.

Now, standing before Cassie and thrumming with a toxic cocktail of adrenaline and regret, I realize the true cost of my choices.

The frayed tether between us, the tenuous link of shared blood and fractured memories, has finally snapped. I see it in the ferocious, desperate gleam in Cassie's eyes, the way she twitches as she assesses her new, unexpected situation.

Cassie's too far gone, consumed by an evil I can no longer hope to pull her out of.

I stalk toward her, my boots squelching on the wet carpet. My heart breaks on each breath I suffer through to get closer to her.

Cassie stays where she is, a line forming between her brows as she takes in the carnage.

"What's wrong, Cassandra?" My voice is velvet wrapped in barbed wire. "Isn't this what you wanted? To see what your father is really capable of?"

Cassie tenses, her arm shifting to reveal a gun she must have grabbed off one of her men. But she doesn't fire.

"It's over, Cassie," I say, my voice calm and even despite the raging inferno of grief simmering beneath my skin. "You've lost."

"I still have her," she hisses, jerking the gun toward Layla. "I can still kill her."

A weary smile tugs at the corner of my mouth. "No, you can't. You had your chance. You didn't take it. Because deep down, beneath all that anger and pain, you know the truth. You know I never abandoned you. I never stopped loving you."

Cassie sniffs hard, avoiding my eye. "You left me to rot. You moved on and forgot all about your broken little girl."

"I never forgot you. Not for one moment. You were always with me, haunting my every step, driving me to push harder, go further—"

"To become this?" she spits, gesturing at my blood-drenched form. "The Scythe, Greycliff's own Reaper? You didn't do this for me. You did it for yourself, to bury your guilt, to forget the daughter you failed!"

"I never wanted this for you," I say softly. "I never wanted you to become like me. Like him."

"No," she whispers, her voice cracking. "Papa loved me. He's the only one who ever did."

I'm close enough to touch her now, close enough to see myself reflected in her eyes. The horror I've become. The man who would do anything, sacrifice anyone, to protect what's his.

Even if it means destroying a piece of myself.

"Cassie-girl," I say, my voice breaking. "It's not too late. We can still fix this, still find a way back to each other."

Her finger tightens on the trigger, her hand trembling. "There's no going back. You made sure of that when you chose your whore over me."

She jerks her chin toward Layla, who is now standing in front of Ethan's prone form as some form of protection. Her hands are fisted at her sides, obviously uncomfortable and terrified, but also pushing herself to become a knock-down fighter if she has to.

She's loyal, my Wraithling. Devoted. Even though her light is slowly being eaten away by the dark tendrils of the Black family.

If I stop Cassie from going any further, Layla is the promise of a future untainted. Of lazy mornings tangled in silk sheets, of shared laughter and gentle touches, of a love that has weathered the worst tempest imaginable. She is my beacon. My lighthouse. The one pure thing in a life drenched in gore and agony.

At a blur of movement in my periphery, I catch Cassie's wrist, preventing Cassie from firing her gun at Layla, but Cassie just laughs.

"You think you can be happy with her? That you can just take a nice warm shower and everything you are, everything *I* am, can be cleaned off? I'll kill her. I'll kill anyone you care about, and then you'll see. You'll finally understand what it's like to have everything ripped away."

"I'm well-versed in that feeling, sweetheart." I keep a firm hold on her wrist while using my other hand to reach into my back pocket and pull out another knife I borrowed from a dead man. "Layla is the first person in a decade I've allowed to get close to me. I won't let you hurt her any longer, or anyone else for that matter. I won't let Morelli's poison spread any further."

I twist Cassie's wrist, the bones grinding together as I force her to drop the gun. It clatters to the floor, lost amid the broken bodies and spilled blood. In a flash, I have her pinned against the wall, my knife pressed to the delicate skin of her throat. My daughter's pulse hammers against the blade. I've imagined this moment countless times over the days. Not out of hatred but despair. Each time I discovered another atrocity she'd committed, another innocent she'd crushed, I wondered if death would be kinder to her than continuing to live as Morelli's creation.

"Do it," she whispers while smiling. "Prove Papa right. Show me how easily a father can kill his daughter."

The knife bites deeper. Blood wells around the blade.

"Kaden, wait." Layla's voice cuts through the haze of grief. "Look at her eyes."

I don't want to. I can't bear to see Morelli staring back at me. But when I do...

I see my twelve-year-old girl. Terrified. Contrite. Still searching for her father's love even as she tries to destroy it.

"Look at her," Layla repeats softly. "Really look."

When I do, something shifts in Cassie's eyes—that hateful gleam splintering down the middle to reveal what lies beneath. The knife at her throat draws another bead of blood.

"He'd hold me down," she says, her voice wavering. "Make me stare into mirrors while he carved away everything soft. Everything weak. Said I had to learn to love what I'd become, just like you did."

My hold on the blade turns ironclad, promising no escape. But her confession peels back another layer of Morelli's corruption.

"*'The Scythe leaves no survivors,'*" Cassie continues, mimicking Morelli's voice. "*'Your father understands that mercy is a weakness.'* So I learned. He'd describe your kills in detail. How efficient you were. Said that's how I should be, too. That anything else was a failure." A harsh laugh. "And look at me now, Daddy. Aren't I everything the Scythe's daughter should be? I learned to be apathetic and efficient. Perfect. When I tattooed your precious Layla, I used the same precision you're famous for. Made art of her pain, just like you would."

"No." Another droplet of blood against the tip of my knife. "You're everything he wanted you to be. His perfect weapon against me."

Cassie doesn't flinch. Instead, she presses forward, forcing me to cut deeper or pull back.

The truth hits harder than any bullet. Morelli used my reputation, my methods, to convince my daughter that cruelty was her birthright. That becoming this warped reflection of me would finally earn my love.

Cassie's face contorts. "But you still choose *her*. Still try to protect her when you should be proud of what I've become."

The blade nicks her pale skin, and this time, it wasn't deliberate. I'm no longer the hardened killer, the ruthless Scythe. I am a father facing the insurmountable: I must look into the eyes of my own child and extinguish the life I once cherished above all else.

I feel the weight of Layla's gaze at the center of my back, her silent plea for mercy despite what Cassie has done to her. After all, she sees the good in *me*, the man I could be if I just let myself feel something other than rage and vengeance. But right now, with Cassie's life in my hands and the weight of my sins bearing down, I don't know if that man exists anymore.

"All those years perfecting my technique," Cassie continues. "Making each cut deeper, each break cleaner. I wanted you to see..." Her voice catches. "I wanted you to know I was worthy of being the Scythe's legacy."

I want to tell her that I am proud, in some sick, perverted way. Proud of her strength, her resilience, even as it manifests in acts of unspeakable cruelty. She survived horrors that would have shattered a lesser person, emerging from the flames tempered by anguish and fury. But that pride is a bitter pill.

"You don't need to prove anything to me," I say. The knife trembles against her skin. "Every kill, every broken body I left behind, it was all to find you."

"Then why didn't you?" Her voice fractures. "Why didn't you save me before I became this?"

I croak, "I'm trying to save you now."

I shift my grip, knuckles whitening as I prepare to make the killing blow. Cassie's eyes widen, a flicker of fear breaking through.

"Daddy..." she whispers, her voice small and feeble, a terrified child pleading for mercy.

A single tear escapes from the tangle of her lashes, carving a clean line through the blood and grime.

I falter.

I'm transported back to a time when she was my entire world, when her laughter was the sweetest sound and her smile could chase away the darkest of nights. I remember teaching her to ride a bike, bandaging skinned knees, and chasing away imaginary monsters from under the bed. I remember the fierce, protective love that consumed me, the vow I made to always keep her safe.

My mind races, desperately searching for another way—some miraculous third option that will spare me the agony of this choice. But there is no deus ex machina waiting in the wings, no last-minute reprieve from the machinations of fate. There is only the cold, hard truth:

Sometimes the only way to save someone is to let them go.

# 19
## LAYLA

The sound of a daughter begging her father not to kill her will haunt me for the rest of my life.

That single tear cutting through the gore on Cassie's face transforms her from villain to child in an instant. Her whispered "Daddy" carries the same desperate need I once felt, crying out for a father who never came.

I should want her dead. After everything Cassie's done—the torture, the mind games, forcing me to watch Kaden destroy Ethan—I should be begging Kaden to finish this so we can go home.

Instead, I'm frozen, watching two broken pieces of my heart tear at each other.

"Sometimes," Cassie whispers, her voice small, "when Papa would hurt me, I'd pretend you were coming to save me. I'd imagine all the ways the Scythe would make him suffer for touching your little girl."

Kaden shifts his stance. For the first time since I've known him, indecision marks every line of his body. But I know him well enough to understand that indecision won't stop him from doing what he thinks is necessary.

I surge forward, my hand outstretched. "*Wait*."

Kaden's eyes snap to mine, his pupils blown from all the restraint he's using.

I touch his wrist, feeling the tension humming through him. "It doesn't have to end like this."

Cassie jerks against the blade, fresh blood welling, directing her next question at me. "You think you can fix this, kitten? Fix me?"

I step closer despite Kaden's warning growl. "There has to be. Because if there isn't…" My hand stays on his arm as if I could funnel all my warmth through my palm and into him. "If there isn't, then what hope is there for any of us?"

"Hope?" Cassie spits the word. "Was there hope when Papa split my fingers one by one? When he made me thank him for teaching me strength?" Her eyes lock with mine. "When I did the same to your friend?"

The mention of Ethan slices through me, but I hold her gaze and deadpan, "There's hope as long as your father's blade hasn't moved."

Kaden moves into my hand, silently shifting me out of the danger zone, but I squeeze back, begging him to let me keep trying.

"Maybe there's even a future where you're more than Morelli's discarded toy," I say to her. "Where you get to decide who you want to be."

"Pretty words," Cassie sneers. "But we all know I'll never be anything else."

I shake my head vehemently. "Your father is here, Cassie. He came for you, just like you always dreamed he would."

Kaden's muscles are rock hard beneath my palm, his gaze locked on Cassie. I don't need to feel his chest to know his heart is hammering, the rapid beat matching my own.

I use magic powers I don't possess to *will* Cassie into seeing the truth. To recognize that this moment, right here, is what she's been waiting for from the second she was taken from her childhood home. A chance to be saved. To be chosen.

I will her to understand that Kaden's soul hangs in the balance. That if he takes her life, even to protect me, even to save countless others from her cruelty, it will shatter something vital inside him. A fracture that will slowly bleed him dry until the man I love is nothing more than a corpse himself.

Slowly, deliberately, I reach out my other hand to brush a lock of blood-matted hair from Cassie's face. She hisses but doesn't pull away, her eyes darting between me and Kaden.

"Your father loves you, Cassie," I say. "Believe me, I know what it's like to have a father who doesn't give a shit about you, and that's not Kaden. He's always loved you. Even when he thought he'd lost you forever. Even as he's holding a knife to your throat. *Especially* when he's holding a knife to your throat."

It took me too long to realize that Kaden's capacity for violence doesn't negate his capacity for love. Just the opposite. His ruthlessness is born from the depths of his devotion, a willingness to sacrifice everything, even his own soul, for those he holds dear.

It's a darkness I recognize because it lives inside me too. The willingness to blow the world up for the people I love.

To raze cities and salt the earth if it means keeping them safe.

Cassie sees it too, her eyelids lowering with tentative understanding.

"You really do love her, don't you?" she whispers. "Enough to kill your own daughter."

Kaden's voice is rough as gravel. "Enough to die for her. Enough to live for her. Even when living hurts like hell."

Cassie's lips tremble, a war of emotions playing out across her face. Hope and fear. Longing and despair. The desperate desire to believe wars with the certainty that she's too far gone to be saved.

Her longing is so acute that I almost start crying. I realize that beneath the madness and cruelty, this is what she's always wanted. Not to take Kaden's love from me but to know she never lost it in the first place.

Beside me, Kaden is a statue, every muscle locked tight. But I feel the change in him. The slight loosening of his hold on the knife. The almost imperceptible lean toward his daughter.

I slide my hand down Kaden's arm until my fingers brush the hilt of the knife. He tenses, but I keep my eyes on Cassie.

"Let me," I say to him.

Kaden's hand spasms once before he releases the blade into my grip. I feel the weight of it, the responsibility. The power to take a life. To spare one.

Cassie's eyes fly wide as she feels the knife change hands. Her gaze meets mine. In the depths of her steel-blue eyes, so like her father's, I see my own darkness reflected back at me. The part of me that understands the seductive call of violence. The twisted pleasure of making someone else hurt the way you do.

I press the knife harder against the fresh cuts on her throat, just enough to make her feel it. To remind her of her precarious position.

"I could kill you," I say softly. "I could make you suffer the way you made Ethan suffer. The way you tried to make me suffer."

Cassie swallows, the movement causing the knife to move.

"But I won't," I continue, my voice somehow steady. "Because that's not who I am. It's not who your father is either, no matter how much you try to convince yourself otherwise."

I lean in closer until our faces are mere inches apart. Until I can feel the ragged flutter of her breath against my skin.

A muffled sound escapes her, halfway between a sob and a snarl.

"It's not too late," I say. "You can still choose to be more than what Morelli made you. More than the Ghost Leader's daughter. You can choose to be Kaden's daughter instead."

For a long, stretched-out moment, I'm not sure which way she'll go.

"Let us help you, Cassie," I add, my voice cracking with emotion. "Let your father be the man he always wanted to be for you. Let me be the friend you never had."

Another tear escapes.

"I don't know how," she rasps, small and broken. "I don't know *how*."

"We'll figure it out together," I promise. "Because I don't

know how to be part of a family, either. But that was always, *always*, the most important thing to your dad. So we'll do it for him. One day at a time. One choice at a time."

Kaden releases a shuddering exhale, and I pull the knife away from Cassie's throat. In a movement almost too fast to track, he hauls Cassie into his arms, crushing her against his chest.

"I'm sorry," he rasps, his voice drenched in torment. "I'm so damn sorry, Cassie-girl."

I step back, giving them space, my own heart aching. I know this isn't the end, and we still have a long way to go. But for now, at this moment, a father and daughter are reunited.

And that's a start.

# 20
## LAYLA

Getting two killers and one half-dead man out of a Mafia-owned nightclub without drawing attention requires a special kind of skill.

Not to mention the pile of bodies we're leaving behind in the VIP suite.

I massage the back of my neck as Kaden finally breaks his embrace with Cassie. Bodies litter the floor around us, her men stained in a shade of red brighter than the plush maroon carpeting. The metallic scent of blood clogs the air. I'm not sure a window has ever been opened in this room. Definitely not while I've been held in here.

"We need to move," Kaden says, his voice still thick with a storm he refuses to release. He moves to Ethan's limp form, checking his pulse before hauling him up in a fireman's carry.

I wince at the way Ethan sags over Kaden's shoulder while Cassie chews on the side of her cheek and surveys our environment with new eyes. Abruptly, she hops over two of her former bodyguards with a ballerina's grace and moves to the panel of monitors.

Kaden shifts Ethan's weight on his shoulder, his free hand moving to his knife. "What are you doing?"

"Making sure the other *mafiosi* don't see this." She pauses, her fingers hovering over the keyboard. "They've been circling since Papa died, waiting for his heir to show weakness."

"And this isn't weakness?" I ask, eyeing the dead men at our feet.

Cassie shrugs but still doesn't press any keys. "If they see me leaving with the Scythe, some of Papa's most loyal dogs would love an excuse to put me down."

Kaden makes an annoyed sound in his throat. "We'll have to deal with them eventually."

"Maybe not now," I suggest, all too aware that Kaden is ready and willing to dole out more death, even with a comatose friend hanging off his shoulder, a newly turned daughter and ... me.

"There are lieutenants in the club charged with supervising me during the transition of control. They were Morelli's first made men. His most loyal." Cassie's fingers brush her throat where Kaden's knife drew blood. "If they see me with you, they'll view it as betrayal. And Papa made sure they knew exactly how to deal with traitors."

Kaden's patience wears thin, the tension visible in his strained posture as he bears Ethan's drooping form. "All right, erase our tracks by shutting down surveillance."

Cassie starts typing.

"We can't leave through normal means," Kaden adds as he carefully watches what Cassie pulls up on the screens and the prompts she's entering. "Ethan and I studied the blueprints of this place. An old prohibition tunnel should run under the club to the harbor. We couldn't pinpoint where the access point was or if an exit from this building existed anymore."

Cassie lifts her attention to the monitor where she pulls up a schematic of the Siren's Call. "Yes. It used to be for smuggling booze, but Papa repurposed it."

She points at a bottom section of the blueprint. "Access is hidden in the wine cellar behind a false wall. It leads to a series of underground passages that come out in a sea cave by the old fishing docks."

Kaden frowns. "The tide will be high soon. It'll be a tight window before the tunnel floods."

"Papa liked his insurance policies." Cassie's voice is dry. "Nothing like the threat of drowning to keep his mules motivated to move the merchandise quickly."

"How is it possible that the Mafia had such a firm grip on Greycliff? We're just a small fishing town," I ask, folding my arms and studying the screens.

"This was a perfect location for smuggling contraband. Tiny population, bare-bones police force, and abandoned warehouses galore. That is, until a bunch of twenty and thirty-somethings moved in and messed with the real estate." Cassie stares at me pointedly.

Kaden's too busy searching for threats to notice Cassie's and my exchange, though I'm focused on the obvious threat in front of me. Cassie's switch from Morelli to Black is tenuous, at best, and I'm reluctant to make her the leader orchestrating our escape. Ethan's life hangs in the balance, and while Kaden is lethal and terrific to have on my side, he's blinded by the idea of getting his daughter back.

Cassie hits the final key, and the monitors wink out. "The cameras are now showing a loop. As far as the security team knows, I'm still in this room with you, conducting business as usual."

I shudder, remembering her version of "business," and my precarious faith in her thins further.

She strides across the room, her steps precise even as she avoids the splayed limbs of the fallen men. At the door, she pauses, one hand on the knob as she listens.

Kaden moves up behind her, Ethan's dead weight on his shoulder. "Well?"

"Give me a second," Cassie sing-songs. "Unless you want to explain to the Family why you're absconding with their newly minted boss."

I hover behind them, my heart in my throat. The copper tang of blood is thick in my nose. I want out of this room, out of this building, but a shaky alliance with Cassie is almost worse than no alliance at all.

Cassie eases the door open, flooding the room with the thumping bass from the nightclub's music below. The music bombards us now that we're leaving our hellscape, but the hallway is empty. She gestures for us to follow.

After taking a deep breath, I do.

We move swiftly, Kaden's heavy boots nearly silent on the carpet runner. "Don't suppose you can give me my weapons back?"

Cassie flicks her hair to peer at Kaden over her shoulder. "I doubt there's time. I'm a hot commodity. They'll be checking on my progress soon."

She leads us down a maze of corridors, taking sudden turns that disorient me. Just as I'm starting to wonder if she's leading us into a trap, she stops in front of a nondescript door.

"The cellar," she says, keying in a code on a hidden panel. "Stay close and keep quiet."

The door swings open on well-oiled hinges, revealing a dimly lit staircase. The air that wafts up is cool and damp, with a hint of must.

Cassie starts down, her fingers dancing along the railing to a hidden tune.

I follow, trying to breathe through my mouth. The stairs are narrow, forcing Kaden to angle Ethan across both shoulders like a hunter with a fresh kill.

At the bottom, Cassie flips a switch. Overhead lights flicker on, illuminating rows of dusty wine racks. She weaves between them with purpose, heading for the back wall.

I hurry to keep up, my eyes darting to the shadows pooling between the racks. It would be all too easy for Cassie to order someone to hide there, waiting to strike.

Kaden's breathing is harsh behind me, Ethan's added weight taking its toll. When I glance back, his face is set in grim lines, a sheen of sweat on his forehead, but his eyes are just as alert as mine.

"Here," Cassie says, stopping so abruptly I nearly run into her. She's facing a blank stretch of stone wall, her hands skimming over the surface.

"I don't see anything," I say, my voice hushed. The sounds of the club are muted down here, but I'm all too aware of how thin a barrier a single door is.

With a soft click, a section of the wall swings inward, revealing a dark, gaping maw. The musty smell intensifies, mixed with the briny scent of the sea.

Cassie steps through without hesitation.

"Watch your step," she warns without glancing back. "The ground's uneven."

I follow her into the tunnel, my heart hammering against my ribs. The darkness is absolute, broken only by the thin beam of light from Cassie's phone. Behind me, Kaden's breathing is labored as he maneuvers Ethan's limp form through the narrow opening.

The low tunnel is cramped, the walls slick with moisture. I have to duck my head to avoid hitting it on the rough-hewn ceiling. Water drips steadily, echoing in the confined space.

Cassie moves with confidence, her steps sure even in the dark. I stumble along behind her, trying not to think about the tons of earth and stone above us or the rising tide that could flood the tunnel at any moment.

"How much farther?" I ask in a strained voice.

"Not far," Cassie replies. "Maybe a hundred yards."

A hundred yards. In the dark, in the damp, with the weight of the club above us and the sea waiting to swallow us.

I've never considered myself claustrophobic, but at this moment, I'm acutely aware of how much stone separates me from open sky.

I focus on putting one foot in front of the other, on the sound of Cassie's steady breathing ahead of me. If she's not concerned, then I shouldn't be either, because if I drown, so does she. Then again, I'm not sure *what* concerns her, if anything at all.

Minutes trickle by, marked only by the dripping water and our rasping breaths. The passage twists and turns, leading us deeper beneath the earth.

"Hear that?" Kaden says behind me.

I strain my ears, trying to listen past the frantic thud of my pulse. There. A distant roar, like the rush of waves against the shore.

"The sea cave," Cassie says. "We're almost there."

I pick up my pace, spurred on by the sweet promise of escape.

The roar grows louder with each step until it fills the tunnel, drowning out all other sounds. Cassie rounds a final bend and stops dead, forcing me to pull up short behind her.

Before us, the passage opens into a yawning cavern. Choppy seawater sloshes against a narrow strip of rock, with the tang of salt heavy in the air.

Cassie steps out onto the narrow ledge, her lithe form silhouetted against the mouth of the cave.

"We'll have to time it right," she says over the roar of the waves. "The tide's coming in fast."

I peer out at the churning water, wondering which is worse, being buried alive or drowning?

Kaden comes up beside me, then sidesteps closer to Cassie, Ethan's limbs dangling like a puppet's. He edges forward, scanning the waves for a break in the swells. I try to calm my breathing and steady my nerves.

"Get ready," Kaden says, his voice tight.

On his other side, Cassie grins, ready to leap.

A heartbeat passes. Two. Then Kaden barks, "Now!"

We surge forward as one, sprinting across the slick rock. The ledge is narrow, barely wide enough for a single person. One misstep, one slip, and we'll be swallowed by the hungry sea.

Kaden charges ahead, Ethan bouncing limply on his shoulders. I'm hot on his heels, my lungs burning with the cold, salty air. Cassie brings up the rear, her breath coming in sharp bursts.

We're halfway across when a rogue wave crashes over the ledge, drenching us in icy brine. I gasp, blinded by the salt spray. My foot skids on the wet rock, and I stumble.

A hand grabs my arm, yanking me upright. Cassie. Her grip is like iron, her eyes glinting with mirth in her phone's light. "Saved ya."

I blink away the stinging salt. "Am I—do you want me to thank you?"

She laughs. "Of course not."

She skips around me and continues on.

Once I recover, I notice that the ledge curves sharply to the left, angling up toward a fissure in the cavern wall.

Kaden reaches it first, ducking into the crevice without hesitation. Cassie follows, slipping into the narrow gap. The rock is cool and damp against my skin as I squeeze through, scratching my palms on the jagged stone.

Then we're through, stumbling out onto a rocky beach. The night sky stretches overhead, the stars blurred by a thin veil of fog. The crash of the waves is muffled now, the sea kept at bay by the towering cliff face at our backs.

Kaden lays Ethan down on the sand, his chest heaving.

"Now what?" I ask, my voice nearly lost to the wind.

Cassie scans the beach, her dark hair whipping across her face.

"There's a path. It leads up to the old docks." She points at a faint track snaking up the cliffside.

Kaden crouches beside Ethan, checking his pulse again. "That path's too steep to carry him."

I chew on my lip. Kaden's right. He cannot manage Ethan's dead weight up that incline. Not after the toll the tunnel took.

"We need a boat," Kaden says, pushing to his feet.

"There." Cassie points at the tip of a small skiff bobbing just out of sight and camouflaged with underbrush. Had she not pointed it out, I would never have seen it.

"It's one of Papa's," she explains, reading my mind. "For emergencies."

I don't question what kind of emergencies a Mafia boss might need an escape boat for. I'm just glad it's there.

We hurry toward it, Kaden carrying Ethan in his arms like a damsel now. When we reach the boat, I clamber in and try to make Ethan as comfortable as possible when Kaden sets him down on the bottom of the boat while Cassie unties the mooring line.

"L ... Layla?" Ethan rasps, his brows scrunching together while I toss a scratchy wool blanket over him.

"Ethan?" My hands still. "*Ethan?*"

Relief crashes over me, so powerful I nearly collapse beside him.

"What happened?"

His voice is a hoarse whisper, barely audible over the lapping of the waves against the boat. I grip the side for support.

"You're okay," I say, reaching out to brush his hair back from his forehead. "We got you out."

He frowns, his gaze drifting past me to take in the boat, the stars, and the fog-shrouded cliffs. "Out?"

Kaden comes into view, taking up position at the outboard motor. Ethan notices.

Ethan struggles to sit up, wincing as the movement pulls at his injuries. I hover, torn between the urge to help him and the knowledge that he probably doesn't want to be touched right now.

"You broke my neck." Ethan's mangled hand goes to his throat. He grimaces when his broken fingers take the pressure. "I felt it. I was dying. How...?"

"A trick. A very convincing one." Kaden shifts his weight, the boat rocking beneath him. "I'm sorry. I had to make it look real."

A hoarse laugh bubbles up Ethan's throat. "Real? My broken fingers are sure as hell real."

"Hey," I say softly, finally giving in to the urge to touch him, my hand resting on his shoulder. "I know. What Kaden did ... it's a lot. But he did it to save you. To save us both."

Ethan catches my eye, searching. For what, I'm not sure. Reassurance? Sanity? An explanation for the nightmare he's just woken up from?

"You're really okay?" he asks, his voice small and uncertain.

I nod, not trusting myself to speak around the lump in my throat.

Ethan's attention slides suddenly to the left and over my shoulder. I follow his movement in time to see Cassie flutter a wave at him from her seat.

"The *fuck*?" Ethan goes ramrod straight.

I wince at Ethan's reaction, glancing between him and Cassie. Her smile is sharp with amusement as she watches Ethan's confusion morph into panic.

"It's okay," I say quickly, trying to draw his attention back to me. "She's with us now. Sort of."

Ethan's gaze darts from Cassie to Kaden, his breath coming in short, sharp bursts. "With us? She's Morelli's daughter. She's the one who kidnapped you in the first place!"

"Things have changed," Kaden says, his voice low and even.

Cassie's smile widens. "I've had a change of heart."

Ethan barks out a harsh laugh. "A change of heart? Is that what we're calling it when the daughter of a psychotic mob boss decides to switch teams?"

Kaden's head snaps around.

"Watch your mouth," he growls.

"Homicidal tendencies must be genetic," Ethan mutters.

Cassie leans back, crossing her arms over her chest. "To be fair, I wasn't going to kill Layla. Not permanently, anyway."

I shoot her a sharp look, silently begging her not to make this worse. She rolls her eyes, then settles back against the side of the boat like she's on a pleasure cruise.

"Ethan, please," I say, turning back to him. "I know it's a lot to take in, but we don't have time for this right now. We need to get out of here before Cassie's men realize we're gone."

Ethan scrunches his eyes shut, then opens them again, as if forcing himself to realize this is his new reality. "Are we just setting sail into the sunset with the Scythe and his long-lost daughter, hoping they don't slit our throats in our sleep?"

"Kaden saved our lives back there," I say softly. "And Cassie ... she's the reason we made it out. We have to trust her. At least for now."

The motor roars to life under Kaden's direction, startlingly loud. The little boat surges forward, cutting through the waves toward the hazy glow of lights that mark Greycliff's harbor.

I huddle against Ethan, providing him with my warmth, and I'm relieved, *so* relieved, that he's alert, pissed off, and talking. As the boat skims over the choppy waves and the salt spray cleanses my face, I press my hands against my stomach, feeling the damp fabric of my shirt. It's sticky with blood—my blood, other men's blood, and Kaden's.

I glance down at my wrists, rubbed raw from the ties that bound me. The skin is broken and bleeding in places, a tangible reminder of the horrors I endured. Every breath aches in my bruised ribs, and I can feel the sting of cuts on my face from Cassie's precise blade work.

But I'm alive. Against all odds, I survived. We survived.

My gaze drifts to Kaden, his dark form rimmed with stars. The man who tortured Ethan, who threatened to end his life in front of my eyes. The same man who whispered reassurances to me in the dark, who stepped between me and certain death. I know it's wrong, this pull I feel toward him. He's dangerous, lethal, a killer forged in the fires of a hell I can't even imagine. But in a world that has shown me nothing but cruelty, his fierce protectiveness feels like shelter, like safety.

As if sensing my attention, Kaden glances my way, his arctic eyes finding mine unerringly in the dark.

I bite my lip and hug my knees to my chest, trying to steady my racing heart. It's wrong, I know, to crave the feeling of safety that comes with being his.

He looks at me like he wants to devour me, like he would lay waste to this boat and let us drown so long as he was inside me while we did.

I know I should look away, should focus on Ethan's battered form huddled beside me or the dark stretch of coastline looming ahead. But I can't seem to tear my gaze from Kaden's or stop the heat from pooling low in my belly at the unspoken vow in his eyes.

It's a reckless desire, a dangerous longing. But as the boat races toward the distant shore and the dark spires of Greycliff loom out of the fog, I can't find it in myself to care.

At last, I'm able to tear my gaze away and drift to Cassie instead, perched at the prow like a figurehead, her long black hair tangling in the wind.

She looks back at me and winks.

# 21
## LAYLA

The lighthouse stands against the coming storm the way it always does, its beam cutting through darkness just like the choker tattoo slices across my throat.

Kaden kills the motor, and we drift the last few yards, the hull scraping bottom. He vaults over the side, splashing into the shallow surf.

I stare numbly at Ethan slumped beside me, his blood seeping through the makeshift wrappings I made from the spare blanket. He groans, his head resting heavily on my shoulder.

"Almost there," I whisper, more to myself than him. "Just hold on."

Cassie sits at the bow, her steel-blue eyes reflecting the beam of the lighthouse as she stares up at the weathered tower. She doesn't move to help as Kaden lifts Ethan from the boat, cradling his skinny form like a child.

"We need to move," Kaden says gruffly.

I snap out of my stupor and stumble onto land, legs

unsteady. I half drag myself across the rocks and sand toward the weathered cottage, its whitewashed walls and faded blue shutters appearing out of the mist like it's heaven-sent. It's a far cry from the opulent decadence of the Siren's Call, and I couldn't be more thankful.

When I realize Cassie hasn't followed, I turn back, noticing that she hasn't moved from the boat.

"Come on," I say over the growing thunder. "We need to get inside."

She looks at me, her expression so colorless and blank she might as well be a corpse. Slowly, she climbs out of the boat.

Cassie stalks past me, heading not for the cottage but for the lighthouse.

"Cassie, wait—" I start, but she's already gone, disappearing into the shadows at the base of the tower. I hear the groan of rusty hinges as she forces open the door, then the echo of her footsteps spiraling up, up, up.

I glance back at the cottage, torn. Ethan needs me. But something behind Cassie's cold affect, a dent in her steel, pulls at me. Sighing, I follow her into the lighthouse.

The stairs are narrow and steep, the metal railings flaking with rust. Cassie's form flickers through the gaps ahead of me, her footsteps light and quick. We climb in silence, the only sound the wail of the wind and the distant crash of waves.

At the top, the watch room is a circle of shattered glass and peeling paint. Cassie stands at the center, her face tilted up to the domed ceiling where faded murals fight to stay noticeable. There's a section that's brighter than the rest, probably an attempt by my father to bring it back to life, but he never finished, and I still can't tell what the mural's meant to be.

The beam of the lighthouse sweeps over Cassie, casting her in stark light and shadow.

"I'm staying here," she says, her voice flat.

It's not a question.

I open my mouth to protest, but the sheer relief that she won't be in my home stops me. She looks almost small against the vast expanse of the sea, but I know how vindictive and petty she can be. It's probably best that she starts here, in an abandoned lighthouse that belongs to no one and whose gloom and doom matches hers.

"Okay," I say softly. "Okay."

I leave her there, a solitary figure in a solitary tower, and make my way back to Kaden and Ethan. The wind howls as I stumble down the lighthouse stairs, the metal railings cold under my hands. Outside, the storm now rages. Dressed in the simple black sweater and pants, I know I'm going to suffer, but the alternative is to stay here until the storm passes.

With Cassie.

I'm outside in an instant, crossing the rocky terrain toward the cottage, when a particularly violent gust of wind nearly knocks me off my feet.

A jagged bolt of lightning rips across the sky, blinding white. The thunderclap that follows is deafening, shaking the very earth. In that instant, I'm back in the suite, tied up, naked, and beaten by boots and fists.

I freeze, paralyzed, my breath coming out in choked gasps. The metallic scent of blood fills my nostrils. My vision blurs, the cottage and the rocks and the sea bleeding together into a swirl of colors. Another flash of lightning and I flinch violently, a whimper escaping my lips.

I stumble and fall, my palms scraping against the sharp rocks. The pain jolts me back to the present, but only for a moment. The next bolt of lightning sends me spiraling into another flashback, this one of me being torn from Kaden's arms and thrown into a van, mocked by fully clothed men while they ogled my naked body. Touching me where I didn't want them to. Threatening to do worse.

I curl into a ball, my body shaking with sobs. The memories keep coming, each one more vivid and terrifying than the last. I'm drowning in them, suffocating under the weight of my own trauma. The wind moans like it's grieving and knows my pain. Each gust feels like hands on my skin, harsh and bruising.

Then, through the haze of fear and panic, strong arms wrap around me, lifting me off the ground. I thrash and fight, but the arms don't loosen and hold me close to a wet, solid chest.

"Wraithling." Kaden's voice cuts through the chaos. "You're safe. You're safe now."

I try to bury my face in his chest, but he shifts me in his arms so I have to look at him. Rain streams down his face, carving lines through the devil's beauty.

"No one will ever hurt you like that again," he vows. "Not even my own blood."

Lightning splits the sky again, and I flinch. Kaden tightens his hold.

"Look at me," he says. "Show me those gorgeous eyes that haunt my dreams."

I do. I keep my attention focused on his scar—the only

flaw in a face designed to distract. I wouldn't even call it a flaw, actually. It's just ... him.

Kaden shields me from the worst of the wind and rain, using steady strides to get us to the cottage's porch. Once inside, he gently sets me on the worn sofa, his hands lingering on my arms. I look up at him through wet lashes.

"I'm sorry," I say. "I don't know what happened. I just ... I couldn't..."

He brushes a strand of wet hair from my face. "Breathe. In and out. Slowly."

I try to obey, but my lungs feel like they're filled with ocean water. I choke on a sob, my fingers tangling in my hair, tugging painfully.

Kaden's hands cover mine, gently untangling my fingers. He guides my hands to his chest, pressing my palms against the steady thrum of his heartbeat.

"Focus on me," he says. "You seem to be awed into silence every time you look at my face, anyway."

That gets a small smile out of me.

"You're okay," he murmurs. "You're home."

I lean into his touch, exhaustion sweeping over me. The cottage blurs again, but it's not from panic this time.

Kaden pulls me into his arms, and I let myself sink into his strength. I let myself believe, just for a moment, that he's right. That I'm okay.

"Ethan?" I ask against Kaden's chest.

"In the bedroom. I splinted his fingers the best I could and cleaned his opened wounds. He's stable."

I exhale shakily, relief mixing with the residual terror still coursing through my veins.

"I need to check on him. And change out of these

clothes." I pull away, wrapping my arms around myself as I stand on unsteady legs.

Kaden nods, his eyes never leaving mine. "I'll secure the perimeter. Make sure we weren't followed and that every security measure I set up before is working."

Shivering, I hug myself tighter. It stands to reason that Morelli's men—or Cassie's men—would know to come here to get Cassie back. But the hardened resolve in Kaden's eyes tells me that we're exactly where he wants us to be. When they come, which they will, it will be on Kaden's terms. His turf.

Kaden's gaze lingers on me for a moment longer before he turns and strides out into the storm, the door clicking shut behind him.

I make my way up the stairs and down the short hallway, stopping at the doorway to my bedroom. Ethan lies on the faded quilt with Reaper curled against his side. I smile at the sleek feline, glad she's safe and that Cassie never actually caught her, then go back to Ethan. His glasses are missing, making him look so much younger.

"Hey," I say softly, perching on the edge of the bed. "How are you feeling?"

Ethan turns to the sound of my voice and opens his hazy eyes. "Kaden found opioids. I'm a happy boy."

A soft laugh escapes me. "I'm glad you get to hang out in the clouds for a while." I carefully take one of his hands in mine. His skin feels clammy. "Do you forgive me?"

In my attempt to hold back my tears, they leak into my voice when I ask the question.

Ethan's brow furrows, his uninjured hand squeezing mine weakly. "For what?"

I swallow past the thickness in my throat. "For getting you involved in this. For putting you in danger. If I hadn't listened in and recorded Dawson's conversation about Oracle, if I'd just minded my own business…"

My voice cracks, and I look away, blinking rapidly. The tears come anyway, sliding down my cheeks in hot, shameful trails.

"Hey, hey…" Ethan tugs on my hand until I meet his gaze again. Even drugged and in pain, his eyes are earnest, full of a steadfast devotion I don't deserve. "You didn't do this to me, Layla. You're my best friend. I'd walk through hell for you."

A sob escapes me, and I press my forehead to our joined hands. "I think that's exactly where I've led you."

"Well, you didn't leave me there to burn alone. That's what matters."

I lift my head, managing a wobbly smile. I let his words wash over me, let myself believe them, if only for a moment. Then I pull back, wiping at my tears. "I should let you rest."

Ethan nods, his eyelids drooping. "Stay with me? Just until I fall asleep?"

"Of course."

He's snoring within seconds. I gently kiss his forehead before quietly grabbing some dry clothes from the dresser and slipping into the bathroom across the hall.

I shut the bathroom door behind me and lean against it heavily, exhaling a shuddering breath. In the harsh light of the bare bulb, I catch sight of my reflection in the mirror above the sink.

My hair hangs in limp, wet strands around my face, the once vibrant blond now dull and matted. The bruises and cuts littering my skin stand out in stark contrast, a morbid collage of purples, blues, and angry reds. I look like a water-color painting gone horribly wrong, everything bleeding together in a grotesque imitation of art.

But the tattoo draws my eye, as it always does. The intricate design wraps around my throat like a noose, black ink against pale skin. I reach up to trace it with trembling fingers, remembering the burn of the needle. I try to remember if Harris was one of the men slaughtered when we escaped, and I can't.

A shudder runs through me, and I have to grip the sink to keep from collapsing. My knuckles turn white from the force of it, the chipped porcelain biting into my palms.

I force myself to look, to really see the extent of the damage. A particularly nasty gash runs along my jawline, the edges jagged and inflamed. I think I got that one from the serrated edge of a knife.

With shaking fingers, I peel off my wet clothes, wincing as the fabric sticks to the cuts and bruises littering my skin. Each article falls to the floor with a heavy plop, revealing more of my abused body.

The bruises on my ribs are a mottled mess of colors, some fresh and others fading into sickly yellows and greens. Each one is a reminder of a boot or a fist, of pain exploding through my body like a supernova.

And then there are the marks you can't see, the ones that run soul-deep. The feeling of hands where they shouldn't be, of hot breath and hissed threats. The humiliation and degradation sinking into my bones like venom.

I meet my own gaze in the mirror, hardly recognizing myself. Then I tear my eyes away and turn on the shower, the pipes groaning in protest. Under the spray of the shower, I scrub my skin until it's raw and my entire body is as red as my wounds.

When I emerge, dressed in my favorite oversized T-shirt and leggings, Kaden waits for me in the living room. He's stripped off his wet shirt, his chest bare and gleaming in the low light.

On him, scars are beautiful. I couldn't picture him any other way.

And I wonder what he thinks about my body now.

"I forgot to tell you," I say after clearing my throat. "Cassie's staying in the lighthouse."

He nods. "I know. It's probably for the best. I don't expect her to play nice with others right now."

Kaden gives me a slow survey, taking in the T-shirt that hangs off one shoulder and the leggings that cling to me. I feel exposed under his scrutiny, all too aware of the marks marring my skin underneath the fabric.

But I don't see disgust or pity in his eyes. Only a fierce protectiveness and insatiable desire that always manages to stop me from remembering to meet my basic needs, like breathing.

He takes a step closer, his hand reaching out to brush against the tattoo on my throat. I shiver at his touch even as I recoil.

"I wish I could kill the person who did this to you," he says. "Make them suffer for every bruise, every cut they put on your body."

"Don't." I turn my face away. "We both know you'd burn the world down to protect what's yours. But she's yours, too."

His fingers trace the tattoo, possession competing with fury in his touch. "And that's why she's still breathing. But if she ever touches you again..."

The threat lingers unfinished because the Scythe doesn't need words to drive his point home.

"The lighthouse keeps her close," he says, his hand sliding to my hip. "Anything she plans, every movement. She lives because she's mine." His grip turns bruising. "You're protected because you're mine."

His thumb retraces where the tattoo begins, transforming Cassie's mark of ownership into his own claim. Where her touch brought pain, his brands pleasure into my skin.

This man carved his way through empires to find his daughter. Now he's carved a place in my soul, too.

I raise my eyes to his.

He tilts his head slightly as he uses his innate talent to decipher the emotions swirling inside me. His stare narrows.

"If you think I'm not yours in return, Wraithling, then I haven't done nearly enough to prove that to you."

<h1 style="text-align:center">22</h1>
<h2 style="text-align:center">LAYLA</h2>

It astounds me that Kaden doesn't think he's proven his obsession over me.

"You turned my cottage into a fortress so you could watch me at all hours," I argue. "You willingly imprisoned yourself so you could stay with me. You've killed men for me—"

"Not nearly enough."

"I know you're mine," I say at the same time.

"Do you?"

He grabs one of my wrists, and I wince at the rub of his grip against the barely healed scrapes. But the slice of pain is quickly forgotten when he pushes my palm against the length of his dick through his pants.

"This heat, this pulse that's throbbing so hard it's painful, this cock, is all fucking yours."

I bite my lip at his delicious, dirty words, unused to hearing them but desperate to hear them again.

"Take me, Layla. Grab me and hold on. I'm yours to control. Claim your power over me."

I stare up at him, my own pulse racing, desire rivaling my trepidation.

Without looking away, I slide into his pants and curl my fingers around the hard length of him.

Kaden's eyes darken, his jaw clenching as he fights for control.

"That's it," he rasps. "Don't be afraid to take what you want."

Emboldened, I squeeze harder, relishing the low groan that escapes his lips and the way he tips his head back.

Kaden's hand slides into my damp hair, his fingers tangling just shy of pain. He pulls my head back, exposing the inked column of my throat.

I shudder, my grip on him faltering. He notices.

"Too much?" he asks.

I shake my head, not trusting my voice. I want this, want him. I want that control he's so willing to give when I feel like I've lost all of mine.

"We go at your pace," Kaden murmurs.

Tears prick at my eyes, gratitude and affection swelling in my chest. "Thank you."

"You never have to thank me for respecting your boundaries. It's the bare fucking minimum."

A watery laugh escapes me. "Such a romantic."

"I have my moments."

Smiling, I test my effect on him again, feeling him twitch against my palm. A thrill shoots through me at the power he's offering. After being at the mercy of others for so long, it's intoxicating.

I stroke him slowly, watching his pupils expand with lust. His breath stalls when I increase the pressure.

"Is this what you want?" I ask.

"That's it," he rasps. "Take what's yours."

I pump harder, reveling in his surrender. This deadly, dangerous man, reduced to a shuddering mess by my touch alone.

With my free hand, I tug on the waistband of his pants, pushing them down until he's completely bare. Kaden is hot and silky smooth, pre-cum beading at the tip.

I swipe my thumb over it, spreading the wetness down his shaft.

"Fuck, Wraithling." He grunts, his hips bucking into my fist.

I stroke him faster, tighter, spurred on by the broken sounds spilling from his lips. His hands come up to grip my hips, digging into my flesh, but this pain is welcome. Grounding, even. A reminder that I'm alive and he's here with me.

"I want to taste you," I proclaim, surprised by my own boldness.

His eyes fly open, locking onto mine. "Then get on your knees and take what you want."

I sink to the floor without hesitation, wrapping my hand around the base of his cock and holding him steady as I lean in to flick my tongue over the weeping tip.

He makes a strangled sound, his fingers tangling further in my damp hair. I take him into my mouth inch by inch, savoring the heavy weight of him on my tongue. He's too big to take all the way, but I hollow my cheeks and suck hard, bobbing my head in a steady rhythm.

"Just like that," he groans, guiding my movements with the hand fisted in my hair. "Take all of me, Wraithling."

I relax my throat and take him deeper, fighting my gag reflex. Tears threaten at the corners of my eyes, but I don't stop, determined to give him as much pleasure as he's given me.

"Look up," he commands.

I obey, gazing up at him through my lashes as I work his length with my mouth.

"You're so fucking beautiful like this," he murmurs. "On your knees for me, looking up at me with those bewitching eyes while you suck my cock."

Heat floods my core at his filthy praise. I moan around him, and he curses, his grip on my hair tightening. He throbs against my tongue, growing impossibly harder.

"I'm close," he warns, his voice strained. "Pull off if you don't want to swallow."

But I do want to. I want to taste every part of him, to consume him the way he's consumed me, body and soul. So I redouble my efforts, sucking harder, taking him as deep as I can.

"Fuck, Layla, I'm going to—"

His words cut off with a guttural groan as he spills into my mouth, his release hot and salty on my tongue. I swallow every drop, savoring the intimacy of it, the power.

Kaden's chest heaves as he tries to catch his breath, but I'm not done yet. I release him, but my hand is covered in his spillover. When I'm confident his eyes are back on me, I lick from the bottom of my palm to the tip of my fingers, relishing every drop.

Kaden's eyes flash with renewed hunger.

"You're going to be the death of me," he growls.

I release my fingers with a wet pop, a small smirk playing on my lips. "But what a way to go."

He hauls me to my feet and crashes his mouth against mine in a bruising kiss, all teeth and tongue. I melt into him, my hands sliding over the hard planes of his chest, tracing the scars that map his skin.

Kaden lifts me until my legs wrap around his waist, then backs us up against the wall, caging me in with his arms. He breaks the kiss, keeping his lips a hairbreadth from mine.

"If it gets to be too much, if you need to stop, you tell me," he says. "No matter what. Understand?"

"Yes," I breathe.

"Good girl."

Then his mouth is on me again, all-consuming and overwhelming in the best way. He trails his lips down my jaw and my neck, nipping at the sensitive skin. When he reaches the tattoo, he pauses, his breath hot against my throat.

"I want to mark you as mine," he rasps. "Cover this brand with my own claim on you."

I shudder at his words, my inner thighs going slick with want.

"Then do it," I say. "Make me yours."

Kaden growls, and it vibrates right through me. He bites down on the juncture where my neck meets my shoulder, sucking hard enough to leave a mark. I cry out, my nails digging into his back as pleasure-pain sparks through me.

He soothes the sting with his tongue before trailing lower, pushing the T-shirt off my shoulder to expose more skin for his lips and teeth to explore. Each scrape of his teeth, each bruising kiss, sends another aching bolt straight to my core.

Impatient, I tug at his hair, bringing his mouth back to mine. He kisses me deeply, desperately, like he's trying to crawl inside me and make a home there. Like he already has.

I'm panting when he pulls back, my lips swollen and tingling. Kaden looks as wrecked as I feel, his eyes wild and feverishly bright. He's a fallen angel, a dark god, and he's all mine.

His hands slip under my shirt again, this time to peel it up and off, baring my upper body to his hungry gaze.

For a moment, I tense, acutely aware of the bruises painting my skin.

"These are badges of your strength," he says, pressing a kiss to a particularly lurid bruise between my breasts. "They show the world you can take a hit and get back up."

My eyes go hot at his reassurance, at the unwavering acceptance and adoration in his gaze.

He kisses a path down the valley of my breasts while I'm pressed against the wall, his hand coming up to palm one, his thumb brushing over the pebbled nipple. I arch into his touch with a gasp.

Kaden's mouth closes around my other nipple, his tongue swirling and teasing the sensitive bud. I moan, my head falling back against the wall with a thud. He lavishes attention on my breasts, sucking and nipping until I'm writhing.

"Please, Kaden," I whimper, not even sure what I'm begging for.

He seems to know anyway. His other hand drifts lower, slipping beneath the waistband of my leggings. I squirm as his fingers brush against my most sensitive flesh, slick with desire. Kaden circles my clit, making me buck against his hand with a needy whine.

I'm aching for more, my body singing with want.

"Please," I gasp out.

"Please what, Wraithling? Tell me what you need."

"I need you. Inside me. Filling me."

Kaden's eyes darken further at my breathless plea. My feet hit the floor in one swift motion, and he rips my leggings away, the fabric giving easily under his strength. Cool air hits my overheated skin, and I shiver.

He drops to his knees, throwing one of my legs over his shoulder. Then his mouth is on me, his tongue delving between my folds to lap at the wetness there. I cry out, my head thudding back against the wall.

Kaden grips my thighs, holding me open. He traces patterns on my clit, flicking and circling and sucking until the pressure starts building.

"Kaden, I'm going to ... I'm close..." I pant, my fingers sinking into his hair.

He doubles his efforts, sealing his lips around my clit and sucking hard as he thrusts two fingers deep inside me, curling to hit that perfect spot. With a hoarse scream, I shatter. Kaden works me through it, prolonging my pleasure until I'm limp and trembling.

Before I can catch my breath, he's surging up to recapture my mouth. I taste myself on his tongue, and it makes me throb with renewed desire. I feel him, hard and insistent, pressing against my belly.

Kaden lifts me again, and I wrap my legs around his waist. His cock notches at my entrance, teasing me.

"Take what's yours," he rasps against my lips. "Take all of me."

With a roll of my hips, I sink onto him, taking him to the hilt in one smooth glide. We groan in unison at the exquisite stretch and fullness. For a moment, we're both still, foreheads pressed together, just savoring the feel of each other.

Then Kaden starts to move, withdrawing almost all the way before slamming back in.

The ancient cottage walls rattle with the force of our passion, absorbing the echoes of my cries and his grunts. Kaden's hands grip my hips hard enough to leave fresh bruises, branding me in a way that feels like worship rather than violence.

My nails rake down his back, my heels digging into his ass to pull him deeper.

Kaden seems to have the same idea. He shifts the angle of his hips, hitting a spot so deep I see stars. I throw my head back with a keening cry, the tendons of my neck straining.

"That's it, let me hear you," he pants. "Let the whole fucking town know who you belong to."

I'm too lost in sensation to be self-conscious. Let them hear. Let the world know I'm his and he's mine.

"Yours," I gasp out. "Only yours."

Those words seem to spur him on. He's chasing his release as much as he's driving me toward my own.

"Let go," he commands in a gravelly rasp. "I've got you."

And I do. I let go with a silent scream, my body bowing in his hold as rapture crashes over me in unrelenting waves. I clench rhythmically around him, pulling him over the edge with me.

Kaden buries himself to the hilt with a guttural groan,

spilling deep inside me and rocking us through the aftershocks.

We stay like that for a while, joined, hearts pounding in sync, breathing each other's air.

"Mine," he murmurs, cupping my cheek.

I turn into his palm, pressing a kiss to the calloused skin.

"Yours," I affirm.

# 23
## KADEN

Teaching my lover to kill feels like foreplay.

Layla positions her body exactly the way I instructed, her feet placed just so on the dewy morning grass and a giant scowl on her face.

"Kaden, I just got my warm home back. I didn't sign up for boot camp the very next morning," Layla grumbles, blowing a stray blond strand out of her eyes.

The rising sun casts a halo around her delicate features, making her appear both fierce and fragile.

I circle her, my footsteps silent on the damp earth. "Keep your weight centered. Don't let your guard drop."

She pivots with me, keeping me in her sights. "I'm not a soldier."

"No, you're not." I step closer, invading her space. "But you are a target. As am I, as is Cassie. We need to be prepared for when they come for her. If they try to take you this time, you'll be ready. That is, if they can get past me."

My voice is harsher than I intend, but the thought of

Layla facing danger alone again makes my hands clench into fists. I need my Wraithling to be strong. I need her to survive.

I step behind her, my chest nearly brushing her back.

"Widen your stance," I command, my breath ghosting over her ear. She shivers despite the warmth of a sunrise after a storm.

Layla adjusts her feet, her movements precise yet hesitant. I place my hands on either side of her stomach, guiding her into the proper position. My touch lingers, savoring the way her body molds to mine.

"Good," I murmur, my lips grazing the shell of her ear. "Now, show me how you'd disarm me."

Layla mirrors my movements, her supple body whirling. She lunges forward, her fist aimed at my jaw. I catch her wrist easily, pulling her off balance and into my chest. She gasps, her free hand splaying across my chest. We both halt, our breaths mingling. Her pulse beats rapidly beneath my fingertips, the heat of her seeping through my shirt.

My arm snakes around her waist, holding her firmly in place. She struggles for a moment before going still, her breath coming in shallow pants.

"You're not trying hard enough," I growl, nipping at her lower lip.

I release her abruptly, and she stumbles backward, catching herself at the last second. Layla lifts her head, that adorable scowl returning.

"I am trying! I've sat in front of a computer most of my life. This is me trying," she says with her hands on her hips.

I stalk toward her in two long strides. Layla stands her ground, tilting her chin up. The fire in her eyes makes me harder than I already was. This is the fighter I'm certain lurks beneath her soft exterior. This is the woman I need her to be.

"I want you to survive," I tell her, capturing her face between my palms, my thumbs caressing her cheekbones. "I will always kill for you, Wraithling. But I need to know you can hold your own, even as I haunt your every step."

Layla's expression softens, and she leans into my touch, her eyes fluttering closed. "Okay. Keep showing me how."

"Anticipate my movements," I instruct. "Use my momentum against me."

Layla nods, her brow furrowed in concentration. I shift my weight forward, and she reacts instantly, twisting to the side. Her elbow jabs into my ribs, and I grunt in approval.

"Good. Again."

We fall into a lethal dance, strike and counterstrike, advance and retreat. Layla's movements grow more fluid and more confident. She meets my attacks with a relentless determination that makes my blood sing.

I lunge for her, and she ducks, sweeping my legs out from under me. I allow myself to hit the ground hard, the air rushing from my lungs. Before I can roll, Layla is on top of me, straddling my waist. She pins my wrists above my head, her grip surprisingly strong.

"Yield," she demands, her face inches from mine. Her golden hair falls around us like a curtain.

One corner of my mouth tips up. "Keep thinking you can dominate me. It'll make breaking you in a lot more fun."

I could easily overpower her, but the weight of her body on top of mine, the heat of her pussy against my rock-hard cock, makes me all too willing to draw this out.

A triumphant smile curves her lips as she feels my cock twitch beneath her. She lowers her mouth to mine, sucking on my lower lip and pulling it into her mouth. I groan against her tongue, meeting her desire with a roaring, primal need.

I know we should keep training, keep our guards up...

But in this stolen sunrise, with Layla warm and willing on top of me, all I want is to lose myself in her. The rest of the world can fucking burn.

I deepen the kiss hungrily, my hands roaming her sweat-slicked skin as the sun climbs higher, burning away the morning dew. But before I can ruin another pair of her leggings, a shadow falls over us.

Layla breaks our kiss, her grip on my wrists spasming as she turns her head, and I follow her gaze.

Cassie stands at the edge of the clearing. Her expression is shrouded in the lighthouse's shadow, but there's no disguising the weight of her stare.

Layla scrambles off me, her cheeks flushed with more than just exertion. I rise to my feet and take my time dusting off my clothes.

I use that time to assess my daughter's mood. She's both a potential threat and a broken soul. I'm torn between the need to protect her and the fear that she'll betray us.

"Morning, Cassandra," I say calmly. "How did you sleep?"

"I made breakfast," she replies, then turns on her heel and strides toward the cottage.

I wipe my mouth with the back of my hand and nod at Layla to follow Cassie.

Layla clears her throat. "Are we sure she didn't pick some poisonous mushrooms on her way to the kitchen?"

"Only one way to find out," I say with a deep sigh and lead the way.

As we enter the cottage, the aroma of coffee and something sweet fills the air. Cassie stands at the stove, her back to us as she flips pancakes with a spatula.

Ethan is already seated at the rickety wooden table, hunched over a steaming mug, his broken fingers taped together and his other arm wrapped protectively around his stomach. The angry red bruise on his neck must be giving him hell, too.

"How was combat training?" Ethan asks Layla.

Layla offers him a tired smile. "Good. It's a lot, though."

He reaches out with his good hand, giving Layla's fingers a squeeze. "Hey, if you ever need to talk or, you know, learn some moves to go with those shiny new battle skills, I've been known to throw down in *Call of Duty*."

That startles a laugh out of Layla. "I don't think video game reflexes translate to real-life knife fights, but I appreciate the offer."

"You never know," Ethan says with a tired grin. "I'm pretty lethal with a joystick."

"I'm sure you are," I deadpan, arching a brow.

Ethan flushes scarlet, choking on his coffee. "That's not —I didn't mean—"

Layla giggles, the sound brightening the whole damn room, then takes the chair beside him, offering a smile of reassurance. Ethan returns it with a grimace, his gaze darting between Cassie and me warily. I remain standing, my back against the wall, arms crossed over my chest as I survey the room.

Cassie sets the platter of pancakes in the center of the table with a thud. She drops into the remaining chair, her movements sharp yet unhurried.

Silence descends as they each take a pancake, the scrape of forks against plates unnaturally loud.

My attention is on Cassie. She's watching Layla, her focus intense and unblinking. Layla squirms under the scrutiny, her knuckles whitening around her fork.

"Thanks, Cassie," Layla says. "This looks … great."

Cassie's lips twist into something that might be a smile. "Don't thank me yet. You haven't tasted them." She gestures idly with her fork. "Go ahead."

When nobody complies, I stride over to the table and swipe a pancake off Cassie's plate, taking a bite. The pancake is fluffy and sweet, with no hint of poison.

"It's good," I say in a low voice. "Eat, Layla."

Layla takes a tentative bite, her shoulders relaxing as the flavors hit her tongue. "Wow, these are actually amazing."

Cassie's smirk fades, replaced by a shuddered expression. "If I didn't make Papa's breakfast delicious every day, I'd be punished."

An uncomfortable silence follows.

"Oh, thank God," Ethan says, breaking the tension. "I was wondering how long we were gonna be forced to act like a bizarro family sitting down for a meal."

Cassie barks out a laugh. "The grub with glasses is right. There's nothing quaint about sleeping on the same property you were buried alive under. Are those your books?"

Layla's jarred out of her uneasy expression by the rapid

change in subject. "You mean the bookshelf over there? Yeah, they are."

"Excuse me, *grub*?" Ethan asks.

"Romance, huh?" Cassie ignores Ethan and eases out of her chair mid-chew. She sidles out of the open kitchen and toward the bookcase.

Cassie runs her finger along the spines of the books, her nail catching on the embossed titles. She tilts her head, reading the titles aloud in a mocking tone. "*The Duke's Forbidden Desire, Scandalous Seduction, Ravished by the Rogue ...*"

She plucks a well-worn paperback from the shelf, flipping through the pages with a snort.

"*Love's Eternal Embrace,*" she reads aloud, her voice dripping with disdain. "Sounds like a real page-turner."

Layla's cheeks flush, and she stiffens in her chair. "There's nothing wrong with a little escapism. Those books got me through some tough times."

"An escape from what?" Cassie scoffs. "Your perfect little life?"

She tosses the paperback carelessly onto the couch and pulls another one from the shelf, this one a hardcover with a glossy dust jacket.

"Cassie," I warn.

"News flash, princess," Cassie says to Layla. "There's no escape from the real world."

With a sudden, violent motion, Cassie rips the dust jacket off the book, tearing it cleanly in half. Layla gasps, jumping to her feet.

"What are you *doing*?" Layla cries.

Cassie ignores her, tossing the ruined dust jacket to the

floor. She flips open the book again, this time pulling a wicked-looking knife from her boot.

"Romance is dead," Cassie says, then plunges the knife into the pages, twisting it savagely. Bits of paper flutter to the floor like confetti.

Layla races into the den. "What is *wrong* with you?"

I'm fighting like hell not to intervene. In a way, an argument between these two could be healthy—like two piranhas going at each other could be healthy. Ethan is looking at me like I should've stepped between them already, but I meet his horrified look with hooded eyes. This needs to happen, whether we want it to or not.

Cassie dances out of Layla's reach, holding the book above her head. "Oh, I'm sorry. Did I ruin your little fantasy world?"

She rips out another handful of pages, crumpling them in her fist.

"Give it back!"

"Please," Cassie sneers. "You don't know the first thing about romance. About love. Your just a little blond whore playing house with monsters."

Something in Cassie's statement makes Layla snap. With a scream of fury, she charges at Cassie, shoving her hard. Caught off guard, Cassie stumbles, the book falling from her grasp.

Meanwhile, I'm focused on what my daughter plans to do with that fucking knife.

"You don't know anything about me," Layla snarls, advancing on Cassie. "Or about Kaden. You're just a bitter, twisted shell of a person who wants to destroy anything good."

Cassie's blue eyes flash with a dangerous light as she regains her footing, the knife glinting in her hand.

"Oh, kitten's got claws," she purrs. "But do you really think you can take me on? I was raised by a *lion*."

Layla doesn't back down, her contrasting eyes blazing with a fury I've never seen before.

"You don't get to come into my home and destroy the things I love," Layla spits through gritted teeth. "You don't get to poison everything you touch just because you're hurting inside."

Cassie's smirk falters, a glimmer of pain passing over her face before it hardens into a mask of cold anger. "Keep talking, princess. See what happens."

Cassie lunges with a feral snarl, the knife slashing through the air. I'm mid-leap when Layla reacts instinctively, twisting to the side just as I taught her. The blade misses her by a hairbreadth.

In a flash, Layla grabs Cassie's wrist and wrenches it hard, slamming it against the bookshelf. Cassie cries out in pain and surprise, the knife clattering to the floor.

Layla doesn't hesitate. She shoves Cassie hard, sending her stumbling back into the shelf. Books rain down around them as Cassie crashes to the floor.

Breathing hard, Layla stands over her, hands still clenched into fists. "I may not have had your childhood, Cassie, but don't for a second think you know what I've been through. I'm a survivor, just like you. The difference is, I didn't let it turn me into a vindictive bitch."

Cassie glares up at her, chest heaving. For one hot second, I think she might try to stab Layla in the neck. My muscles tense, ready to intercept.

But then Cassie laughs, heartless and edged with hysteria.

"Well, well, well," she gasps out. "Looks like Daddy's new pet has some bite after all."

As much as a part of me wants to let this continue to play out, to let Layla put Cassie in her place, I know I can't allow it to escalate further. Not with my daughter's fragile state of mind or Layla's safety on the line.

In less than two strides, I'm behind Layla, my hand closing in a firm but gentle grip around her upper arm. She startles at my touch, her head whipping around to meet my gaze.

"Enough," I say. "Both of you."

Slowly, I turn my gaze to Cassie, still sprawled on the floor amid the scattered books. My daughter meets my eyes with a defiant glare, but there's a flicker of fear behind the bravado. She knows the consequences of pushing too far.

"Get up," I order, my tone as hard and cold as steel. "Now."

Cassie hesitates for a fraction of a second before obeying, pushing herself to her feet with a wince. She stands before me, chin lifted, a challenge in her eyes even as she favors her bruised wrist. I crouch down beside her, picking up the discarded knife. Cassie flinches almost imperceptibly as I rise, twirling the blade between my fingers, examining it. It's a good knife, well-balanced and razor-sharp. A weapon befitting the daughter of an assassin.

"Let me make one thing perfectly clear," I say, my voice deceptively soft.

I throw the knife into the wall, burying it to the hilt barely an inch from Cassie's shoulder. She goes utterly still.

"Layla is not a pet or a plaything for you to torment. She is mine to protect, just as you are. You are here because I allow it. Because despite your abuse of people I care about, I still believe there is a shred of humanity left in you worth saving."

Cassie flinches as if I've struck her, her mask of arrogance cracking for the briefest of moments. But I'm not finished.

"But make no mistake, Cassandra. If you ever, *ever* threaten Layla again, if you so much as look at her wrong ... I will put you down like the rabid dog you've become. Daughter or not."

The words taste like ash in my mouth, but I force them out, knowing they need to be said. Knowing it's the only kind of threat Cassie responds to, as well as the certainty that Layla's safety, Layla's very life, is in my hands.

Cassie's eyes widen, genuine humiliation and something akin to hurt mingling in their blue depths. For a moment, she looks achingly young, a lost little girl playing at being a bad guy.

Then her face hardens, the vulnerability vanishing behind a sneer. "Understood, *Father*."

She turns on her heel and stalks out of the room. The front door slams, echoing through the cottage like a gunshot.

I close my eyes briefly, exhaustion settling into my bones. When I open them again, Layla is watching me, her expression concerned. "Kaden, you didn't have to—"

I shake my head, cutting her off. "Not now, Wraithling."

I turn away from Layla, needing a moment to collect myself. Striding over to the wall, I yank the switchblade free, then tuck it into my boot. The weight of my words to Cassie settle like lead in my gut. Am I prepared to kill my own flesh and blood? I'd come to terms with it at Siren's Call when I thought all was lost, but Layla helped me see the light. See my daughter again. Though I'm beginning to realize the daughter I once had is no longer a possibility. Cassandra Morelli is who she is now, and I either have to kill her or learn to accept the woman she's become.

"Let's finish breakfast," I murmur, guiding Layla back to the kitchen where Ethan still sits frozen, a forkful of pancake hovering near his open mouth.

When we're seated, he raises his mug in a mock toast. "To dysfunctional breakfast bonding. May we not be murdered before lunch."

# 24

## LAYLA

After fighting with your kidnapper-turned-housemate, nothing clears your head like a walk along the shore. At least, that's what I tell myself as I shut the cottage door behind me.

The walls have suffocated since my return, and now, after Cassie's latest mind game and Kaden's cold lecture, I need air, need space—but the moment I step outside, something feels wrong.

Kaden's outfitted my property with the latest tech, relying on security measures like triggers, motion sensors, and possibly bombs to alert us to trespassers. I feel safe inside his fortress, knowing it spreads far outside the brick and mortar of my home, so that can't be what nags at me.

As I walk, my eyes scan the shoreline, taking in the familiar sights—the weathered driftwood, the scattered seashells, the tufts of beach grass swaying in the wind. But then something catches my eye. At first, I mistake it for the random scribblings of a child or perhaps the meandering trail of a shore crab. But as I move closer, the lines take on a jagged, deliberate shape. Letters. Words.

**WE FOUND YOU.**

I blink, half expecting the message to disappear, but it remains crisp and clear. I take a step closer, my eyes tracing each letter. A sudden gust of wind whips across the beach, and I shiver, wrapping my arms around myself. The once-comforting sound of the waves now seems ominous.

I glance back at the cottage, its windows glinting in the sunlight. Inside, Kaden is likely still fuming while Cassie's retreated to the top of the lighthouse. Ethan is trying to stay out of all of it by keeping to my room and drowning himself in pain pills. I don't blame him.

Turning, I run back toward my home, my feet slipping in the shifting sand.

I need to tell Kaden. Need to warn him that despite his precautions, despite the layers of security and secrecy, the remaining Morelli family breached it.

But as I hurry across the sand, a faint buzzing sound catches my attention. At first, I dismiss it as the hum of a distant boat or the whir of insects. But the noise grows louder, closer, until it's impossible to ignore.

I scan the sky, searching for the source of the sound, and spot a small, sleek drone hovering above my cottage. My blood runs cold as the reality of the situation sinks in.

I shoot into a sprint, desperate to warn Kaden and

Ethan. But even as I run past the lighthouse, I can't shake the feeling that the real danger isn't out here.

It's already inside.

With one last glance at the drone, I burst through the door. "Kaden!"

Kaden's head snaps toward me at the sound of my voice, where he was staring at the lighthouse through the front window.

"What is it?" His voice is low, but the tone is urgent.

"A drone," I gasp out. "Outside, watching the cottage. And—a message. In the sand. They found us."

Kaden responds with a closed-mouth smile. "That quickly? Good."

He strides past me, and I follow him outside. The drone still hovers above, its sleek black body almost invisible against the gray sky. Kaden tracks its movements with a cold, calculating gaze.

This is the Kaden I first met—the lethal, unforgiving killer.

He reaches behind him, pulling a sleek black handgun from the waistband of his jeans. The metal gleams as he levels it at the drone. There's no hesitation, no flicker of doubt. Only a chilling, single-minded focus.

Cassie suddenly appears at my side, having silently prowled out of the lighthouse and toward us. "What's going on?"

"Stay back," Kaden orders. "Both of you."

The drone buzzes closer, its camera swiveling to track our movements. Kaden's finger tightens on the trigger, his stance immovable. He doesn't flinch as the drone darts forward, a clear provocation. Instead, a slow, deliberate smile curls his lips.

*Crack.*

The drone explodes. Pieces rain down at our feet while Kaden lowers his weapon, his expression impassive as he surveys the destruction.

"You shot their invitation," Cassie says. "Rude."

Kaden kneels beside the mangled remains of the drone, his hands carefully sifting through the debris. He extracts a small, black device from the wreckage—a camera, its lens cracked and splintered.

"Did you have anything to do with this?" he asks her.

Cassie raises her hands. "I'm not stupid enough to put a drone in your face."

Kaden studies her for a long moment. Finally, he nods, apparently satisfied with her answer.

He returns to sifting through the debris, his fingers closing around a small, rectangular object.

"What is it?" I ask, stepping closer.

Kaden doesn't answer. Instead, he stands, holding it up to the light. It's a photograph, edges singed and curling from the heat of the explosion. My breath catches in my throat as I realize what I'm seeing.

It's me—naked, bound, and beaten. My skin is mottled with bruises, and my hair is matted with blood. The picture is grainy, but the setting is unmistakable—the VIP suite at Siren's Call.

Bile chokes me as the memories flood back—the plush carpeting, the zip ties biting my wrists raw, the searing pain of each blow, the sickening smell of my own blood.

I force myself to look away, my stomach churning.

Kaden's jaw clenches as he studies the photograph. When he speaks, it's with barely held in restraint. "Cassandra?"

Cassie's eyes go wide with innocence. "I didn't take any pictures. That was all them."

Kaden moves his murderous stare to her, searching for any hint of deception. I stand frozen, my arms wrapped tightly around myself as if I can physically hold together the shattered pieces of my composure. All I can focus on is the photograph in Kaden's hand, the tangible proof of my darkest, most vulnerable moments.

Cassie's gaze flicks to me.

"I only did what I was taught," she says, her voice soft, almost pitying.

The words hit me like a physical blow, and I flinch, my nails digging into the flesh of my arms.

"We need to go," I say, my voice shaking. "Now. Before they send something worse than a drone."

Kaden's eyes meet mine. "No."

"No?" I echo, disbelief coloring my tone. "Kaden, they found us. They know where we are. We're not safe here anymore."

He shakes his head in a slow, deliberate motion. "Running won't solve anything. It'll only delay the inevitable."

Cassie shifts her weight, her lips curving into a sly smile. "Listen to the man, Layla. He knows what he's doing."

I shoot her a withering glare before turning back to Kaden.

"But the message in the sand, the drone, the photograph..." My voice wavers, the weight of each piece of evidence bearing down on me. "I can't go back there, Kaden. Please, don't let them take me again."

Kaden's expression turns hard, but it's not directed at me. He fuels all that hatred toward the photograph still clutched in his hand.

"This photo reminds me how you wore pain like armor." Kaden's voice carries deadly intent. "Now let me show you how to wear it like a crown."

With his other hand, he reaches into his pocket and pulls out a lighter. The flame dances to life, and he throws it on the wrecked drone. The grass and dried leaves underneath it catch fire instantly, igniting with a *whoosh*, flames licking angrily at the mangled components.

The intense heat sends shimmering waves rising from the ground. I take an involuntary step back, shielding my face with my arm.

Kaden stands motionless, the flames casting a hellish glow across his features, painting him in shades of red and orange. He looks every inch the demon I once believed him to be.

Cassie sidles up beside me, her shoulder brushing mine.

"Looks like we're in for one hell of a show," she murmurs, her voice laced with dark amusement before she saunters away.

---

I feel safe in Kaden's presence. Protected. Like nothing can touch me as long as he's by my side.

But that safety comes at a price. Kaden's walls are high and impenetrable, his emotions locked away behind a facade of cold detachment. He's a puzzle I can't solve, a labyrinth I can't navigate. And the more he shuts me out, the more I feel like I'm losing myself in the process.

"Kaden," I venture, my voice barely audible over the crackling of the flames. "What is your plan?"

He doesn't answer immediately, his attention still focused on the burning wreckage.

Finally, he says, "I'm going to end this."

There's a finality to his words, a grim determination that leaves no room for argument. But I can't shake the unease.

"And how exactly do you plan on doing that?" I press, taking a step closer to him.

A muscle ticks beneath his scar. "I have my ways."

It's not an answer, not really, and frustration surges through me. I've trusted him this far, put my life in his hands time and time again. But now, with the threat looming closer than ever, his evasiveness feels like a betrayal.

"Dammit, Kaden!" I explode, my voice rising with each word. "You can't keep shutting me out like this! Not now, not after everything we've been through."

He rounds on me, his eyes flashing.

"You think I'm shutting you out?" he growls, his voice low and rough. "I'm ensuring no one ever touches you again. No one but me."

"By keeping me in the dark?" I counter, refusing to back down. "By making decisions for me without even consulting me?"

He steps forward, closing the distance between us until we're mere heartbeats apart.

"You want to know what I'm planning?" he asks, his

voice a rumble in his chest. "I'm going to make them pay for what they did to you. For every bruise, every cut, every moment of pain they inflicted on you. And I'm going to keep this photo as a reminder of just how much they deserve to hurt."

I turn to the side, hugging myself.

He catches my chin and forces me to keep looking at him. "Those men who helped break you—who stood there watching, who held you down? They're about to learn exactly why they call me the Scythe."

"And Cassie?" I force myself to ask.

His jaw tightens. "She's my blood. My responsibility. But her men?" A deadly smile curves his lips. "They're fair game. And they will suffer for every mark on both my women."

# 25
## LAYLA

Lighthouses guide ships to safety. Tonight, ours will guide killers straight to us.

With Cassie's help, Kaden arms the perimeter of my property with explosives, trip wires, acoustic sensors ... I couldn't keep up with Kaden's list as he explained to Cassie what he intended to do.

He also isn't letting me out of his sight. Anywhere he goes, he demands that I follow. I can't say I'm upset about it for so many reasons. When Kaden assumes command, he's even sexier than normal. His confidence, arrogance, and skill all meld together to form the Scythe, a lethal combination that always gets my salivary glands going, even when at the center of danger. Ever since I met him, my hormones are out of control. And with the way his attention never leaves me for more than a few seconds at a time, he's feeling the same. The thought of Kaden morphing into that brutal, merciless assassin tonight actually turns me on, and I'm not sure what that says about me.

Maybe that I belong to him.

Kaden's hands move with practiced precision as he sets the final explosive charge near the shoreline in case they decide to come by boat. He threads his fingers in mine when we make our way back to the cottage, and I glance at the lighthouse as we pass. Cassie will be up there with one of Kaden's long-range guns, shooting to kill. I try not to think about Cassie on her own with a dangerous weapon. Kaden seems to have faith that she'll be on our side, but I'm not sure if it's based on hope or certainty.

Taking a deep breath, I try not to think about it too hard. There's enough on my plate as it is.

Inside, Kaden leads me to the living room, his hand never leaving the small of my back. Cassie wanders in behind us, her footsteps so silent, I don't notice her until she falls onto the couch and lets out a dramatic yawn. "As much as I love watching you two eye fuck each other, don't we have more pressing matters to attend to? Like, what's the plan? Now we just sit here and wait for them to come to us?"

Kaden doesn't take the bait. "You know your position. Get up there and keep watch. Radio me immediately if you see any movement."

Cassie rolls her eyes but gets to her feet, grabbing the sleek sniper rifle propped against the wall. She heads for the door, then pauses and looks back at me. "Hey Layla, try not to get killed, okay? I'm just starting to enjoy our special time together."

Her voice drips with insincerity, but I sense an undercurrent of ... something else. Before I can respond, she disappears outside.

Kaden turns to me, his eyes roaming over my body as if

committing every inch to memory. Electricity rushes through my veins, and I wish we had the time for him to *really* commit to my body.

"No matter what happens," he says, "I won't let anything happen to you. Understand?"

I nod, my mouth suddenly dry.

"When they come, it will get bad fast," he warns, his expression grim. "The things I'll have to do ... I need you to trust me. Don't interfere, no matter what it looks like. Let me handle it my way."

His eyes search mine, seeking obedience.

"I trust you," I say rather than answering directly.

Seemingly satisfied, Kaden nods curtly and steps back, all business once more as he checks his weapons again with methodical focus. I pace the room, already missing his touch, and glance around the cozy den, my mind struggling to reconcile the homey furnishings with the arsenal of guns and knives laid out with ruthless precision.

I never asked for any of this—but then again, I never asked to fall for a gorgeous, deadly hitman either. Yet here we are, our fates intertwined as we stare down the barrel of a gun together. Multiple ones.

Kaden spins a knife in his hands, and it's so sharp, it whistles with his movements. "Do you think Ethan is up for surveillance in the computer room upstairs?"

I take my time answering. Ethan would want to help in whatever way he could, but he's having a more difficult time coming to terms with Cassie's presence than I am. Maybe because he's not in love with her sire and willing to overlook extreme red flags in order to be with him. I cringe at the thought, but I also can't deny it. I'm not fully evil, but I'm not fully good anymore, either. Not if I can love a man like this and accept his murderous spawn.

Sighing, I rub my eyes. Ethan's skills would give us a tactical advantage I'm not willing to pass up. "I'll go get him set up."

I hurry upstairs to my bedroom, knocking softly before entering.

Ethan's sitting cross-legged in bed, one of Reaper's kittens spinning in circles on his lap as Ethan dangles a piece of dental floss.

"Hey," I say as I come in and shut the door.

Ethan replies without looking up. "Let me guess, Tall, Dark, and Deadly wants me to hack into some satellite feeds and get eyes on the surrounding area."

Though his tone is wry, the undercurrent of defeat breaks my heart.

I perch on the edge of the bed, drawing the attention of another kitten, this one a puffball gray color who's secretly become my favorite. I pick her up, nuzzling her nose with mine.

Ethan glances up, watching. "Has Kaden named them?"

"The kittens? Not that I know of." I set the puffball down in order for her to join her siblings, attacking shreds of toilet paper in the corner. "Why, do you have suggestions?"

"Well, lying in here high on pain meds had me thinking all sorts of things. So let's see. Satan." He gestures to the one in his lap, currently chewing on the hem of his sweater, then points at the others. "Beelzebub, Lucifer, Dark Lord, and ... Hades."

"You named my puffball Dark Lord?"

Ethan squints at me. "You wanted Kaden to own a cat named Puffball?"

That gets a smile out of me.

But just as quickly, Ethan's amusement fades. "Is helping them the only way for me to get out of here?"

"Oh, Ethan." I reach for his hand. "I'm so sorry I got you into this."

"I don't know how many times I have to say it, but I'll keep saying it. It was my choice to help you. It's still my choice. I don't blame you."

"Well, I'm still sorry. I'm sure you thought assisting me would involve significantly fewer near-death experiences."

His expression softens. "I just ... I worry about you, Layla. This guy, his *daughter* ... are you sure you can trust them?"

I think of the way Kaden's eyes follow my every move, even before he officially introduced himself. The firm possessiveness in his touch, the obsessive intensity of his protection.

"I trust Kaden with my life," I answer honestly.

Ethan studies me for a long moment, then nods. "Okay, then. I'll do it."

I flash him a grateful smile. "Thank you. Really. You'll be safe up here, too. Kaden's set up a bank of computers across the hall."

"Thank me when we're not about to have our asses shot at."

He sets Satan on the floor and stands, brushing cat hair off his pants. Fast, before I can second-guess it, I pull him into a tight hug.

"You're my best friend. The only friend I have. Thank you. For everything," I say into his shoulder.

Ethan responds with a wheeze.

"Shit! Your ribs!" I jump back, curling my fingers against my mouth. "I'm s—"

"Say that again, and I'll tell Kaden you named one of his cats Puffball." Ethan shakes his head with a tiny smile. "Be gone, Layla. Go be with Batman down there."

I leave him to it and dash back downstairs. Kaden is exactly where I left him, cataloging his weapons. He looks up as I approach.

"Ethan's on board," I report. "He'll keep a bird's-eye view on the property."

"Good." Kaden sheaths a knife and steps closer, his presence enveloping me. I tilt my head back, never wanting to stop staring at his face. "Put this on. Stay behind me and keep your head down at all times."

I take the tactical vest from his hands. "Okay."

My voice comes out breathier than intended. Damn him and his overwhelming masculinity.

His eyelids lower, and for a charged moment, I think he's going to give me my last erotic wish before we face the inevitable, but Cassie's staticky voice coming through his radio interrupts us, her usual snark replaced by terse urgency.

"*We have company.*"

Kaden whips his attention toward the window, his whole body tensing.

"Before sunset," he muses. "Already, they're making a mistake."

As I fumble with the vest's straps, my fingers clumsy

with adrenaline, Kaden's hands close over mine, efficiently securing the Velcro and cinching it tight. His touch lingers for a charged moment, his fingers trailing electricity across my collarbone. In his eyes I see the war between the man he once was and the ruthless killer. I pray to any dark gods listening that both sides of him survive this night.

A teeth-rattling boom shatters the thick silence, and the cottage windows rattle in their panes. Kaden spins to his weapons and grabs his mask. It settles onto his face with an electronic hiss, and then I'm standing in front of the Scythe.

"You have a spare mask?" is all I can think to ask as my brain shuts down and reboots in simple survival mode. Kaden's original one was removed at the Siren's Call. As I eye the armory my couch has become, he lost his mask along with a litany of weapons he also seemingly had multiple spares of.

Another explosion rocks the cottage, this time from the opposite side of the property.

Kaden presses his earpiece. "Cassie, report."

As he listens to Cassie's response, he settles another earpiece in my ear. "*...hostiles approaching from the north shore. Armed to the teeth. These are just mercenaries. I don't recognize them as any of Papa's men.*"

"They'll wait until the mercs have me cornered. Take out as many as you can."

Kaden's voice is a menacing growl, all traces of his morals slipping away as he becomes the Scythe.

Staccato gunfire erupts outside, the walls shuddering as if in fear. I flinch, my heart threatening to flee, but I force my breaths to even out.

Kaden stalks to the door. He pauses and looks back at

me, those eerie neon slits sending a delicious frisson down my spine. "Last time, I had you barricade yourself in a room, and they still found you. Come here."

I do as he says, allowing him to wrap my arms around his waist until one side of my face is pressed against his back.

"Keep holding on to me. Do *not* let go. I'm taking you to an area Cassie and I scouted earlier where they won't find you."

Gasping, I abruptly release Kaden and run for the stairs. "What about Ethan—"

Kaden hooks my waist, my feet flying off the ground as he slams me against his solid chest. "Do *not* disobey me again, Wraithling."

"I can't leave him, Kaden. Ethan's hurt and exposed—"

"I'll come back for him."

"Do you promise?"

I hate how small my voice sounds, but I'm *scared*, and I've made Ethan face enough hazards.

Kaden spins me around until I'm face-to-face with his cold, metal persona. "On my life."

He pushes me behind him again, locking my arms around his torso and kicking open the door.

The setting horizon explodes with light and sound as we step outside, tracer rounds and muzzle flashes strobing through the darkening sky.

I press into Kaden's broad back, my breaths coming fast and shallow. He moves with fluid grace, his body an instrument of death as he leads us away from the cottage.

Another explosion occurs nearby, and I stumble, but Kaden's iron hold keeps me upright.

"Almost there," he says, his voice distorted by the mask. "Hold on to me, Layla."

As if I'm about to let go.

The stench of smoke and gunpowder assaults my senses. Orange flames lick at the tree line, casting menacing shadows across the lawn.

"Keep your head down," Kaden orders as he picks up speed, heading toward the old fishing docks.

Bullets zing past us. Kaden returns fire with one hand, his other pressing protectively against mine around his stomach.

Smoke stings my eyes and fills my lungs, but I focus on putting one foot in front of the other, trusting Kaden to get us through this nightmare. His scent envelops me, gunpowder and musk, danger and safety all at once. It shouldn't comfort me the way it does.

We reach the old fishing docks, rotting planks creaking beneath our feet. Kaden pulls me around to face him, his hands gripping my shoulders. Even through the mask, I can feel the seriousness of his expression.

"I need you to get in the water and hide under the dock. Don't come out until I come for you, no matter what you hear. Understand?"

Fear makes it hard to speak, but I nod.

Kaden threads his fingers through my hair, a fleeting caress. "That's my girl. Now go."

I slip into the dark, frigid water, gasping as it bites into my skin. Kaden watches me disappear beneath the planks before he turns back to the fight, a phantom in the night.

Treading water, I press myself against the slimy support post, trying to control my chattering teeth. Above me, the battle rages on. The dock shudders with each impact, showering me with debris.

My heart pounds in my ears, nearly drowning out the gunfire and shouts. Every fiber of my being screams to go to Kaden, to help him somehow, but I gave him my word. I have to trust that he knows what he's doing.

Cold seeps into my bones, numbing my limbs, but I barely notice. All I can think about is Kaden. The coppery scent of blood mingles with brine, turning my stomach. Was he hurt? Killed?

I'm distracted when the glow of a searchlight seeps through the gaps in the planks. I peek through one section, spotting a sleek black speedboat slicing through the waves and heading straight for my dock. Its powerful light sweeps the shore, seeking its prey.

As the boat glides closer, I make out the cruel, chiseled features of the men on board. They're dressed in black tactical gear, bristling with weapons. A heavy dread settles in my gut.

Morelli's men have come.

My heart thrashes painfully against my ribs as I think of Kaden out there facing them alone. Ruthless assassin or not, he's outnumbered and outgunned. Cassie's sniper support can only do so much against this sheer firepower.

I'm shaking now, and not just from the cold. Hot tears mingle with the salt water on my face. I bite my knuckles until I taste blood as if the physical pain can overshadow the agony shredding my chest.

*He's not going to die. He won't leave me. Kaden will be okay. Ethan will be okay. We're all going to be fine.*

The boat slows at the side of the dock. I shrink back, praying the inky water conceals me.

Heavy boots thud on the planks with gruff voices barking orders in Italian, followed by the ominous click of guns being cocked.

My heart pounds so loudly, I'm certain they can hear it. I barely dare to breathe. The water laps against my chin, so cold it burns. My muscles scream in protest as I force myself to remain still.

One pair of boots stops directly above me. Through the rotting planks, I catch a glimpse of cruel eyes in a brutish face. It's one of the men who loved watching me while I was naked and tied down, the kind of man who paints his rape-like thoughts on his face without shame.

"Jesus Christ, it took you guys long enough."

I cover my mouth to stifle the gasp that almost escapes.

That was a woman's voice. One I recognize all too well.

Cassie's.

# 26

## LAYLA

Kaden taught me how to kill a man fifteen different ways, but he never mentioned how to stay silent while freezing to death under a dock.

My teeth chatter violently as I crouch in the frigid, murky water. The cold seeps into my bones, my muscles cramping and spasming. I clench my jaw, trying to still the involuntary shudders wracking my body, terrified that even the slightest ripple will give away my position.

Above me, footsteps thud heavily on the weathered wooden planks, sending vibrations through the rotting posts that surround me like a cage. I press myself deeper into the shadows, my back scraping against the algae-slick pilings. The brine stings my eyes and fills my nostrils with its pungent decay.

Through the narrow gaps between the boards, I catch glimpses of tight jeans and a leather jacket—clothes I've lent Cassie while we were stuck in a fortress.

A fortress of *her* doing.

One she always planned to crumble to dust.

She must have followed Kaden and me, allegedly watching his back while waiting for her men to come get her.

My lungs burn as I hold my breath, straining to hear the conversation above.

"You've done well, Cassie." A man's tone turns appraising. "If he were alive, Morelli would be pleased. You've passed his final test to become the rightful heir."

"I'm so glad I had to let them go when I already had them, then *re*capture them, all to prove Papa's posthumous love," Cassie drawls. "Can we get the rest over with and kill them now? I'd love to sleep in my own bed again instead of a rat-infested lighthouse."

The man chuckles as if accustomed to Cassie's prissy behavior. "Where is the Scythe hiding?"

"Not far," Cassie replies. "He wouldn't stray too far from her. He's gone soft."

*Oh, Kaden.* My heart breaks for him.

"We'll keep our word then, Miss Morelli," the man says, his voice now directly overhead. "Once we tie up these loose ends, we're your lieutenants to command."

"Wonderful," Cassie says, applauding. "Because I'm tired of Papa's games and have my own shit to take care of."

Cassie's betrayal cuts deep even though I never truly trusted her. But the ease with which these men agree to her terms sets off warning bells in my head.

"Now, where exactly is the girl hiding?" the man asks, his tone dripping with false sincerity,

Planks above my head creak as she shifts her weight. "She's currently cowering like a drowned rat."

*She knows where I am!*

I hold my breath, not daring to even blink, as her movements pause. The boots pivot slowly, deliberately, as if she can sense my presence beneath her feet. A shaft of wan sunlight filters through the slats, casting the last bars of illumination across my face. I remain perfectly still.

Suddenly, Cassie drops to a crouch.

I shrink back, pressing my spine against the slimy wood, but it's too late. Her chipped, sapphire eyes lock onto mine through the narrow crack, widening with triumphant malice.

Wicked red lips curve into a smile as cruel as it is beautiful.

"Oh, hey, future stepmom," she purrs. "Found you."

I press myself farther into the shadows, my hand closing around the knife strapped to my thigh. Kaden's parting words echo in my mind. *"If they corner you, don't hesitate. Strike fast and true. Go for the kill."*

I tighten my grip on the hilt, steeling myself. I may not survive this, but I'll be damned if I go down without a fight.

A hand plunges into the water, grasping for me. I lash out blindly with the knife, feeling it connect with flesh and bone. The man screams, recoiling.

Gunshots explode above me, splintering the wood. I flinch and cry out as shards rain down.

Cassie's voice rises above the onslaught. "I said she was under there, idiots! Don't kill her yet!"

In the confusion, I seize my chance. Sucking in a breath, I dive under the water, knifing through the murk. I surface on the other side of the dock, gasping for air. It's just dark enough that maybe I can float to shore without them noticing.

I take one stroke, then another, trying to be silent as I cut through the icy black water. My muscles scream in protest, cramping from the cold, but I grit my teeth and push on. The shoreline beckons, a distant haven shrouded in mist and shadow. If I can just reach it...

Shouts erupt behind me, followed by the thunder of boots on the dock.

"There! In the water!" a man bellows.

My heart leaps into my throat. I don't dare look back, my strokes becoming frantic and graceless. The water churns around me, choked with seaweed that tangles around my limbs like grasping fingers.

A gunshot cracks the air, the bullet slicing into the water inches from my head. I yelp and dive under, the frigid brine enveloping me. I swim blind, lungs aching, praying I'm heading the right way.

A hand clamps around my ankle like a vise, dragging me backward. I thrash and kick, but more hands grasp at me, seizing my arms, my hair, the back of my vest. They haul me roughly from the water, throwing me onto the dock.

I land hard on the weathered planks, coughing and sputtering. A boot presses into the small of my back, pinning me in place. I struggle weakly, but the man above me just laughs, grinding my stomach into the splintery wood.

"Not so fast, cutie pie," he sneers. "Miss Morelli wants a word with you before we slit your pretty throat."

The other men laugh, the ugly sound rolling over the black water. I squeeze my eyes shut, trembling with cold and fear.

Cassie's boots appear in my line of sight. She lowers to her haunches and grabs a fistful of my hair, wrenching my head back.

"Layla, Layla," she tsks. "You've been a very naughty girl."

One of the men kicks me in the ribs, sending blinding pain shooting through my body. I curl in on myself as much as I can, gasping.

"Where's your attack dog now?" another taunts.

A knife kisses my throat, biting into my skin under Cassie's watchful observation.

"Kaden will kill you," I rasp out. "All of you."

The men laugh, but there's an uneasy edge to it. They've seen the state in which he left the VIP suite.

I say to Cassie, "When he finds out what you've done..."

Cassie throws her head back and laughs.

"Oh, that's precious. You think my father will keep saving you?" She pauses to smile at me, slow and vicious. "News flash, Layla—Daddy's not the white knight you've built him up to be. He's just as broken and fucked up as I am. And when he finds your body washed up on shore? He'll do what he always does—"

Cassie cuts herself off when one of the lieutenants uses a meaty hand to grope along my side, undoing my vest and going under my shirt.

"Just like old times with the boss, eh?" he says to Cassie, or maybe the other men. "Teaching bad little girls their place."

The man's hand starts to wander, his touch invasive and sickeningly familiar. Bile rises in my throat as I realize what he's implying, the horrors Cassie must have endured at Morelli's hands.

I meet her gaze, seeing my own revulsion reflected back at me.

"What did you just say?" Cassie asks him, her voice a deadly whisper.

The man laughs, ugly and unaware. "Come on, Cass. We all know how Morelli liked to break in the new—"

Cassie moves like a striking viper. One moment, she's poised with her fingers tangled in my hair, and the next, she's on the man, a blur of black leather and fury. She slams him to the dock with a force that rattles the boards.

Savage, animalistic snarls rip from her throat as she straddles his chest, pinning him.

"Don't you EVER say that again!" she screams.

She snatches a knife from her belt and buries it in his eye with a savage twist. The man's scream cuts off with a wet gurgle as she rips the blade free, a gout of blood and sclera splattering her face.

The other men stand paralyzed, eyes wide with shock and dawning horror. They exchange uncertain glances, hands creeping toward weapons.

Cassie's chin snaps up, those ferocious eyes fixing on them. "None of you move, or I swear to God I'll renovate this dock with your fucking insides."

They freeze, cowed by the sheer, unhinged savagery in her gaze. She refocuses on the man pinned beneath her, fingers curling into claws.

"You don't know what he did," she hisses, spittle flying from her lips. "The things he made me..."

She leaps to her feet, and the other men shout in alarm,

the last one releasing me as he scrambles for his gun. But Cassie is a hurricane of rage, unstoppable in her onslaught.

Cassie slashes the throat of one man, his blood arcing through the air in a crimson spray. Another shoots at her, but she sidesteps nimbly, hamstringing him with a vicious swipe of her blade. He crumples, howling, and she silences him with a brutal stomp to his windpipe.

Through it all, Cassie screams, a sound of pure anguish torn from the depths of her traumatized psyche. Tears streak her blood-splattered face, her eyes dark and unfocused.

This isn't the calculated violence I've come to expect from her. This is the deranged viciousness of a wounded animal, lashing out at a world that has only ever brought her pain.

Finally, she stops, chest heaving, standing amid the carnage. Her knife clatters to the dock, slick with blood. She stares at her shaking hands, then at me, her eyes wide and lost.

"Cassie," I whisper, slowly pushing myself upright. Every inch of me throbs, my throat raw from the icy water. "Cassie, it's over."

The night explodes with the roar of an engine. Tires screech, followed by the slam of a truck's door. I see Ethan's pallid face in the back seat before the interior light goes off.

Heavy footsteps pound down the dock, the boards shuddering under their force.

Kaden appears like the harbinger of death, his mask molten silver in the moonlight. In his hand, a gun smokes.

Cassie tenses, her hand twitching toward her fallen knife, but she doesn't move. Even she knows better than to stand in the way of the Scythe's wrath.

Kaden reaches me in a heartbeat, gathering me into his arms.

"Are you hurt?" he asks, his free hand skimming down my body, checking for injuries.

I shake my head, fighting back a sob. His warm touch is grounding, chasing away the god-awful hands that pawed at me.

Cassie makes a disgusted noise. We both look at her. She's glaring at us, her face a mask of blood and contempt.

"I hate that I couldn't let them hurt you," she spits at me. "I hate that I saved your pathetic life."

"You," Kaden growls, the word loaded with threat.

Cassie winces as if he'd struck her but quickly covers it with a sneer. "What? No thank you for saving your most prized kitten?"

Kaden releases me with the utmost care before stalking toward her. She holds her ground, but I catch the way her throat bobs at his approach.

"You led them here," Kaden snarls, circling her. "You set this up."

"And I finished it," Cassie snaps, gesturing to the bodies littering the dock.

"For us? Or for yourself?"

"Fuck you," she hisses. "You have no idea what I've been through, what I've had to..."

She chokes on the words. Cassie's voice breaks, a strangled sound that's half sob, half snarl. She staggers back from Kaden, nearly slipping in the slick of blood pooling at her feet. Her eyes dart between the carnage she's wrought and some distant, horrifying point in her past.

She shakes her head violently, sending droplets of blood flying from her ponytail.

"I was just a kid," she whispers, her voice tiny and fractured. "I thought ... I thought if I was good, if I did what he wanted..."

A shudder wracks her frame, so violent it's almost a convulsion. She falls to her knees.

Tears mix with the blood on her face, cutting tracks through the grime. She looks at Kaden, really looks at him.

"I didn't want this," she tells him, her voice cracking. "I didn't want to be this. But he made me. He carved out everything good and filled me up with hate. And I can't... I can't get it out."

She presses a hand to her chest as if she can physically feel the rot inside her. Her breath comes in sharp, painful gasps, each one a struggle.

"I'm sorry," she chokes out, the words foreign and awkward on her tongue. "I'm sorry I'm not ... I can't be what you wanted. I can't be saved."

Kaden stares at her, his expression unreadable behind the mask.

Until he takes it off and it drops with a clang at his feet.

Cassie meets his gaze, her own bleak and haunted. "You should've put me down the minute you saw I was alive. You knew these ten years wouldn't have been kind to me. It would've been kinder for you to end me."

He takes a step toward her, then another. Cassie flinches but doesn't retreat, watching him warily. He lowers himself until they're eye to eye and reaches out as if approaching a wounded animal, until his hand hovers just inches from her blood-streaked face.

Cassie trembles, a full-body shudder that seems to originate from her very core.

"You didn't let them hurt Layla the way you were hurt. That means something, Cassie."

Cassie's gaze flicks to me, a trace of grief in her eyes. Then she looks back at Kaden, her lower lip trembling.

Kaden's hand finally makes contact, cupping her cheek with a gentleness at odds with the brutality of our surroundings. Cassie stiffens but doesn't pull away, her eyes scrunching closed as if she can't bear to see the tenderness in his gaze.

Kaden's thumb brushes over a small scar on her cheekbone, tracing the remnant of violence. "I see you, Cassie. I see the strength it took to survive what he did to you. I see the light in you, even when you can't see it yourself."

My vision turns hot. My eyes well up, and I allow the tears to fall because that is exactly the way I feel about *him*.

Cassie searches his face as if trying to find the lie, the trick, the inevitable betrayal. But there is only open honesty in Kaden's gaze, a vulnerability he so rarely shows.

"I don't know how to be anything else," she says. "I don't know how to be ... good."

Kaden's hand slides to the back of her neck, pulling her forward until she's pressed against his chest. "Neither do I. But you can start by choosing, every day, to be better than what he made you. And when you can't, when the darkness feels like it's swallowing you whole, you lean on the people who love you. You let me help you."

Cassie's hand comes up to clutch his wrist. "You—you still love me? After everything I've done?"

"Always," Kaden says fiercely. "You're my daughter. Nothing will ever change that."

A splintered sound escapes her, halfway between a laugh and a breakdown. She buries her face in his chest as great, heaving sobs wrack her body. Kaden's arms come around her, holding her tight as she falls apart.

"I'm sorry," she gasps out between sobs. "I'm sorry I didn't fight harder, that I let him turn me into this. I'm sorry I hurt you, that I hurt Layla. I'm just … I'm so sorry, Daddy."

Kaden's eyes close at the heartsick endearment, a single tear slipping free.

"I forgive you," he tells her. "You hear me, baby girl? I forgive you. You're not poison; you're not rotten. You're my daughter, and I love you, no matter what."

Cassie clings to him like a lifeline, like he's the only thing keeping her from shattering.

And maybe he is.

# 27
## LAYLA

**1 Week Later**

When I wake up, Kaden's side of the bed is cold, but the bruises he left behind still burn like promises. His pillow still holds the indentation of his head, and I stroke my hand over it and smile.

Rubbing sleep from my eyes, I sit up, pulling the duvet around my naked form.

I spot Kaden standing in front of the circular window, his muscular frame carved out against the pale dawn light. He's watching the lighthouse, as he does every morning, ensuring that there's a small golden light indicating that Cassie's still there. That she's staying.

I pad across the room, the duvet trailing behind me like a regal cape. Kaden doesn't turn, but I know he senses my approach. I press myself against his back, my breasts flat-tening against his hot, bare skin.

Snaking my arms around his waist, I place a tender kiss between his shoulder blades.

"Come back to bed," I murmur, my lips brushing against his spine.

Kaden spins, pinning me against the cool glass. His large hand encircles my throat, applying just enough pressure to remind me of his strength, his control.

"Or we can just stay here," he says with a growl—and a grin.

His mouth crashes against mine, claiming me with a hard kiss. I melt into him, surrendering to his dominance, the duvet falling off my shoulders and pooling at our feet. Kaden nudges my legs apart, but I stop him with a hand on his sculpted chest. "Wait."

Kaden pulls back with an arched brow that stretches his scar. "That's a dangerous request, Wraithling."

"Well, I-I kind of ... want to try something new."

"Oh?"

I bite my lower lip. The sight of it makes his cock jump against my stomach, and his chest rumbles with a warning that my wait time is almost up.

"Do you, um, do you think you can wear your mask?" I ask.

His lips curve into a wicked smile as he regards me, his eyes scorching a path down my body.

"Wait here," he commands.

He strides across the room to the antique armoire, the muscles of his back rippling with each step. Anticipation coils tight in my belly as he retrieves something from the top drawer. When he turns back to face me, he's holding his sleek gunmetal mask, simple yet undeniably menacing.

With deliberate slowness, Kaden slips it over his face. It molds perfectly to his chiseled features, leaving only his piercing blue eyes exposed. He doesn't turn on the neon-green night vision.

The effect of a mask on top and nothing but a sexy, masculine, hard body underneath is striking and reckless. My pulse quickens, desire pooling hot and heavy between my thighs.

In three long strides, he's on me, slamming me back against the window. The cold glass bites into my bare skin.

"Is this what you wanted, Wraithling?" he asks quietly. "To be fucked by a dangerous man in a mask?"

"No," I breathe, aching for his touch. "I want the Scythe to fuck me."

Kaden laughs darkly beneath the mask. His hands skim down my sides, his fingers digging into my flesh. With a sharp tug, he hoists me up, urging me to wrap my legs around his waist. I comply eagerly, locking my ankles at the small of his back.

He thrusts his hips, grinding the thick ridge of his erection against my slick folds. I moan, biting my lip.

"You're mine," he warns. "You'll always be mine. No matter what mask I wear."

"Yours," I gasp as he positions himself at my entrance. "Only yours."

But he holds me there, suspended in anticipation. "Beg for it."

"Please," I whimper. "Please fuck me. Take what belongs to you."

A deep, rumbling growl emanates from beneath the mask. "You want the Scythe to take you hard and rough against this window? Where anyone could see what a wanton little thing you are for me?"

"Yes," I practically wail. "Take me. Use me. I'm yours."

With a feral grunt, he slams into me, burying himself. I cry out, my walls clenching around his thick length.

"Is this what you wanted?" he snarls, punctuating each word with a sharp snap of his hips. "To be fucked raw by a monster in a mask?"

"You're *my* monster," I gasp out between moans. "You're mine. My protector, my lover, my—"

He sets a punishing pace, slamming into me over and over, the force of his thrusts rattling the window at my back.

"Look at you," he snarls. "So desperate for a madman."

"Yes," I keen, the degradation only heightening my arousal. "Keep using me. Ruin me for anyone else."

Kaden drives into me relentlessly, his masked face a terrifying, thrilling sight above me as I'm pinned and ravaged against the window.

"You're a twisted little thing, aren't you? Getting off on being taken by a masked killer."

"Only for you," I husk out. "I want you in any form. Monster or man."

His pace turns savage, each ruthless thrust shoving me up the glass. The cold press of it against my heated skin makes me shiver and clench around him.

"Fuck, just like that," he grunts. "Take it all, greedy girl."

I'm lost to the brutal rhythm, my world narrowed to the ferocious pleasure ripping through me with every thrust.

Kaden shifts, angling his hips to hit that perfect spot inside me. I cry out, my legs tightening around him.

One hand moves to my throat, squeezing just hard enough to make my head swim with euphoric lightheadedness. His other hand snakes between our sweat-slicked bodies to find my clit. He rubs the sensitive nub in harsh, merciless circles that have me seeing heaven.

"Kaden," I say, my inner muscles fluttering around his length. "I'm going to—"

"Not yet." He fists my hair, pulling my head back. "You come when I allow it."

He rewards me with a particularly deep thrust, grinding against my clit. My body bows into his. I writhe against him, chasing my release. The rough scars and old burns on his chest rub deliciously against my sensitive nipples, the dual sensations pushing me closer to the edge.

"Come for me," he commands, his voice a dark rasp. "Milk my cock like the good girl you are."

His words send me hurtling over the edge. My orgasm crashes over me in shuddering waves as my pussy spasms almost violently around him. With a final snap of his hips, he spills himself deep inside me, marking me from the inside out as his.

We stay joined for a long moment, both struggling to catch our breath.

Kaden reaches up and removes the mask, tossing it carelessly to the side. He cups my face in his large hands, his touch almost unbearably tender after the brutal fucking.

"I love you, Layla," he says solemnly. "You're my whole fucking world. Never forget that."

I place my hands over his. "I love you, too. All of you. With or without the mask."

Foreign emotion ripples across his scarred, jaded face before he lets his head fall forward to rest his forehead against mine. "Even when the darkest parts of myself want you for their own, you always obey me."

We stand there, wrapped in each other, as the rising sun bathes us in its warm golden glow.

A loud honk shatters the moment. I jerk away from Kaden, peering out the window to see a familiar sedan pulling up the gravel drive.

Kaden stills, his body going rigid against mine.

"Expecting someone?" he asks, his tone dangerously calm.

I shake my head, panting. "No, I—" The realization hits me. "Oh God. It's Ethan."

Kaden's eyes narrow to slits. "And what is he doing here at this very moment when I plan to fuck you again?"

"He mentioned coming by to say goodbye. He's leaving Greycliff, remember? Starting his new job in Millhaven next week."

Kaden mutters a curse under his breath. For a moment, he looks like he might march out there naked, cock still hard and ready, and physically remove Ethan from the property. But then he glances down at me, his gaze softening imperceptibly.

After a few more bonus strokes of his perfect cock inside me, Kaden slips out with a reluctant hiss. "Let's go say farewell, then."

———

I hastily throw on a robe while Kaden pulls on a pair of low-slung sweatpants, not bothering with a shirt. We head downstairs to the kitchen, where the scent of freshly brewed coffee permeates the air.

Ethan waits by the front door, shifting his weight from foot to foot. He looks up as we approach, his hazel eyes widening slightly at the sight of Kaden's imposing figure despite seeing it many times.

"Hey, E." I greet him with a smile. "Come on in."

He steps inside hesitantly, his gaze darting between Kaden and me. "I don't mean to intrude. I just wanted to come by and say goodbye before I head out."

Kaden remains silent and unmoving, his usual default setting.

I usher Ethan into the kitchen, where Cassie is already seated at the table, nursing a mug of black coffee while Reaper laps at a small bowl of milk beside her. Cassie looks up as we enter.

"Well, isn't this cozy," she says. "The whole gang together again."

I bristle at her tone, but Ethan just offers her a tight smile and gives Reaper a long stroke from head to tail. She arches into it with a happy purr.

Ethan and I settle around the table while Kaden remains standing, arms crossed over his broad chest.

I clear my throat. "So, Ethan, you're all set for Millhaven?"

He nods, his fingers fidgeting with the handle of a coffee mug Cassie filled and pushed toward him. "Yeah, I start at the new firm next Monday. It's a good opportunity."

"I'm happy for you," I say with sincerity. "You deserve a fresh start after everything that's happened."

Cassie snorts. "Running away from your problems won't solve anything."

"I'm not running away," Ethan retorts, a hint of steel in his voice. "I'm choosing to move on. To build a life that's not defined by violence and death."

Ethan pales, his eyes darting to Kaden before dropping to the table as if worried Kaden will retaliate for snapping at Cassie.

Kaden shifts, drawing everyone's attention.

"We've all done things we regret," he says quietly. "What matters is what we do going forward."

"I just ... I can't stay here anymore," Ethan admits.

Guilt twists at my insides as I regard Ethan and how much he's changed since I entered his life. How much he fights the darkness rather than accepts it. It's the decent, moral thing to do, a natural rejection of evil. And while I'll miss him desperately, I'm certain he doesn't belong in this world. My new world that will forever include violence and death.

So I nod in understanding. "And the job? You'll be doing IT work for a software company, right?"

A glimmer of his old enthusiasm sparks in his eyes. "Yeah, it's a good opportunity. A chance to do something normal, you know? Something that doesn't involve ... well, all of this."

Cassie leans back in her chair, eyeing Ethan with a mix of disdain and grudging respect. "Well, look at you, Rutledge. Finally growing a pair and striking out on your own. Never thought I'd see the day."

Ethan's jaw tightens, but he doesn't rise to her bait. Instead, he turns to me, his expression softening. "I'm going to miss you, Layla. You've been a true friend through all of this insanity. I don't know how I would have survived without you."

Tears prick at the corners of my eyes. "I'm going to miss you too, E. But I'm so proud of you for doing what's best for you. You deserve happiness and peace."

"We all do," he says quietly, his gaze encompassing Kaden and Cassie as well. "I hope you find yours in whatever form it takes."

Kaden clears his throat, drawing our attention. "Millhaven isn't that far. Don't be a stranger. You're welcome here anytime."

Ethan blinks in surprise at the unprecedented invitation. "I ... thanks. That means a lot."

The hint of a smile tugs at the corner of Kaden's mouth before his expression turns serious again. "I owe you for everything you've done for Layla. If you ever need anything, say the word."

Ethan nods, swallowing hard. "I appreciate that."

An awkward silence descends until Cassie abruptly stands, her chair scraping against the floor.

"Well, this has been touching, really. But some of us have actual work to do." She drains the last of her coffee and sets the mug in the sink with a clatter. "I'll be at the lighthouse if anyone needs me. Try not to."

She stalks out without a backward glance, Reaper trotting at her heels. Ethan sighs, pushing back from the table as well.

"I should get going too. I have a long drive ahead of me."

He hesitates, then pulls me into a tight hug. "Take care of yourself, okay? And him." He nods toward Kaden.

"I will," I promise, my voice muffled against his shoulder. "You take care of yourself too. And keep in touch."

"I will." Ethan pulls back, swiping surreptitiously at his eyes. He extends a hand to Kaden. "Mr. Black."

Kaden clasps his hand firmly. "Drive safe. Remember what I said."

"If it's all the same to you, I hope I never need your kind of help," Ethan replies.

Kaden's lips twitch into an almost smile in response.

"Now go," I say to Ethan, shooing him before I really do cry. "Live a good life. Find a nice, normal girl and fall stupidly in love. You deserve that happiness."

Ethan huffs a quiet laugh. With a final squeeze of my hand, he walks out the door and down the steps to his car. I watch until the vehicle disappears down the fog-shrouded drive, an odd mix of sadness and relief swirling inside me.

Strong arms wrap around my waist from behind, pulling my back flush against a solid wall of muscle. Kaden nuzzles into my neck.

"You're not having second thoughts, are you, Wraithling?" he murmurs, a hint of tension beneath his seemingly casual tone.

I turn in his embrace, looping my arms around his neck. "Never. You're stuck with me, Mr. Black. For better or worse."

His eyes search mine intently before he crushes me to him, his mouth commanding mine.

When he finally pulls back, we're both panting.

"Your black heart is mine," I say.

He kisses me again, more gently this time, a silent seal of our dark covenant. Then he takes my hand, lacing our fingers together. "Let's go back to bed."

I grin at him, mischief sparking in my mind. "Race you."

I take off running, laughing as I hear Kaden's growl of outrage behind me. I make it halfway up the stairs before strong arms scoop me up. Kaden tosses me over his shoulder like a sack of flour, giving my ass a stinging smack.

"Brat," he scolds.

He carries me into our bedroom and tosses me onto the bed. I bounce once before he's on me, caging me beneath his much larger body.

"It looks like I've captured a naughty little Wraithling," he rumbles, nipping at my bottom lip. "Whatever should I do with her?"

I squirm beneath him, rubbing wantonly against the thick ridge of his erection through his sweats. "Whatever you want."

"Careful, love," he warns, his voice a dark purr. "You know I'll take you at your word. And I have very wicked things in mind for you."

"Do your worst," I challenge, my core already slick and aching for him.

"First, I think some punishment is in order for that little stunt you pulled."

He flips me onto my stomach, yanking my hips up and tossing the bottom half of my robe over my back so my bare ass is in the air.

I yelp at the sudden change in position, my fingers clutching at the sheets.

The first smack of his hand against my rear makes me

jolt. The sting quickly melts into a warmth that spreads through my blood. The second blow wrings a whimper from my lips. By the fifth, I'm writhing and mewling, shameless in my need.

"Look at you," Kaden marvels, massaging my reddened cheeks. "Taking your punishment so beautifully. Ass in the air for me like a proper lady ready to be put in her place."

"Yes," I gasp out, arching into his touch. "I love it. I love you."

He rewards me by keeping his eyes locked on mine while he lowers himself until I can't see him anymore. Then he slowly, deliberately licks a broad stripe up my slit.

My hips buck off the bed, but he pins them down with a forearm across the backs of my calves, then seals his mouth over my aching sex, his tongue delving and swirling as he devours me like a man starved.

I fist the sheets and moan while on all fours, my thighs quaking, lost to the decadent pleasure of his mouth.

He adds two fingers, pumping them in time with his lapping tongue.

"That's it," he coaxes as my walls begin to flutter. "Come on my tongue. Soak my face with it."

After a few more skillful flicks, I'm shattering, my orgasm hitting me like a freight train. I scream his name as I come, my vision whiting out at the edges.

Kaden works me through it, stroking me through the release until I'm boneless and whimpering from the intensity. Only then does he raise his head, his lips and chin glistening obscenely.

He peels my robe away before pushing me down on all fours again and shrugging out of his sweatpants. Kaden's erection springs free, the tip glistening. He kisses his way down my spine, his stubble rasping deliciously against my sensitive skin.

"Always so wet for me," he marvels. "Such a good pussy."

He presses the tip of his finger into my entrance, teasing me with shallow thrusts. I try to push back against him, but a large hand at the small of my back holds me in place.

"Ah, ah," he chides. "Naughty girls who don't wait their turn get punished, remember?"

I still beneath him, trembling with the effort of holding back. "Please, Kaden..."

He hums, considering. "Since you asked so nicely..."

The blunt head of his cock nudges against my entrance. With one smooth thrust, he sheaths himself.

"Fuck, I'll never get tired of this," he groans.

Kaden pounds into me from behind, the slap of skin against skin filling the room and mingling with my wanton cries.

He reaches around, finding my clit and rubbing merciless circles, and commands me to milk him dry.

"Come on my cock," he orders.

His filthy command is my undoing. My orgasm crashes over me.

With a guttural groan, Kaden stills, spilling himself deep inside me.

We collapse onto the bed, our limbs tangled and sweat-slicked. Kaden rolls to the side, pulling me against his chest.

We lie like that for a long while, basking in the afterglow and the quiet intimacy of the moment. The golden light of late morning spills through the windows, painting our entwined bodies in a soft, honeyed glow.

Eventually, Kaden breaks the comfortable silence.

"Marry me," he says, his voice a low rumble against my cheek.

I still. Slowly, I lift my head. His blue eyes are earnest and unwavering as they hold mine.

"What?" I whisper, hardly daring to believe what I heard.

He cups my face in his large, calloused hand. "Marry me, Layla. Be mine, in every way, forever."

Kaden's arms come around me, crushing me to his chest as if he can absorb me into himself and make us as one in body as we are in spirit.

They say monsters don't get happy endings. But as Kaden's hold tightens, I realize they never met a monster worth loving.

I say into the warmth of his skin, "Yes."

# EPILOGUE

KADEN

"Delete it," I order Cassie. "Show me you've learned there's more power in your hands than any AI."

The three of us stand at the top of the stairs leading to the server room at Siren's Call. It took me days to even get Cassie to admit the AI that started this whole mess was ready and waiting to be activated. Honesty is taking her much longer to learn than deceit ever did.

I stare at Cassie, waiting. Her eyes narrow against mine, a silent battle of wills before we descend.

"Cassie," I warn. "Don't make me tell you again."

Layla's hand slips into mine, steadying me. Her throat tattoo peeks out from her black turtleneck—once a mark of captivity, now a sign of her power. At her touch, some of the tension eases from my shoulders. The bite of her engagement ring, a three-carat black diamond with a ruby halo on a white gold band, cuts into my palm when I squeeze. I smile, glad that both the ring and my Wraithling can draw blood.

With a huff, Cassie turns on her heel and stalks down the metal stairs. I keep my grip on Layla's hand as we follow. The last time the three of us were in a server room together, Cassie put a bullet in my shoulder before abducting Layla. The spot still aches, a reminder of how close I came to losing everything.

"Let's not have a repeat of last time, shall we?" I mutter, my voice echoing off the concrete walls. "I'm rather fond of this suit, and I'd prefer not to get blood on it."

The door to the server room hisses open, a blast of cold air hitting us as we step inside. The space is cavernous with rows upon rows of sleek black servers stretching out before us. Blue-and-green lights blink in rhythm, and the only sound is the gentle whir of cooling fans.

Cassie strides over to the main terminal. She pulls up the AI interface, and lines of code scroll past, reflecting in her slitted eyes. I watch her with one hand resting on the knife at my belt.

Old habits die hard.

"It's almost a shame to destroy it," Cassie muses, studying the screen. "The power the Oracle could have given us ... we could have been gods."

"We're already gods," I counter, pulling Layla closer to my side. "This is our kingdom now. The Siren's Call belongs to us."

A smirk tugs at Cassie's red lips. "Does it? You're not just warming my throne?"

Rage flares through me, but Layla pulls at my hand, grounding me. I take a breath, holding my temper at bay.

"Thank you for giving me the perfect opportunity to tell you that you're going to college in the fall."

"*Excuse* me? College? You've got to be kidding me."

"I assure you, I'm not." My tone is calm but as hard as Layla's black diamond. "You need structure. Direction. A chance to develop your skills beyond Morelli's teachings."

"And you think shuffling me off to some stuffy university is the answer?" She snorts. "I have an empire to run."

"Had an empire," I correct. "The Siren's Call is under new management now. And part of that management includes ensuring you receive a proper education."

Layla chimes in, "It's not a punishment, Cassie. It's a chance to grow, to acclimate into normal life."

"My path is right here!" Cassie gestures around the server room, desperation creeping into her voice. "This is what I was made for. Molded for. You can't just take that away from me."

I step forward, capturing her chin and forcing her gaze to mine. "I can and I will. Because despite what Morelli drilled into you, there is more to life than this. Than him. You have a brilliant mind, Cassie. It's time you learned to use it for something other than destruction."

She wrenches out of my grip, breathing hard. "What, you want me to join the debate team? Run for student council?"

Layla says, "Campuses have a lot of predators. Women are assaulted constantly. You can help put an end to that with your, uh, talents."

"We were thinking along the lines of a controlled hunting ground," I say, agreeing with Layla. "A place to channel all that rage into something productive."

Cassie's eyes widen for a fraction of a second before narrowing again. "I don't need your permission or your direction."

"No, you don't," I agree. "But you do need a purpose. Something more than this vendetta that's consumed you. So what's it going to be, daughter? Delete the Oracle and forge your own path, or cling to the ghost of a man who never deserved your loyalty in the first place?"

Cassie harrumphs, but it's obvious that wheels are turning in her head. She has a hunger for a new challenge. It's a look I know well.

"And you think I'll, what, start attending frat parties and tailgates?" Cassie hedges, arching a brow.

"No, I think you'll do what you've always done. Observe. Manipulate. Destroy." I lower my voice. "Only this time, you'll do it on your own terms. Not Morelli's. Not mine. Yours."

The silence stretches between us, broken only by the hum of the servers. Finally, Cassie turns back to the terminal. With a few swift keystrokes, the lines of code vanish from the screen.

Cassie steps back, a mixture of loss and liberation rippling across her features. She looks at me, then Layla, as if searching for approval or condemnation. But she'll find neither in our expressions. This was her choice to make. Her first real one, perhaps ever.

"It's done," Cassie says, her voice steady despite the magnitude of what she's just done. "The Oracle is gone. Along with any backups or traces of the code."

I nod once, pride blooming in my chest. It's a foreign

feeling when it comes to Cassie. One I could get used to. "You made the right call."

"Did I?" she challenges, crossing her arms. "Or did I just prove that you can manipulate me as easily as Morelli ever could?"

"The difference," Layla interjects softly, "is that we want you to grow beyond need for manipulation at all. Morelli wanted to keep you dependent on him. We want you to be your own woman."

Cassie digests that, gaze flicking between us before landing back on the blank terminal screen.

"I've never been my own anything," she admits.

I survey the dark servers, now purged of Morelli's poisonous legacy. A kingdom of circuits and wires, ripe for the taking. My kingdom. Our kingdom.

We exit the server room, the chill of the space replaced by the warmth of possibility. Layla's hip brushes mine as we climb the stairs, a silent promise of things to come.

As we emerge from the subterranean depths of the Siren's Call, the revelry of the club swirls around us— pulsing music, clinking glasses, laughter both false and genuine. But there is another sound, faint beneath the din. The sound of muffled cries and rattling chains.

I lead Cassie and Layla down a hidden hallway, the plush crimson carpet giving way to rough stone as we descend into the bowels of the building. The dank air fills my nostrils, the scent of desperation and fear almost tangible.

We reach a heavy iron door, a single flickering light casting ominous shadows. Cassie retrieves an ancient-looking key from her pocket and unlocks it with a resounding clang. The door swings open, revealing a dimly lit chamber that was once use for illegal rum runs and now harbors captives.

Cages line the walls, and within them, the hunched figures of Cassie's prisoners.

Fathers and daughters, their faces gaunt and haunted, their eyes hollow from the unspeakable horrors Cassie subjected them to under Morelli's command. They flinch as we enter, cowering against the far walls of their cells.

Layla makes a choked sound beside me, her hand flying to her mouth. I glance at her, seeing the shock and revulsion in her mismatched eyes. For her, these broken souls were just images on a screen, distant and unreal.

"I know," I murmur, brushing my thumb across her knuckles. "But you're not a captive audience this time. You're here as a liberator."

She nods, pressing into my side.

"There's one more thing you need to do," I tell Cassie as she observes these people in her usual nonplussed fashion. "These fathers and daughters you imprisoned. It's time to let them go."

Cassie's eyes flash. "Why? They're leverage. Insurance."

"No, they're innocents that you tortured to manipulate me and teach the Oracle's algorithm. If you truly want to step out of Morelli's shadow, this is how you do it. Prove that you can let go of his methods, not just his tech."

"But they've seen our faces. They could report us." Cassie taps a finger against her chin in thought. "I should just kill them."

Cassie's benign tone causes the girl nearest us to mewl and scramble back, clutching her knees to her chest.

I fix Cassie with a hard stare. "No. You will not. They will each be paid handsomely for their silence. And I have connections in the police force and FBI who will bury any attempt to report us."

Cassie regards me for a long moment. With a sigh, she reaches for the key ring. "Fine. But if this bites us in the ass later, remember it was your call."

She moves to the first cage, unlocking it with a metallic click. "You're free to go. Courtesy of the Scythe's bleeding heart."

The father inside stumbles out, blinking rapidly in the dim light. He reaches a trembling hand toward his daughter in the adjacent cell.

Cassie makes quick work of the other locks, the prisoners emerging one by one. They huddle together, clinging to each other like lifelines in a storm-tossed sea.

I turn to address them. "You're free to go. But let me make one thing abundantly clear. If any of you breathes a word of what happened here, I will find you. And I promise, my methods will make you yearn for the mercy of Cassie's cages. Understood?"

A chorus of frantic nods and whispered assents meets my words. I gesture for them to leave through a back exit, and they scramble toward it, the echoes of their retreating footsteps soon swallowed by the damp air.

One of the fathers, a grizzled man with a beard flecked in gray, pauses at the threshold. He looks back at Layla, his gaze lingering on the tattoo at her throat.

A growl builds in my chest, and I step forward, placing a possessive hand on Layla's shoulder and grazing the handle of my knife with my other hand.

The man's eyes snap to mine, and he blanches at the lethal promise in my gaze. He quickly turns and disappears into the dark tunnel, his footsteps fading.

"I don't like the way he looked at you," I mutter, pulling Layla flush against me. She tilts her head back, a teasing glint in her eyes despite our macabre environment.

"I'm yours, Kaden. Thoroughly and completely. No wayward glance from a broken man will ever change that."

The truth of her words sinks into my marrow, and I seal my lips against hers. She opens for me, our tongues entwining with the rhythm of desire and dominance.

I stop kissing her long enough to say against her lips, "You've come a long way from the frightened girl in the lighthouse. You're a force to be reckoned with now."

A smile tugs at her lips. "I had a good teacher."

Cassie audibly gags, but there's less venom in her response to our intimacy.

"If you two are quite finished, I need a drink. Or five," she says.

She stalks past us, heading back up into the main level of the club. Layla and I follow, my hand resting on the small of her back.

We emerge out of the muted anguish of the dungeon to the pulsing vibrancy of the nightclub.

Gothic arches of weathered driftwood entwine above the dance floor, their keystones carved into snarling sea monsters. Antique ship lanterns in the ceiling cast a seductive glow. The bar is carved from the bow of an old schooner, its sails repurposed into artful canopies. Bartenders in tight black shirts and nautical tattoos slide drinks across the polished surface to the patrons perched on salvaged boat seats, and sheer curtains billow in an artificial breeze, giving the impression of sails whipped by a tempestuous wind.

It's a far cry from when I broke into it and was surrounded by Morelli's men, laying waste to them on the very floor so many of Greycliff's residents are now gyrating on.

Cassie bellies up to the bar, signaling for a whiskey, neat. She tosses it back in one fluid motion, the amber liquid catching the light before disappearing down her throat. She orders another, and I watch as she tries to drown whatever feelings were stirred up in the dungeon below.

"Should we be worried?" Layla asks, nodding toward Cassie as she throws back a third drink.

I shake my head. "She needs to numb herself for a bit. At her age, facing the atrocities she committed, even if they were under Morelli's influence, isn't easy."

"I had no idea a conscience survived in that head of hers," Layla says.

Cassie's shift from Morelli to Black is a subject that's taken up many of our weeks. My daughter is always a priority, but so is my future wife. I look down at her. At the face that astounds me in any light.

I step in front of her until I dominate her entire view. "Dance with me."

Layla's mismatched eyes sparkle as a slow, sensual beat pulses through the club. "I thought you'd never ask."

I lead her onto the dance floor, the sea of bodies parting before us. The scent of her, citrus with a hint of vanilla, fills my senses as I pull her close.

A pulsing beat thrums through our bodies as I spin her out, then back into my arms. She molds herself to my chest, her hips swaying. I'm not much of a dancer, but it's as natural as breathing with Layla. My hands skim down her sides, relishing the dip of her waist and flare of her hips. I pull her back against me, letting her feel the hard ridge of my arousal pressing insistently against her backside.

Layla rolls her hips, grinding against me in a move that makes me grit my teeth against a groan. My fingers dig into her hips as I guide her movements, setting a tempo that borders on indecent for such a public venue. But I can't bring myself to care. Not when she feels this good in my arms.

I lean down, my lips brushing the shell of her ear. "You're playing with fire, Wraithling."

She tilts her head back, her blue eye darkening almost as much as her brown one. "Take me to your hell, Scythe, because I like how it burns."

A growl rumbles in my chest, and I nip at her earlobe. "You feel what you do to me? How much I want you?"

She reaches back, threading her fingers into my hair.

"Always," she breathes. "I always feel how much you want me."

I turn her in my arms until we're face-to-face, chest to chest. My thigh slips between her legs, hiking her dress up. She grinds down on it, her eyes fluttering shut at the friction. My hands skim down her sides, fingers digging into the supple flesh of her ass as I guide her movements.

My lips find hers, and she kisses me back just as fiercely, her nails raking down my scalp. I groan into her mouth, the sound swallowed by the music.

"You drive me fucking crazy," I say, moving to nip at her

throat. "I can never get enough of you. I'm fucking obsessed with you."

Layla arches into me, her head falling back to expose more of her throat. I trail my lips down the slender column, pausing to lave my tongue over her tattoo. The black ink stands out starkly against her fair skin, a beautiful reminder of how far we've come.

"Kaden," she gasps, dragging my name out like the sound of it alone will bring her to orgasm.

Her fingers fist in my hair as I suck at her pulse point, determined to leave my mark on her. To stake my claim for all to see.

The music changes to a slower beat. I slide my hands down to her thighs, hitching her legs up around my waist. She locks her ankles at the small of my back, pressing herself intimately against me. I can feel the heat of her pussy through the thin fabric of her panties and my slacks. My blood boils with want.

I capture her lips again, devouring her mouth with a kiss that is all tongues and teeth. She matches me, stroke for stroke, pouring every ounce of her desire into the slant of her lips against mine.

The rest of the world falls away until there is only her. Her scent, her taste, her touch. She is my beginning and my end, my salvation and my damnation.

I pull back just enough to rasp against her lips, "Marry me. Tonight. Right now."

Layla's eyes widen, her breath catching. "What? But we already have a date set for next month."

"I don't want to wait another moment to call you my wife. To vow myself to you entirely."

Joy, fierce and bright, surges through my veins. I capture her face between my hands and kiss her deeply, reverently.

The vow I give Layla tonight won't be spoken in front of gods or witnesses—it will be carved into the marrow of her bones, seared into her soul, just as she's burned into mine. I'll claim her in every way a man like me can—without mercy, without repentance, without end.

When she nods, her smile bright but trembling, I take her hand. The weight of her trust is staggering, her love as brutal as the man she chose. And as I lead her toward the only ceremony I'll ever deserve, I catch Cassie's eye. She smirks, lifting her glass with a mix of disgust and grudging approval.

This isn't the beginning of a happy ending.

But it is the beginning of our forever—unforgiving, unyielding, and ours.

# LAYLA'S PLAYLIST

Revenge (DBSC) - tan feelz

Some Say - Adam Ulanicki

Marble - Neptunica, Shockz, Rebecca Helena

Zombie - The Cranberries

Survivor - 2WEI, Edda Hayes

Let Her Go - lost, Honeyfox, Pop Mage

The Blackmoor Mansion (3 AM) - Martin Egger

you should see me in a crown - Billie Eilish

Saints - Echoes

Doin' Time - Lana Del Ray

*Listen to the rest of the playlist on Spotify:*

# ALSO BY KETLEY ALLISON

**all in kindle unlimited**

*If you want more secret societies, read:*

Rival

Virtue

Fiend

Reign

*The Thorne of Winthorpe:*

Thorne

Crush

Liar

*If you want mafia with dark, why choose romance:*

Cruel Promise (M/F)

Broken Beauty (Why Choose)

Loyal Vows (Why Choose)

*Masked stalker romance*

The Reaper Duet

**also writing as S.K. Allison,**

**contemporary romance:**

*If you like your bad boys and bullies as standalones (no series, one book,
a happy ending), read:*

Rebel

Crave

*If you like a grump turned into a protector for his woman, read:*

Rock

Lover

*If you like your playboys with tormented hearts and scars, read:*

Trust

Dare

Play

*If you like grumpy billionaire and a small town, sassy heroine, read:*

You Will Want Me